DIRTY PUCKING PLAYER

THE FURY FAMILY SERIES
BOOK 1

GWYN MCNAMEE

Dirty Pucking Player
by
Gwyn McNamee © 2020 © 2023 (previously published as Dirty Player)

Cover Design: Tiffany Black at TE Black Designs
Cover Model: Zack Salaun
Photographer: Wander Aguiar
Editor: Stephie Walls

1

BASH

Blood splatters across the Plexiglass from Miller's split lip, and I shove his face against it, keeping him pinned to the boards with my hips. It's not my fault the fucker lost his helmet and opened himself up to an ass-kicking he deserves. After what he did to King on that last play, he needs a serious reminder never to touch our tendy.

The crowd roars, the sound reverberating through the arena at an almost deafening level. My ears ring, the noise only causing my blood to pump harder, my anger to rise more.

Miller twists and shoves back his body, trying to buck me off him. I swing, and my fist connects with the side of his head. He roars, pushes off the boards, and manages to get enough space between us to free himself from my hold.

Rage flares through my veins as he skates toward me, tugging off his gloves. Mine are long gone somewhere on the ice where I tossed them before I took him down.

The second he's close enough, my strike lands on his face. The crack of his nose breaking doesn't give me any pause. Not after the way he's been pushing for a confrontation all night.

I swing again and hit his jaw this time. His head whips back, sending blood from his mouth and nose flying through the air and splattering across the ice.

He recovers a second later and responds with a shot to my jaw. Pain spreads through the side of my face.

Motherfucker!

That sharp bite of pain acts as gasoline on the already blazing inferno inside of me, and I unleash on him.

Shot after shot.

Blow after blow.

I rain my aggression down on him until he's on his back on the ice, and I'm straddling him, my bare hands covered in his blood.

Someone grabs me from behind and tugs on my shoulder. It's nothing but a fruitless attempt to pull me off and away from him.

They shouldn't bother.

It's futile.

When I'm in *Bash* mode, there's no stopping me. And this douchebag has been asking for it all game. It was only a matter of time before it was going to come to blows. Every chance he got, he was taking cheap shots on one of us, and the fucking refs seem to be blind to it tonight. But you touch King, you *dare* lay a fucking finger on our goalie, and you will suffer the consequences.

I pull my arm back for another blow, but a set of hands grabs my wrist and a forearm wraps around my neck and jerks me backward. The familiar black and silver of our team's jersey flashes in my peripheral vision—the only reason I don't swing at them, too.

"Bash! Stop!" Larsson's voice comes from directly behind

me. He tightens his hold on my neck for emphasis. "It's fucking over."

Whoever was holding my arm releases it, and a ref skates between me and where Miller still lies on the ice, bloodied and whining like the fucking pussy he is.

He loves to dish it out but can't take it without turning into a blubbering baby.

It's part of the game, asshole. Grow the fuck up.

Larsson releases me, and I glance back at him. "The asshole fucking deserved it. He's been up my ass all game, and he hit King." Another cheap shot when the ref wasn't looking, so he got away with it.

It was time someone taught him a fucking lesson.

Miller climbs to his feet, pressing a hand over the gush of blood from his nose. His dark, hard eyes find mine, and he sneers and skates right past the useless ref toward me.

Ready for a second round, dickwad? BRING IT!

I skate toward him, but strong arms pull me back, and his teammates grab him before we can reach each other. We both struggle against the holds, but neither team is letting us go.

"Bash, man, chill."

"Lars"—I thrash but can't manage to free myself—"let me go."

He shakes his head. "It's not worth it, and you don't have any more free passes, dude."

The words instantly chill the anger burning through my blood.

Shit. He's right.

I look over to the bench and into the stone-cold eyes of Coach Spencer.

Fuck.

I've been skating on thin ice with him and the GM all season. Every penalty is another mark against me, and every suspension might as well be another step out the fucking door.

They warned me they weren't going to put up with much more after what happened last season. That they couldn't risk having me on the team going into the second half of this season when we're so close to making it to the playoffs. They said my attitude and the constant penalties were a hindrance to the team, and no matter how well I played, no matter how many goals I scored and assists I racked up, I couldn't make up for it.

Five damn years busting my ass for this team, helping them make it to the top of the Central Division every single damn season, All-Star Team five times, voted fan favorite three times, and *this* is how they repay me. By making threats to trade me if I don't fall in line like a good little boy.

It was so condescending and insulting. I should have told them to go fuck themselves and asked to be traded, but Chicago has become my home. These guys are my friends, my family. I don't want to get shipped off to some shit team somewhere, so I promised I'd be "good."

I swore up and down I'd reel myself in.

It was a fucking lie.

And they knew it.

Bash Fury doesn't have an off switch. Even now, my hands fist and open at my sides, ready for more. But it's over. In more ways than one. No way I'll be staying on the Warhawks with what just happened. This is exactly the excuse they need to get rid of me.

The ref skates over to make the announcement. "Number 71. Ten-minute penalty for fighting and a game misconduct."

Motherfucker.

I glare at Miller as I skate off the ice, but I don't bother looking at anyone in the stands or at our bench again.

It's pointless.

They hired me to play the game, and I'm fucking playing. Just because I don't do it like the rest of these pussies doesn't mean I should be repeatedly punished for it.

Fucking bullshit.

I already know where this is heading. And it isn't anywhere good.

What team is gonna pick up my contract on trade after this? Probably one with no hope of ever making it anywhere in the playoffs.

My chance at the Stanley Cup just went down the drain along with my career—and this time, the guy deserved it. But I'll still pay the price.

I storm down the tunnel to the locker room. Every muscle in my body vibrates with the adrenaline from the fight and the rage of knowing the consequences of what I just did.

"This is such fucking bullshit."

I tear off my helmet and chuck it across the room. It slams against the wall of lockers and ricochets back.

This is fucking hockey, not touch football. Violence is part of the game and asshats like Miller need to know they can't play like that, touch our fucking tendy, and expect no response.

What the fuck is going on with these snowflakes?

The wrath building inside me has reached a boiling point. What just went down on the ice was only the tip of the iceberg. I march over to my next target—the water cooler. I grab it and toss it across the room. It smashes into one of the lockers and explodes, water drenching my teammates' personal items and soaking the floor.

"What the hell is going..." Louie, our assistant equipment manager, freezes in the doorway and takes in my handiwork. "Shit."

"Get the fuck out of here." My screamed order echoes through the space, reverberating in my ears. "Now!"

He nods and backs away slowly. The man knows better than to get in my way when I'm like this. It isn't the first time he's seen it, but there's no doubt it *will* be the last.

This will be my last game as a Warhawk.

I flip one of the benches and then drop onto the one across from it and lower my face into my trembling, bloodied hands.

Fuck. Fuck. Fuck.

This is it. The end of my career.

What team is going to take me now?

―――――

GREER

"No. Absolutely not." I try to keep the anger and mild panic out of my words as much as possible, but I fail miserably. Each syllable vibrates with incredulous disdain and borders on wildly inappropriate, considering who I'm sitting across from.

I shouldn't have snapped, but it's just...I can't wrap my head around what he told me.

This cannot be happening.

Fate wouldn't drop such a massive turd on me like this, not when things have been going so well. As far as I can remember, I haven't done anything that would draw the ire of karma to make her demand retribution like this. Although, speaking to the man who is, for all intents and purposes, my boss like that probably hasn't put me on the top of anyone's "nice" list.

It was kind of bitchy.

Borderline cunty, if I'm being honest.

But I couldn't help it.

I've always worn my heart on my sleeve, and even though I should act more deferential and professional right now, this is absolute insanity that calls for something less appropriate.

The man must have totally lost his marbles to be considering this. I would wonder if maybe dementia hit, but Bob seems very clear of mind. At least, he certainly reacts to my snarled response appropriately—with a giant frown and a deeply furrowed brow.

He sighs, a deep, labored sound, and leans forward in his chair to rest his forearms on his desk between us. "Look, Greer, I understand your position, but—"

"But *nothing*." I cut him off without even caring how rude it is anymore. I don't have the patience for placations from a man who made me certain promises to get me here. "When you hired me as head coach, you told me I would have control of my team. *Full* control. And I'm telling you right now, I don't want a dirty player like Bash Fury wearing a Scorpions' jersey or taking the ice under my watch."

Bob offers me a look that could either be condescending or sympathetic—maybe both. Soft, droopy lids hang low over pale-blue eyes surrounded by wrinkles that show his age. He may not be quite up in the years where we need to worry about his mental faculties, but Bob Harmon has been around the block a few times.

More than a few.

He's smart. He was a great coach, and now he's an amazing GM. One of the best, even though this is only his first year. But he's also under a lot of pressure to make the Scorpions successful in their inaugural season. The weight of those expectations practically crushes me, so I can only imagine what that feels like bearing down on his shoulders.

He holds up his hands. "I understand your position, but

it's a done deal. Sebastian Fury's suspension is up today, and the trade is complete. He will be here by practice tomorrow. And he'll be your new first line right winger."

Son of a bitch.

That wasn't a request.

That was a statement of fact.

A done deal.

He went ahead and took Bash without my knowledge. No amount of arguing about what I want can change Bob's mind now. But maybe, just maybe, I can appeal to his desire for success for this team instead of my personal feelings. Maybe there's a *chance* we can get rid of Bash before the trade deadline in a few days.

"What happened to me being able to control my own team?"

Complete control is the only way we'll continue winning. I can't have players who go off at the drop of a glove and spend more time in the penalty box or suspended than on the ice. We'll spend half the game killing off his penalties, and Marty and I will constantly be rearranging the lines while he's serving his time on suspension.

The man who has helped me bring this team this far rises to his feet behind his desk and slowly lumbers around to sit on the edge in front of me. "On the ice, you make the calls, but as GM, I'm the one who makes the big decisions for the team. That's the way it is for every NHL team in the league. You just need to make it work with Mr. Fury."

Make it work? What a fucking joke.

Bob is setting the team up for failure by bringing on a guy like Bash Fury. He may be one of the best wingers in the league, but he's also the biggest liability we could have on the Scorpions right now.

An expansion team in a position to make the playoffs in its first year.

Unheard of.

One coached by a woman.

That sure as hell has never happened before since I'm the first in the league.

We're making history on two fronts.

Which means all eyes are on me.

Everyone's waiting for me to fail so they can point the finger and say, "*See, women shouldn't be coaching men in this sport.*"

There's no doubt I'm a test case, and Bob put a lot of faith in me by bringing me on. He took a massive risk. There were any number of male coaches, with far more experience in the NHL, who would have leaped at the chance to coach this expansion team in Vegas. But he came to *me.* He sought *me* out for this position and talked me up to the media. He lifted me up to head coach after only a year as an NHL assistant coach because he knew what I was capable of.

It never would have happened if we hadn't already worked together so much. He knows me better than just about anyone. After three Olympics coaching me, then bringing me on to help coach the men in Pyeongchang during the last games, we've worked together so much that Bob is basically a second father figure.

That makes times like this frustrating because I don't want to insult the man who has almost single-handedly brought me to where I am today. But he doesn't seem to see the big problem here.

I've already stuck it to the naysayers and demonstrated I know what the hell I'm doing. We're sitting at number three in the division, with only two months left until the playoffs.

We're in shape to do something unheard of—make it to the Stanley Cup Playoffs in our inaugural season—which is precisely why today's news has me so rattled.

We're a well-oiled machine. We've worked out all the

kinks that happen when a team is cobbled together from leftover players no one wanted to protect, many of whom have never played together before. We're plowing through our opponents left and right. And now, a giant wrench like Bash Fury is being thrown into the mix.

I sigh and rub my hands over my face, not even caring if I smear the remnants of my eye makeup and end up looking like a crack-whore raccoon. I'm not trying to impress anyone here. "And what about when he starts up with his usual crap, Bob? The penalties. The suspensions." I raise an eyebrow. "What then?"

He shrugs nonchalantly. "Then we deal with it. Bash knows the Scorpions are taking a big risk picking him up after he just had his third suspension this season. My hope is that he'll calm down a bit, but to be honest, part of the reason I brought him on is how passionately he plays the game."

I snort-laugh. "Passionately? What he does isn't passion. The man is out of control. He's going to hurt somebody really badly one of these days."

And people seeing I have no control over him will only hurt *me*. It will be the proof the haters need to say I don't belong, that the guys don't respect me to captain this ship.

Bob shifts to his feet. "We can only hope that doesn't happen."

Hope. I'm resting the remainder of my fucking season on hope?

I blow out an annoyed breath and stand.

He reaches out and places a reassuring hand on my shoulder. "Try not to worry so much, Greer. From what I hear, he's not all that bad of a guy, actually."

Yeah, right. Not that bad of a guy.

That's what everyone said about Sean, and he ended up

cheating on me with a cocktail waitress while I was away in Pyeongchang for the Olympics.

Sebastian Fury is nothing but a problem to be solved.

And I know how to handle him.

He just needs to know who's boss. Then, he'll fall in line.

2

GREER

The asshole is late.

His first day as a Scorpion, and he can't even make it to practice on time.

This does not bode well.

But I can't say I'm surprised. Everything I've heard about Bash up to this point has led me to believe he's not going to last long on my team. Bob may think he controls everything, but he can't force me to put Bash on the ice. And if my players don't come to practice, they don't play. It's a simple rule. One I've enforced before and won't hesitate to again.

Everyone else managed to get here on time, and Bob said Bash was flying in last night, so there's no excuse for his tardiness. This is deliberate and exactly the type of behavior Bash Fury is famous for.

His arrogance is almost as well-known as his lineage. Being the son of a Hall of Famer like Mike Fury gives Bash that extra "glow" of celebrity even if he weren't an outstanding forward in his own right. But arrogance and skill aren't enough to get what you want on my team—you have to play by the *rules*.

No practice. No play.

As simple as that.

I'll plan to move forward with the current first line. Lebedev, Hayes, and McCormick are one of the best forward combos in the league this year, and breaking them up was going to cause problems. Lebedev has an ego almost as big as Bash's, and it was sure to cause a fight if I moved him to open the way for Fury. At least now, I have a little more time to assess the line-ups, knowing Bash won't be hitting the ice tomorrow.

I watch the guys move through their drills...a little too sluggishly for my liking. It may only be practice, but I like to keep my players sharp and ensure they keep up the energy they need in the game. I clap to get their attention. "Let's go, guys. Strong forecheck. Move your feet. Win the race to the puck. Let's go."

My voice carries out across the ice, and the guys push harder and faster.

If Bash were here, I'd be trying to work him in to see how he fits on the first line—most likely in the position currently occupied by Lebedev at right winger—but the arrogant bastard can't even deign to grace us with his presence, so he's being relegated off first for the foreseeable future when he *does* get put into the line-up. I don't care what Bob has to say about that. He can fire me if he disagrees.

We run the drill over and over, like the efficient team I know we are. There's a reason I've managed to bring this group this far in such a short amount of time. I don't tolerate any crap, and these guys know how to play together. They all know they're good, but they don't let it go to their heads. Even Lebedev manages to reel it in when necessary.

I'm not so sure Bash would fit in with them even if he were here.

"Hey, Coach." Hayes skates over to me. "What—" He looks over my shoulder, and his eyes widen slightly. "Well, look who finally decided to grace us with his presence."

There's only one person he can be talking about. Only one member of the team is missing this morning. And everyone is very aware of his absence.

Bash.

I turn toward the tunnel to the locker room. Bash makes his way up, and even walking in skates and pads, he still manages to swagger like he owns the place.

Conceited son of a bitch...

I glance at my watch. An hour past the start of practice. I clench my jaw to bite back the angry words I have about him being late. Tearing into him in front of the entire team is unnecessary. It's better saved for a private conversation— one I would have been having with him whether he was late for practice or not. One about what I expect from him when he's on *my* team.

He runs a hand back through his thick, dark-blond hair, then shakes it before pulling on his helmet.

Christ...

It really is too bad he's such a cocky asshole because one thing I can't deny about Bash Fury is he is *hot*. The kind of dirty hot that gives you dreams that have you waking up panting with your hand between your legs.

His soft whiskey eyes lock with mine, and he flashes me a grin and winks.

Fucking winks.

He reaches down and adjusts his cup before he jumps out onto the ice and skates straight over to Mac while pulling on his gloves. One of the reasons Bob wanted Bash so much is because Mac played with Bash on the Warhawks before coming to the Scorpions this year. They played well together there, and there's every reason the two of them will fall right back into that rhythm again here in Vegas.

They embrace like old friends, and the other guys on the team skate over to greet him. He didn't even have the decency to come to introduce himself to me...his coach.

Such a douchenozzle.

Anger heats my skin even in the chilled air of the rink. It crawls up my neck and over my cheeks in what is undoubtedly a red flush. I clench my fists at my sides.

Damn my pale complexion.

It makes hiding my reactions to things all that more difficult.

The asshole skates straight over to Lebedev and says something that has my current first line right winger straightening his spine and fisting his hands in his gloves. They get chest to chest, but, thankfully, neither takes a shot.

Fucking Bash...

Already starting shit and he's only been here two minutes. He needs to fall in line, but I'm not going to go off on him in front of the guys. He's just trying to establish he's top dog.

Well, he's in for a mighty rude awakening if he thinks that's the way it's going to be on the Scorpions. There's only room for one alpha, and it's me.

Lebedev skates over to the bench in a huff and throws his stick against the boards. Our equipment manager, Steve, takes care of the discarded stick without a word, then glances at Lebedev with sympathy. Even Steve feels for him.

Poor guy.

He already knows he's been replaced, but Bash is going to have to earn that spot. If he can't keep himself in check and under control, I'm not putting a liability on the ice. Not when we're *this* close to making the playoffs. Not when I'm *this* close to having the most successful first season expansion team in history. Not when I'm the first female coach on top of that.

There's too much at stake and too many people counting on me to let this arrogant bastard ruin my plans with his ego.

———

BASH

Coach Greer Waterson is *pissed*. Maybe the wink and crotch grab were a bit much, but damn, her anger brings a sexy red blush to her cheeks.

I wonder if it's the same one that appears when she's coming?

A grin tugs at my lips.

That's definitely something I want to see.

That woman is a force of nature. Even years ago, when she was just a college student playing on the Olympics team, I couldn't keep my eyes off her when she was on the ice. She played with relentless focus and passion. A passion I would love to experience directed at me...were we in different positions. Mostly horizontal. But I'd take her vertically, too, against the glass, against a locker, anywhere I could.

As it stands, hitting on my new coach is probably not the brightest idea.

I'm quite literally at the end of the road where my playing career is concerned. If this doesn't work out, I may not have another chance at the Cup.

But if I had to be traded somewhere, the Scorpions are probably the best team it could have been. I should count my blessings I'm on the ice at all and be happy I'm with her. Another hot-headed, testosterone-fueled old school coach would have just been another inevitable trade, but her...I can handle *her*.

I've never met a woman I couldn't manage with a grin and some sweet-talking, and Greer will be no different.

God willing.

It's time to stake my claim here. And I've already made that first move with Greer and my competition. Lebedev stands off to the side, eyeing me with fury burning in his gaze. He had to know my coming meant he was going to lose his first-line position.

Sorry, dude. Time's up!

I skate over to him and flash him a grin. "Hit the bench."

He growls and puffs out his chest as he skates right up next to me. "Fuck you, Bash. You couldn't even bother to come to practice on time, and now I'm just supposed to hand over my position?"

"They're paying me a fuckload more than they're paying you to play this position. You really think they're going to put me on the second or third line? Let the big boys play."

I wait for the swing, but it doesn't come. He has more restraint than most of the assholes on the ice these days, or maybe he's just smart enough to know I'm right and there's no point in fighting it.

Save that anger for the ice.

He scowls at me, then skates over toward the bench, throwing his stick. Coach glares at me from across the ice. Her cool-green eyes match the temperature of the rink, sending a slight shiver through me.

She had to have seen the entire exchange.

Good.

She needs to know where I belong on this team. Bob promised me the first line position wouldn't go to anyone else, and I expect that to be true. No one is going to keep me from what I earned. And I *earned* this spot with hard fucking years of work.

I wait for her to approach me, to say or do something to acknowledge my presence and what just went down, but instead, she sucks in a deep breath and glances around the ice.

"What are you all just standing around for? Let's go."

A tiny smile pulls at the corner of my lips. She's not fighting it, either. She knows *exactly* where I belong. It's going to make this a lot easier for both of us if she just accepts who is in control here. And it's the one scoring all the goals.

For now, it's time to work with my new teammates. Things with Coach Waterson can be dealt with off the ice.

She hammers us with drills for almost two hours without letting up. Mac and I fall right back into the groove we had in Chicago, and Hayes, Kasinski, and Grey all seem to be with the program. Lebedev is another matter entirely. The dude has an attitude problem, but just like with Coach, it will work itself out eventually...like when I take the ice tomorrow night first instead of him.

When Greer finally ends practice, I'm more than ready to head back to the hotel and crash. The late-night flight knocked more out of me than I thought, and relaxing and settling into my new digs sounds like absolute bliss.

I make my way off the ice and down the tunnel toward the locker room.

Mac steps up next to me and smacks my shoulder. "Hey, man, I'm happy you're here."

I smirk at him. "I'm glad someone is."

He chuckles, but all humor drains from his face. I follow his line of vision to find Coach standing halfway down the tunnel, her arms crossed over her ample chest, a scowl on her perfect bow lips, and angry heat radiating from her green eyes.

We approach her, and her hand shoots out. She presses it into the center of my chest firmly. "A word, Mr. Fury?"

I stare down at her, my skates giving me an even greater height advantage. "What do you need, Coach?"

She lets the rest of the guys walk past us before she shifts fully in front of me and glowers up. "We need to have a little chat."

"Oh, really?" I do my best to appear clueless and innocent. "About what?"

It doesn't work, given the way her lips twist into a sneer. "About your attitude. You come late to my practice, you don't play. You pull any of the shit that you did back in Chicago, you don't play." She closes the distance between us, her breasts almost brushing my jersey, and pushes her finger harder into my chest. "I don't allow dirty players on my team. Don't for a second think I'm going to let you walk all over me and do whatever you want."

Every word she says drips with disdain that should probably have my balls shriveling up to hide, but instead, my cock twitches and heat spreads through my chest where her finger rests, despite the pads between us.

Coach has some fucking balls. I'll give her that.

She has to be a total badass to have played the way she did. Her impressive stats when she was on the Olympic team and in college mean she probably could've played better in the NHL than half the guys here. If they were going to give any woman a chance to coach us, I'm glad it's her. She's earned it.

But what she hasn't earned is the right to talk down to me like I'm a piece of shit stuck to her shoe. I'm an All-Star player with a multi-million-dollar contract, not some rookie she can intimidate.

I grin down at her. "Let's get one thing clear, Coach. The Scorpions are paying me $9 million to be here this year *alone*. They're paying you...what? Not even a million?"

She flinches slightly and jerks her hand from my chest, so I push in even closer to her. Close enough that I can feel the heat radiating off her and see her fists shaking with rage at her sides.

"I was brought here to do what I do, and I'm going to do what I do best. Win games. Just try to keep me off the ice and see what happens to your job. Whose side do you think they're going to choose if it comes down to the two of us, sweetheart?"

I shift to the right and move past her down the tunnel without a glance back. She doesn't come after me. She doesn't shout some retort.

Hopefully, she got the message.

3

GREER

"That bastard did *what*?" Jill shakes her head, her black bob swinging at her chin. "You can't be serious."

I swallow a big cooling gulp of my wine and set it back on the table to take a second to compose myself before I talk about it anymore. Even thinking about my confrontation with Bash today and what he said to me before he sauntered off gets my blood boiling so hot, I feel like I might explode and send shrapnel across the restaurant.

Though, now that I've told Jill all the dirty details, I don't feel the rush of relief that I thought I would at unloading. Instead, more pent-up rage has worked its way into the knots in my shoulders.

How fucking dare *he speak to me like that?*

I'm his coach, for fuck's sake.

He needs to show me some damn respect, even if he does make almost ten times what I do a year. I'm still the one in charge—at least, as much as Bob lets me be.

I'm the coach. He's just the dirty player. I'm the authority in this professional relationship. And he just walked all over me like he wasn't wearing blades that sliced up my pride and left me standing there bleeding.

Jill watches me from across the table, anger and concern etched on her soft features.

"Yes." I take a deep breath. "He *actually* said that to me and then he pushed past me like I wasn't even there on his way back to the locker room."

"What a fucking dick."

"No shit."

"It's too bad he's hotter than hell." She shakes her head and takes her wine glass in her hand, releasing a little sigh. "Such a fucking waste."

She sips at her pinot grigio, and I bark out a laugh that has the people at the surrounding tables glaring at me.

Oops.

I never was very good at biting my tongue or keeping my mouth under control. It's gotten me into a lot of trouble in the past. But it also means I stand up for myself like I tried to do this morning with Bash. So far, he's the only one who has managed to render me speechless.

Bash fucking Fury.

Already the bane of my existence and he hasn't even been here twenty-four hours.

I twirl my glass between my fingers, that damn cocky grin of his playing in my mind. "I don't think he's that hot."

Jill chuckles and shakes her head. She tilts her glass toward me. "You're a fucking liar. He's exactly your type. Tall. Broad shoulders. Tattoos everywhere. Flowing locks. Lips that are sinful and begging to be kissed. And that grin...*giiiiirrlllllll,* even on television, it's panty-melting. If he weren't Bash Fury, you would be *all* over that."

Shit.

She's not wrong. Not wrong at all.

Sometimes, I hate that the bitch can see right through me so damn well, but because of being almost inseparable in middle school and high school, we know each other nearly as well as we know ourselves. The fact that she moved to Vegas a few years ago and would be here was the ultimate icing on the cake of being offered this job. But it's times like these when she's joking around and taunting me with her knowledge of my deepest desires, that I want to kick her under the table.

Admitting out loud that Bash is exactly the type of guy I've gravitated toward during my adult lifetime would sting almost as much as his words did today.

But he *is* sooooo my type.

Strong. Athletic. Not afraid to have an opinion or challenge me.

It's irrelevant, though. When I took my first job as an assistant coach under Bob, I swore off ever dating a hockey player again. Plus, he's not just *any* player. He plays for *my* team. That makes him doubly off-limits...

And *somehow* that makes him even more appealing.

Why the hell is that?

The old saying, "You always want what you can't have," flashes through my head. That's all it is. Some strange desire to prove my dominance to that man who I know I can't touch.

I stare through the almost-clear wine in my glass and lament my choice in men. "Why am I always attracted to assholes?"

Jill snorts and sips her wine. "Because you want to fix them. You see a tiny bit of good in someone and latch onto that and use it as a reason to ignore all the bad."

Shit. I absolutely do that.

She nods as if she knows I'm mentally admitting she's right. "Bash Fury is no different, Greer. You hate him now, but you'll get to know him and figure out he's not such a bad guy. You can't help but see the good in people. That's not a *bad* thing, hon. You just have to make sure you don't open yourself up to those people who only have a tiny bit of good. The rest is the part that ends up hurting you in the end."

I sigh and lean back in my chair, the active chatter of the restaurant around us helping to drown out the voice in my head that keeps insisting there must be something redeeming in that man. "I don't need to worry about that with Bash Fury, Jill. He's an arrogant prick. He doesn't have a redeeming bone in his body."

Jill waggles her eyebrows. "It isn't his *redeeming bone* I'm worried about. It's the supposedly massive one between his legs. I've seen that look in your eyes before, girl. You want to jump that man."

I jerk upright. "I do *not*. I wouldn't go near that thing with a ten-foot pole."

She grins. "Methinks you doth protest too much."

"Oh, shut up." I wave a hand at her. "Knock it off with the smarty-pants literary bullshit. I'm not getting involved with Bash Fury. I can *guaranfuckingtee* that. All I'm doing is making sure he stays in line."

"And just how do you plan on doing that?"

However I have to...

I chew my lip and consider my options.

Bash is right about one thing...if I try to bench him without reason, Bob will come down on me. But if he keeps up his usual shit on the ice, that will give me a legitimate excuse I can argue to the boss about why he's not out on the first line. The first penalty he gets, I can make sure he spends the rest of the night riding the wood instead of on his skates.

He won't like it, but it will be a necessary return fire. He started this with his shot across the bow this morning. All

I'm doing is staking my claim and ensuring he understands the way the Scorpions run. He may have been able to get away with his bullshit on the Warhawks, but that won't fly here.

That sexy, infuriating man needs to learn his place, and it's not at the head of this team.

"I'm going to do what I've always done, Jill. I'm going to stand my ground and show my authority the moment he steps out of line."

It's what I did when I assisted Bob in coaching the men's Olympic team and during my one year as an assistant coach in the NHL...and it's what I will do here. Just because I have tits instead of balls doesn't mean I'll tuck my tail and run at the first threat.

Bash Fury doesn't scare me. Not one fucking bit.

He's just a man. One controlled by testosterone and ego.

Both need to be put in check.

―――

BASH

The fluffy, white towel brushes softly against my wet skin.

Like fucking Heaven.

I didn't need a second shower after practice, but from the moment I dropped off my bags here last night—or I guess, technically, early this morning—and saw the bathroom in this place, I knew I was going to be spending a lot of time in there.

Wall-to-wall jets and a waterfall showerhead were just too much to pass up. Even if I already cleaned up at the practice facility. I also needed to relieve a little of the tension that had built up during my confrontation with Greer today.

I could have taken care of business in the locker room

showers, but I don't need my new teammates thinking I'm some sort of sick perv who whacks off all the time on the first day.

The shower here did just fine and allowed me to find that release I needed so badly while visions of that pink flush spreading over Greer Waterson's cleavage and across her cheeks danced in my head.

I run the towel over my hair and chest to get the majority of the water off, then wander out into the bedroom and living room area of my hotel suite.

This place really is fucking incredible.

When I heard they were trading me to the Scorpions, I definitely wasn't thrilled to have to fly across the country to join an expansion team—even one with a great record—but the team putting me up at a place like this helps ease some of the adjustment pain. And my five-game suspension after what I did to Miller gave me time to get some of my shit together, more time than most players get when they're traded.

I'll eventually have to find a permanent place here, a condo or something, but for now, my home away from home is pretty fucking sweet.

If I had to be traded, at least it was to one of the poshest places I could've ended up. Fucking five stars on the Strip. Only the best of the best for Bash Fury...

As it should be.

I let the towel drop to the floor and sprawl out on the king-size bed. The soft mattress might as well be a cloud underneath my naked skin. I'll sleep like a baby tonight, but for now, I grab the remote and flip through channels until I land on *Lethal Weapon*. Chuckling to myself, I relax against the headboard, letting the chilly air in the room dry the last of the moisture from my body.

A fucking classic if there ever was one. And exactly what I need to top off my night.

The massive flat-screen's crystal-clear picture flickers in front of me, and surround sound speakers immerse me in the explosions and gunfire in the movie.

I could get used to this life.

Maid service. Room service. Perfect location. Even the flashing lights of the Strip coming in through the floor-to-ceiling windows that make up one wall of the room can't distract from my relaxation.

As far as first days go, I've had worse. Coach was certainly pretty pissed off after our little chat in the tunnel, but she'll get over it if she knows what's good for the team.

And I have no doubt she does.

She has an impressive résumé. Three-time All-American in college. Three Olympic medals—one bronze and two silver. Assistant coach for the men's team that won gold in Pyeongchang...

The woman knows her hockey. It was only a matter of time before they gave the head coaching position to someone without a dick. I'm glad it was her, but I hadn't anticipated her giving me quite so much shit right off the bat. She certainly isn't a push-over. I may have underestimated Coach Greer Waterson. This head-to-head battle may go on longer than I could have anticipated before one of us finally breaks.

And I don't intend for it to be me.

Though she seems determined to stand her ground.

Still, the way her skin flushed...

Christ...

My phone ringing on the nightstand pulls me away from another fantasy about bending Coach over the boards at the bench and against the glass and fucking her senseless.

I glance at the screen and grin as I swipe, instantly eviscerating those images from my head. "How's my favorite little sister doing?"

Rachel chuckles, and is, no doubt, rolling her pale-green eyes at me. "Your only sister is doing great. I was just calling to see how my *favorite* brother did on his first day with the Scorpions."

"Favorite brother? Does Jameson know that he's been demoted?"

We laugh at that because we both know she tells him he's the favorite, even though it's always been me. He can think whatever he wants. We don't want to damage his fragile ego.

"So," she sing-songs, "tell me about your first day with the new coach. How was it?"

I lean back against the headboard again and stare up at the ceiling. "She was pretty much what I expected."

"Oh, really?"

"Yeah. Strong-willed. You'd have to be as a female coach in the league. And to play the way she did."

Rachel hums. "True. It's one of the reasons she's always been one of my idols."

"I know, Rach." Growing up, baby sis always insisted I watch the women's national team games with her. She was in awe of Greer and her teammates even though Rach herself never had any interest in playing. "And she earned that role."

"So...try not to make her hate you too much, Bash. I want her to actually be nice to me when I come to a game."

I bark out a laugh, but I know she's serious.

Little sister knows me too well.

Rubbing the back of my neck, I release a little snort. "Well, we had a bit of an issue this morning, but I think we've cleared the air and things will go a lot more smoothly moving forward."

She sighs. "Oh, God, Bash. What did you do?"

I shrug and replay the conversation in my head. "Nothing, really."

"Bash..."

The way she says that sounds so much like Mom, my chest actually tightens. I rub at it absently. "Really, Rach, it's fine. We came to an understanding."

By an understanding, I mean I told her off and walked away from her, leaving her speechless. But I'm not about to give Rach a play-by-play. She won't grasp why what I said to Greer was necessary.

"I know how you can be, Bash. If you were a dick, you should apologize."

"I wasn't a dick." At least, not until we got into the tunnel and she pushed me to say certain things. "Really. I wasn't."

"Uh huh." Rachel says something to someone in the background. "Hey, Bash, I have to run. I just wanted to check in on you."

"Thank you." I squeeze my eyes shut. "I could use a little mothering every now and then."

A somber mood settles between us on the line, one I hadn't intended but that's there all the same. Mentioning Mom always brings a painful mix of emotions for all of us.

"I miss her, too, Bash. But she'd be proud of you, of what you've accomplished."

"Even though I just got canned, basically?"

She chuckles. "Well, she'd give you shit about that, but she'd still be proud."

I hope she's right.

"I'll talk to you later, sis."

"Bye, Bash...and hey, I'm telling you, if you fucked up on your first day, it's not too late to salvage it. Just apologize."

"You don't even know what I did."

She laughs. "No, but I know you almost as well as you know yourself. Just apologize."

The line goes dead, and I drop the phone next to me on the bed with a sigh. I crank up the volume on the TV and tuck my hands behind my head.

Rach would probably be right about apologizing if I thought I did anything wrong. But...I'm pretty sure I didn't. Every single word I spoke was the truth. And there's absolutely nothing wrong with speaking the truth...even if it might be painful for the person on the receiving end.

I never wanted to hurt Greer, but if that's what needed to happen for us to move forward, then it was a necessary evil. One I can live with.

The phone rings again, and I glance down.

It's probably Rach again.

"Well, shit, will you look at that?" I swipe to open the call. "Caleb fucking Carlson, where the hell have you been, man?"

He laughs, and a car horn honks in the background. The man always seems to be on the go. First, it was jet-setting around the world as a hotshot money manager for the rich and famous, and now it's racing all over with Tara and the kids, trying to balance being a dad and husband with keeping up with his clients. It's been weeks since I heard from him, and that's unusual for us.

I run a hand through my damp hair. "You on the road?"

"Yeah. Sorry I've been MIA for a bit. Things have been insane with the kids. I just wanted to call and wish you luck at your new gig."

New gig.

"Thanks, man." *For not saying I got traded for fucking up again.* "I'm gonna need it."

He laughs again. "I've heard your coach can be a real ball-buster."

I snort and shake my head. "No doubt."

She certainly let me have it today. It was quite impressive, really, standing up to me, getting right in my face to let me know where she stood.

"Well, you should have something arriving at your door any minute now that will help ease the pain of that transition."

I climb from the bed and stretch. "What did you do, Caleb?"

Knowing him, they'll be a bevy of call girls lined up outside the door in a few minutes. He may have cleaned up his own act and settled down, but that doesn't mean he's lost his sense of humor, or his ability to know what will cheer me up.

Knock. Knock. Knock.

Almost as if on cue...

I look down at my naked body. "Hey, I think whatever you sent is here. I have to go."

"Well, enjoy it and think of me, brother."

"Eww. You perv."

He laughs and ends the call. I grab a robe from the closet on my way to answer the door. Plush. Luxurious. I really *could* get used to this. I tie the sash and glance through the peephole. A beautiful brunette stands on the other side of the door.

Oh, God...he didn't.

I tug open the door, and the woman flashes me a brilliant smile. Large breasts squeezed into a tiny top and sky-high heels make her appear far taller than her petite form actually is.

"Bash Fury?"

I lean against the jamb and examine her. "Yes...and you are?"

Those pearly whites make another appearance, and she

presses her arms against her breasts, shoving them even higher. "I'm Bunny."

Of course, you are.

She extends a bag in her hand that I hadn't even noticed. "This is from Caleb. He says to enjoy it but not too much."

I grab the bag and glance inside. A laugh works its way from my chest as I pull the bottle of twenty-five-year Lagavulin from the paper.

That rich fucking bastard.

"Thank you, Bunny. You made my night."

She winks and purses her lips. "You're welcome, Mr. Fury."

I step back into the room and let the door close behind me. Only Caleb would send me a fifteen-hundred-dollar bottle of aged scotch along with a beautiful woman.

There's not a single doubt in my mind if I wanted that girl to come in to enjoy some with me, she would have, but after what went down with Coach today, a mindless fuck with the Mensa candidate tonight just doesn't have the same appeal it once might have.

4

BASH

I don't have enough fingers to count the number of dirty looks Coach gave me during morning skate today. That woman has fire in her eyes burning hotter than any I've ever seen. And frankly, her anger is sexy as hell. Exactly the kind of flames I'd love to get scorched by.

Most women practically, if not literally, throw themselves at me, so her standoffish behavior and obvious distaste for all things Bash Fury is an interesting change of pace.

But I've kept my distance since I arrived.

No need to stir the pot, even though she was beautiful all worked up at practice yesterday.

Christ, the way her cheeks reddened...

I hated starting off on that foot with her, but she needs to know where we stand, and where I am is the best player on this team at this position. I should be the starter. That's why they're paying me all this money. It isn't to be a second or third-line guy who sits on the bench and only fills in when somebody needs a little breather.

If she can't see the past my reputation to understand that this team needs me, then there would be no point in me being here in the first place.

I think she got my message loud and clear because the disdain flooding her gaze this entire day never wavered. She's not a woman who likes to be told what to do. She's strong. She'd have to be to accomplish what she has. It's pretty damn impressive.

Her background as a player and a coach is staggering enough, but add to that an expansion team sitting at third in the division coming into the trade deadline...if she were a man, everyone would be singing her praises, but as it is, people assume it's a fluke.

The pundits on the sports shows keep praising the play of the team while, in the same breath, dismissing how much of their success comes from Greer's role. They can so easily brush aside what she does.

I don't.

Greer has worked her damn ass off to get where she is, and she deserves all the recognition for this team's success. She just needs to *also* recognize its future success will depend on me, too.

Tonight will prove that. We're less than two months from the playoffs. Every game counts. But they brought me onto this team to be Bash Fury, not Bash Fury *Light*. I won't play to please Greer and hold back. I'll do what's best for the team. What's best for the game. Sometimes, that means some head bashing and sticking people into the boards.

I grab my gloves and helmet and shove out of the locker room to find her waiting. She leans back against the opposite wall of the tunnel, watching the door. Her eyes meet mine, and the coolness there washes over me like an ice bath.

Here for me, Coach?

Something tells me she is. She should be on the bench already or in her office, performing whatever her usual pregame ritual is while we go warm-up on the ice. There's only one reason she's standing here staring me down. She has something to say.

No need to guess what.

I let the guys file out around me and slowly scan her from the top of her blond head down to her high-heeled feet as I grab my stick from the rack outside the locker room.

How the hell does she stand in those all game? It's fucking insane.

So is the way they make her legs look absolutely flawless and a mile long in her prim, dark-gray pencil skirt. The fact that she insists on wearing these perfectly tailored suits that show off every curve while still managing to look completely professional is such a cock tease.

She assesses my approach with a scowl and glances over her shoulder toward the door. When she's sure no one else is coming out, she opens those beautiful lips. "No bullshit tonight."

And here we go...

I tighten my hands around my stick and rest it on the ground between my skates. "Did you stand out here all this time just to get up in my face, Coach?"

She pushes off the wall and steps toward me. "If you start with any of your normal stuff tonight, I will pull you and put you on the goddamn bench. Don't think your big contract scares me. This is still *my* team."

Someone put their big girl pants on today.

I like it.

Rather than avoid another unpleasant confrontation, she's opted to go the direct and aggressive route.

Well, two can play at that game, Coach.

I step into her until only a foot separates us. She squares

her shoulders and straightens her spine, trying to appear bigger, since even in her heels, her eyes barely reach my shoulders.

The move is adorable.

"Thanks for the warning, Coach." I move my stick until it's right between us and wrap my right hand around it at her eye-level. "Are you gonna tell me how to handle my *stick*, too?"

Her mouth drops open, and that adorable flush crawls up her neck and across her cheeks. "You are one cocky son of a bitch, you know that?"

I smirk and pull my helmet on. "Thank you for noticing."

With a parting wink, I step around her and make my way toward the ice and the line of my teammates waiting to head out for warm-ups.

The roar of the waiting crowd drowns out everything, but I still sense her approaching me from behind. Hairs on the back of my neck stand up in anticipation—and so does something else—but not for the game.

Well, isn't that interesting?

Bickering with Greer may have just turned into my guilty pleasure.

She brushes past me without a glance in my direction and moves down the line of players before she disappears out into the arena.

I take a deep breath and shake out my legs.

First game as a Scorpion.

This is my chance to show them why taking me wasn't a mistake but rather the best decision they ever made for this team. They need to see that paying me the big bucks is worth it and why Coach's concerns shouldn't matter.

I slam my stick against the ground.

Time to fucking do this.

GREER

"Number 71—two minutes for slashing." The ref's announcement burns my ears, and Bash heads to the penalty box for the third time tonight.

I tighten my hands into fists at my side. "Goddammit."

We've barely started the third period and it already feels like we've been killing penalties for the entire game. If Bash had as many goals as trips to the sin bin, we wouldn't be in this position.

I glance up at the scoreboard, even though I know what it says. Down by two. Nineteen minutes to get our shit together and pull out a win. We haven't been playing all that badly. The Rockets have just been playing better...and Bash's penalties certainly don't help.

He huffs and drops onto the seat in the penalty box and watches the game without even glancing in my direction. The man can't even look me in the eye.

Every second we're short-handed, my anxiety ramps up. Nineteen minutes simultaneously creeps like a snail and whizzes by faster than the blink of an eye with two more penalties for Bash after a cross-check and another slashing call.

When the final buzzer finally sounds, I give my usual required interview then storm back to my office.

Dammit, Bash. I knew he was going to pull this bullshit.

I slam my door shut behind me. Anger rises, curling my hands into fists and causing blood to rush in my ears.

It was deliberate.

He was trying to show me that he can get away with doing whatever he wants here, and Bob won't let me pull him. And he was right. Bob pulled *me* aside between the first

39

and second periods and made it clear he wanted him in, no matter what. But apparently having Bash on the ice for his first game as a Scorpion put butts in the seats and created a media frenzy Bob didn't want to lose out on.

So much for this being my team.

I asked Mac to tell Bash to come to talk to me, but I don't even know what I'm going to say at this point. I just want to throw something—more like everything—at him.

My stapler.

That stack of papers.

My Olympic medals hanging on the wall.

What's left of my fucking *sanity*.

Anything not bolted down is now a weapon, and Bash Fury's head is the smug target.

The door opens without a knock, and the object of my frustration saunters in wearing nothing but a cocky grin and a white towel wrapped around his trim waist. Water droplets glisten across his chiseled, tattooed chest, and rivulets run down the hills and valleys of his perfect abs, over the elegant script etched into his skin there.

Jesus.

Bash Fury is bad for my libido.

I swallow through my dry throat. "Don't you know how to knock?"

"Don't you know my eyes are up here, Coach?"

Shit.

I jerk my focus away from where the towel crosses right in front of his crotch and meet his gaze. He raises a knowing eyebrow and smirks.

There's no way I'm letting him get the last clever jab. I raise an eyebrow in return. "Don't you know how to dry off after a shower?"

God. That was lame, Greer.

Bash shrugs and closes the door behind him. "Mac said

you needed to see me, so, like a good little boy, I came running, Coach."

The sarcasm in his voice hangs thick in the air. It seems like every time Bash and I are in the same vicinity, another showdown happens. It's like we both come into this with our dukes up and no ability to maintain any semblance of professionalism when we're around each other. It doesn't bode well for the future of our communications.

I've dealt with difficult players before. Guys who thought I shouldn't be coaching them and didn't know shit about the game, but Bash is by far the worst. A fact he seems rather *proud* of.

"What the hell was that?" I point toward the ice with a huff.

He offers me another casual shrug and crosses his arms over his chest. His biceps bulge, and another rivulet trails down to the edge of the towel.

My eyes drift over the scrawled verses on his right collarbone and left rib cage, but he shifts and covers the words before I can read them.

"I don't know what you mean, Coach. What was *what*?"

Grrr.

I force myself to take a deep breath that should be cleansing, but all it does is suck the crisp, clean, manly scent of Bash and his soap into my lungs.

Crap.

I shake my head to try to clear out that smell. "That bullshit you pulled out there tonight. We lost the goddamn game because of all your penalties."

He scoffs and moves a few steps closer to the desk. His eyes narrow, and his jaw tightens. "We lost the game because they played better."

I plant my hands on the desktop and lean toward him. "And *we* would've played better if you hadn't spent so much fucking time in the penalty box. We were short-handed five times because of you, alone. Not to mention the other penalties that fucked us."

A muscle in his clenched jaw flexes as he stares me down. His hard amber eyes never waver from mine for even a millisecond.

Don't look away, Greer.

I fight the urge to avert my eyes from his penetrating gaze. The way he looks at me is unnerving, like he can see every tiny weakness I have and is willing to exploit them to get what he wants.

"If you really think we would have won if I hadn't had those penalties, then you've just admitted I'm invaluable to this team and proved my point that you need to let me play and do my thing."

I slam my palm against the desk. "You play dirty."

He sneers. "I play to win."

"Winning doesn't mean anything if you have to hurt people to get there, Bash."

I played *hard* in my days on the ice, but one thing I *never* did was set out to hurt someone else. There's a difference between playing hard and playing dirty. One he apparently doesn't or can't comprehend.

He considers me for a moment and takes a few more steps forward until the only thing separating us is the three feet span of wood on the top of the desk. My eyes automatically track down to where his arms are crossed over his chest again.

Shit.

I jerk them back up before he can comment again, but I've been caught.

He flashes me a smile that probably has had hundreds of women falling into his bed all over the country. "Look, Coach"—he runs a hand back through his wet hair, only

42

accentuating his beautiful, lean muscles—"you and I have different philosophies on the game. That much is clear. It doesn't mean we have to be enemies."

"It doesn't mean you have to be a jerk."

That cocky, panty-melting half-grin returns, and he moves forward and spreads his palms flat against the desk, leaning in until our noses almost touch over it. The clean, cool scent that wrapped around me earlier almost knocks me over now.

"No"—one corner of his lips curls up—"my personality means I have to be. But you don't think I'm a jerk. Not really. You just don't want to admit it to yourself."

I pull back and shake my head.

Unfuckingbelievable.

This guy has an ego bigger than the Grand Canyon.

He doesn't move from his position poised over the desk. "You know how it is, Coach...to be the best player on the team. To be the *best* of the best."

Wait a second...was that a compliment?

His biceps flex, and he glances at the wall where my Olympic medals hang. "I watched you play. I know how talented you were as a player and how good of a coach you must be to have brought the team to where it is today in such a short period of time."

"But..."

Here it comes.

Bash Fury is incapable of giving me a real compliment. I should have known.

"...you're inexperienced. I've played for coaches who have done this for twenty or thirty years. I see a novice like you, and I feel obligated to help you figure it out."

"Figure it out?" I scoff. "Is that what you think you're helping me do? The only thing you've figured out is how to get me to develop high blood pressure."

He jerks back with a grin. "It's nice to know I have that effect on you."

"You don't have any effect on me." My response is a little too quick and a little too sharp. There's no way he didn't notice.

He points at the small *V* in my blouse just above my breasts. "That flush rising up your neck says otherwise, Coach."

And there he goes again.

Paying me a compliment in one second and flipping right back into flirtatious, arrogant Bash the next. Typical behavior given what I've heard about his reputation and already experienced myself in the two days he's been here.

This kind of attitude cannot continue. I won't fight with one of my players for control for the rest of the damn season. "You may come from NHL royalty, Bash, but that doesn't mean you know everything. You are not the god of hockey."

Sex god...maybe...if the swagger he puts out is more than just an act, but I won't ever be finding out if he can live up to the game he plays.

I point at him. "You are *not* the know-all and end-all of the sport. No matter what you think, this is *my* team. You need to remember that. I won't hesitate to bench you if you do this again."

5

BASH

I step back and hold up my hands in mock surrender. "I just play the game, Coach. A game you are really fucking good at." Her already wide green eyes open more and draw my smirk even wider. "What, Coach, you think I don't know who you are? You think I don't know your history? You think I don't know all that you've accomplished?" I wave at her medals. "It's fucking impressive for a man, let alone for a woman. And I'm not some sexist pig. I have a sister. I had a mother."

Those last words are hard to get out. The fact that she's gone still hasn't completely registered in my heart. Maybe it never will.

"This disagreement we're having has nothing to do with the fact that you're a woman. It has to do with the fact that you don't have any experience head coaching at this level."

Greer undoubtedly thinks I'm some sort of misogynist because I've been pushing her, but what she has to realize is, I'd be pushing *anyone*—regardless of what they have between their legs.

It's just who I am. It's who I was raised to be. Mike Fury never backed down from any fight or bent for anyone, and he expected the same from me. It's what drove me to this point in my life, and it's made me the player I am today.

She huffs at me. "And let me guess...you know more about the NHL than anyone, right? Because you were basically raised in it?"

Her earlier comment about being from "NHL royalty" rolls around in my head with her new comment. I should've known it would get brought into this somehow. The man hasn't played in twenty years, but it's still the first thing people bring up when they meet me.

I always swore to myself I wouldn't become him, that I would take only what he taught me about hockey and be a better person than he was off the ice. Because people just don't understand who he really is, who he really *was*. And maybe this isn't the time or place to air my personal family shit, but I don't want her to get it in her pretty head that I think I deserve something because of who my sperm donor happens to be. "I barely knew my father, Greer."

And what I did know isn't anything I would ever want to talk about with anyone, especially my new coach.

Her features soften slightly, but she maintains her defensive stance.

I wave a hand at her. "You know what this life is like. He was always on the road. Always traveling. And when he was traded, there were large portions of time we didn't even live in the same city." I fist my hands at my sides as tension seeps into my body at the memories. "My brother and sister and I went to three different grade schools. We lived in four different houses and had different sets of friends in each city until my mother finally put her foot down and told him we were moving back to Michigan, with or without him. That isn't any way to live. That certainly isn't

46

any way to parent. So, please don't compare me to my father."

He may have been a great player, but he wasn't a great person. He was an angry drunk who beat Jameson and me more times than I could count and never offered me a kind word. Even excelling in this game he loved so much wasn't enough to warrant his praise.

I want to snap at her. I want to explain what a douchebag the man really was, but I can't. I can't tarnish the memory of the *real* Fury, the one everyone worships as a hockey god. The man whose last name I'm forced to share.

So, instead of burdening her with the truth, I sigh and run a hand through my wet hair. "Mike Fury may have been a shit father, but he was a fantastic hockey player, and even though there are those who would accuse me of coasting by on his name, we both know it's not true. I made my own career."

She sighs and crosses her arms over her chest. I can't help but refocus my attention on her breasts and how they heave with her anger.

I raise an eyebrow at her. "Is this the way it's going to be? Am I going to spend the rest of my contract here arguing with you before and after every game?"

A tiny frown line forms in the middle of her brow, and she chews on the corner of her lip. "Until you prove to me that you can play the game without excessive penalties and with some respect for the other players...yes."

"I'm not a bad guy, Coach."

She holds up a hand to stop me. "I don't care if you're a bad guy or not. All I care about is what you bring to the team."

Ouch. That stings.

It's not that I believe anything would ever go anywhere with her—regardless of how attractive I think she is and

47

how entertaining it is to have these arguments with her— but hearing her say she doesn't give a shit about me except for what I can do for the Scorpions is kind of a bruise to my not so fragile ego.

"Is that in debate?" I raise an eyebrow. "What I can do for the team?"

She runs her hands through her silky hair. It falls softly onto her shoulders, and something stirs below the belt that's pretty dangerous. Especially with just a towel covering me.

"I don't want us to be enemies, Coach, but I can't change who or what I am."

I will always play hard. I will always be a physical player because that's what comes naturally to me, the way I was *trained* to play. And despite what she may think, it isn't about trying to hurt people. Pushing around the opposing team is sometimes a necessary evil, one I'm very good at.

She straightens her shoulders and sets her jaw. "Neither can I."

"Fair enough." I step back from the desk and turn toward the door. The question sits on the tip of my tongue, but it isn't until I pull open the door and glance back at her that it finally slips from my lips. "And just what *are* you, Greer?"

Her eyes soften as she considers my question for a moment. She wasn't expecting it. She didn't think I would care. "I'm a woman in a man's sport trying to prove that I belong here. I'm someone who other little girls who love hockey can look up to and see that they can achieve something in this sport. I'm the gateway to getting women accepted into the NHL."

She's right about all of that.

"That seems like a lot of weight to carry on your shoulders alone, don't you think?"

She shrugs. "It is what it is. And it would be a lot easier if you weren't intentionally making it difficult for me."

A grin tugs at the corner of my lips. "Who says I'm doing it intentionally?"

She stands bewildered, and just as I'm about to pull the door closed behind me, I fight the part of my brain telling me to keep going to the locker room, and instead, I turn back toward where she still stands behind her desk.

I have no idea what just happened between us, but I like it far more than I should. And I shouldn't say the words sitting on the tip of my tongue, but I know I will all the same because apparently, I never do what's right.

GREER

His broad shoulders bunch and flex as he turns back to me again.

Christ, he really is hot.

The team should put him on a marketing poster in nothing but his birthday suit and a hockey stick. We would make a killing and sell out every damn game. And something tells me Bash Fury would eat up every second of the attention it would bring him.

Bash scans me from head to toe. "Seems like you might need to relax a little, Coach. You're coiled tighter than a cobra ready to strike." His lips spread into a classic Bash smirk. "If you ever need to relieve a little tension, let me know. I have a few ideas on how we can take care of that."

He pulls the door shut behind him before I have time to even process his words.

What the hell just happened?

My legs shake, and I drop down onto my chair.

Between the compliment and the blatant flirting and the hostility and annoyance, the man is giving me a serious case of whiplash.

Was that a real glimmer of humanity I saw in Bash when he talked about his father? Or was it all just an act? A way to try to smooth over things between us so that his career won't be at risk?

He seems willing to do anything to cement his position on this team, which is why his parting comment couldn't have been said seriously. He couldn't have been insinuating we should hook up. That would be wildly inappropriate, even if I didn't despise the man.

And I do...despise him.

His arrogance is enough to make anyone hate the man.

I grab the bottle of water from my desk and guzzle down half of it. The cool liquid does nothing to calm the heat flooding my body after what just went down between us. Bash's proximity and near nakedness were wreaking havoc on me despite how much he pisses me off.

Because, as much as I hate to admit it, Jill was right. Bash is exactly the type of guy I would usually go for. Under different circumstances. And with a different personality. He's too much like the men who have broken my heart and crushed my spirit in the past.

I want to believe when he says he's not a bad guy. I want to believe he truly has good intentions and is only here to help the team, but men like Bash Fury only do things that benefit themselves.

That's something I learned a long time ago. It's something that has helped me keep this wall of ice around my heart over the years despite the men who have tried to chip away at it.

The one time I let that wall down, that I let someone in and relied on them, let myself believe in happily ever afters, I got burned. And it won't happen again, especially not at the hands of a man like Bash, who doesn't even try to hide who or what he really is. Finding a selfless man is rare in this world. And Bash is about as far from selfless as anyone I've ever met.

So, why does my hand shake thinking about him being here and staring me down with those whiskey eyes?

Maybe because I'm a fucking fool to think I'm going to be able to control him.

There's a reason the Warhawks traded him away, and it wasn't because of lack of performance. The man was one of their highest scorers this season. It was because they can't control him. And if a coach with that much experience and respect in the position couldn't get through to Bash, then I don't stand a fucking chance.

What the hell should I do about him?

I dig my phone out of my purse, scroll through my contacts, and hit send.

It rings three times before the man I need to talk to answers. "Greer? I wasn't expecting to hear from you tonight. I saw the game."

Dad's voice washes over me like a soothing balm. I close my eyes and drop my head back against the chair's headrest. "Yeah. It wasn't good."

He chuckles and turns down the television in the background. "No, it wasn't, sweetheart, but you win some, you lose some."

"That's easy for you to say. Your career doesn't depend on you winning."

"I don't have a career, sweetheart. I'm retired."

"My point exactly." And when he was working as a custodian at the community college, it was to pay for my hockey camps and ice time and everything else that comes with having a daughter obsessed so completely with a sport that's so damn expensive. "So, what's going on, sweetheart? You just called to say hi to your old man?"

I roll the half-full bottle of water between my hands. "I don't know, Dad. I guess I just need a male perspective."

"Then, you've come to the right place. Perspective on what?"

Having to even ask him this is another blow to my ego, but I need help and don't have anywhere else to go. I would bounce it off Bob, but he's already made his position on this particular problem crystal clear. "On what to do with a player who doesn't seem to respect my authority or think I can do the job."

"Who's the asshole who thinks that? That Bash Fury?"

Leave it to Dad to see exactly what's happening right from the beginning, even from five states away and through the television. He always was insightful. It was one of the things Mom loved and hated about him. He always knew when something was bugging her, even when she claimed things were fine, and was able to pick up on the subtle clues in her body language.

"How did you know?"

He snorts. "You should've seen the way the cameras kept zooming in on your face every time he got a penalty. You looked like your head was about ready to pop off."

Shit.

"Here I thought I was doing a pretty good job of controlling my emotions."

"Sweetheart, you have a lot of gifts. Controlling your emotions is not one of them. It's not an insult. It's just a statement of fact. Your mother was the same way. Wore her heart on her sleeve."

He's right. I never have been good at concealing my emotions. But I've never had to. I've never been on a stage with the focus on me like this before. Even during the

Olympics, on a world stage, there were other major players, other teams. Then Bob was the focus when we were coaching. This is completely different.

I'm the one they're watching. I'm the one they're hoping will fail. "Was it that bad?"

"No, sweetheart. I mean, maybe..."

"Great."

He sighs. "I think any coach would have been pissed, honey. Bash was definitely out of line on at least a couple of those penalties."

"You think I should bench him?"

Dad barks out a laugh that rumbles through the phone. "Oh, hell, sweetheart, I can't tell you that. You're the coach, not me."

"Yeah, but you've watched hockey longer than I've been alive and sat through all my practices and games. I trust your opinion."

"The Scorpions didn't hire you for your dad's opinions, Greer. They hired you for your personal experience and for what *you* think. You need to trust your gut."

He makes it sound so easy.

Trust your gut.

It's such a *dad* thing to say. He's been giving me the same advice my entire life, but this feels so different. Maybe because Bash Fury has my gut twisted up in knots.

"What if I don't know what my gut is telling me?"

"Then, you wait 'til you do know."

As if it's that simple.

6

GREER

Thank God.

It seems our little talk after the last game, while uncomfortable and unsettling in so many ways, may have actually gotten through to Bash. Maybe our travel day getting to Seattle gave him time to consider what I said and the ramifications of not cleaning up his game.

I certainly had what he said to me racing through my mind over the last couple of days. It occupied my thoughts far more than it should have. The truth is, he rattled me, more than I even want to admit to myself, let alone to Jill or Dad.

And I'm still not sure if anything I said got through to him or not. But *something* happened. *Something* changed.

I glance up at the scoreboard. Three minutes left, and we're up by one.

Come on, guys. Keep it tight.

Clean passes. Clean shots.

All we need to do is hold it together for three fucking minutes, and we've got this game.

Whenever we play the Whales on their home ice, it's a madhouse in here. These are the kind of conference rivalries that make the fans insane. The crowd cheers and screams so loudly, we can barely hear ourselves think. Some would see it as a problem, but the energy is infectious. It always makes us play harder and faster.

Tonight is no exception. The guys look good. *Really* good. And Bash has managed to stay out of the penalty box the *entire* game. That's practically unheard of for him. The commentators are probably scrambling to find that statistic to give to the viewers at home.

Having him on the ice rather than in the sin bin has been a huge asset. He's scored two of our four goals and has been lightning-fast and precise with his passes tonight. It's incredible to watch a player of Bash's caliber have a good night.

I'd love to see more performances like this, and I hope I'm now a little voice inside his head reminding him that he doesn't have to hurt people to play well.

But who the hell knows with Bash?

This could be a fluke. Or, maybe Dad was right, and this is just what I needed to know what my gut was telling me about Bash. That maybe, just maybe, there's some humanity under all that bravado, arrogance, and grins.

He jumps back out onto the ice after a short break and gets right into the play, knocking the Whales' Orlov to the boards. Orlov struggles to get back to his feet as his teammate Carlson picks up the puck, but it was a good hit. The type of hit hockey is *supposed* to have.

I have no problem with the violence in the sport, but it doesn't mean it needs to go beyond that. A few lost teeth and some blood are expected. It's unchecked tempers that cause problems, and the tensions are always high when we play the Whales, especially on their home ice. It usually leads to more than one scuffle, yet tonight has been surprisingly calm.

Keep up the good work, Bash.

One twenty-five left.

Just hold it together, guys.

Kasinski manages to wrestle the puck away from Carlson and takes off down the ice into the neutral zone with Mac and Bash right behind him. He knocks it back to Mac, and Mac drives the puck to the goal, zigzags around two defenders, and shoots...straight into the net.

Yes! Goal!

It's a little cushion. A little bit of wiggle room that makes the remaining minute seem a slightly more manageable.

The guys celebrate on the ice, and the Scorpion fans who traveled for the game erupt as do the guys on the bench in front of me.

It's the best part about playing the sport or coaching it—the crowds, the fans. The uninhibited joy that a goal and ultimately, a win, can bring to them is something I can't even begin to explain to someone who hasn't experienced it for themselves.

Playing in the Olympics showed me the camaraderie and national pride in the team and the support we got no matter what country we were in is the same when the Scorpions travel. Even at the away games, there are so many fans wearing our jerseys and people cheering for us.

A new team with the Cinderella season. People love cheering for an underdog. And we certainly are one. Now, having a superstar like Bash Fury on the team, it feels like our fan base has only exploded in the last week since the trade announcement.

His jersey is already outselling any other member of the team. That probably rubs a few of the guys—like Lebedev—the wrong way, but that's always going to happen when big egos butt heads. Thankfully, that situation hasn't come to blows, and even though there's definitely still some tension between him and Bash, whether they're on the ice together or not, it hasn't interfered with the game, and that's all I care about.

What's best for this team. And getting the two points gives us a little more space ahead of the Stingrays who are closing in behind us in fourth in the conference right now. It also inches us closer to second place.

The guys line up for the face-off, and Lebedev—in for Hayes who is getting a skate issue fixed by Steve—gets away with the puck. He shoots it over to Mac, who makes his way into the slot and knocks it over to Bash. Orlov takes out Mac right after the pass, and Berglund flies across the ice and slams into Bash, nailing him against the boards.

Bash climbs to his feet, and even from across the ice, I can see his fists clenched in his gloves.

Don't do it, Bash.

A second passes, and he relaxes slightly, apparently reconsidering whatever response action he was about to take.

He let it go.

At least, for the time being. The problem with guys like Bash is you never know when the shit is going to hit the fan. It's the kind of hit that demands some sort of reaction, and with Bash, that means gloves-off.

Berglund skates past him, following the puck, now in Whale possession, back toward the neutral zone. Bash jerks his head toward him as if Berglund said something to him, but from this far away, there's no way to know what was said.

More than ten feet separate us, but the burning rage in Bash's eyes flashes hot enough that it glows enough for me to see even from the bench. He instantly morphs from the "new and improved" Sebastian Fury he's been all night into the one who played in the last game, the one who got traded because he became a liability.

The one who is *dangerous.*

Oh shit.

BASH

The game has been going so damn well. We're playing great, and if it weren't for a few perfectly placed shots that even a stellar performance by our goalie, Pierre, couldn't stop, we would be winning four to zero instead of four to two.

It's the kind of game we needed, not only to help us gain some points on the Stingrays but also to solidify my place on this team. Mac and I have easily fallen back into our roles, and despite our differences, Lebedev has played well with us when he's rotated in.

I thought there would for sure be some animosity, maybe some selfish play on his part, but he's smarter than I gave him credit for. He knows if he pulls any of that bullshit, Greer will call him out and bench him, just like she threatened to do with me.

A threat that hasn't had to come into play tonight. Time's almost up, and somehow, I managed to stay out of the penalty box today.

Miracle of all miracles...

Though not because of Coach's warning the other day. Not because I became a fucking pussy overnight. It's just been a game that hasn't needed that kind of play.

And until Berglund slammed me against the boards a few seconds ago, I thought it was going to stay that way. It was a dirty hit—I know because I make the same move all the time. A cross-check from behind when the refs aren't watching.

Any other night, I might have retaliated immediately, but when Greer's eyes connected with mine, it was like a soothing balm spread over an open wound oozing anger.

Let it go, Bash.

I return my focus to the puck and shift to the right to try to get in on the play.

"I slammed you into those boards almost as hard as I slammed your coach last night." Berglund's taunting words come from my left.

I jerk my head around just as he skates past me with a lecherous grin. He wiggles his eyebrows suggestively, and it's like a bomb detonates inside me.

White-hot rage surges through my veins, and any control I had this entire game disintegrates in a millisecond.

"What the fuck did you just say, asshole?" I charge after him and slam him to the glass with my forearm against his throat.

The game continues on behind us, both of us oblivious to anything other than what's happening in our few square feet of the ice.

He twists his head and laughs. "Your coach was so damn tight. I slammed her all fucking night long."

I drop my gloves in the flash of an eye. My fist whips out and hits his jaw so fast that he never sees it coming. I barely even realize I'm doing it.

The force of my strike drops him to the ice. His head snaps back, and his helmet flies off. It might be enough to stop someone else from taking this any further, but I'm not someone else. And what I just did to him is nowhere near what he deserves for that fucking comment.

He could be dead for all I care.

I don't give a shit.

No one. Fucking *no one* talks about Greer like that.

This motherfucking prick!

My fists connect with his face over and over again, each blow sending the back of his head slamming against the ice. Blood pools under him and trickles from his nose and mouth, but it doesn't stop me. The rage he's unleashed is unlike anything I've ever felt before.

This isn't about defending my team or even defending myself or my own honor. It's about defending *hers*, and the lack of respect this fucker just showed her after everything she's done to make it here can't go unpunished.

It's certainly never a position I thought I'd ever find myself in—the avenging angel defending the honor of my female coach out on the ice—yet here I am, bloodying my hands for a woman who can barely stand to be in the same room as me.

Strong hands tug at my arms, and someone else tries to shove himself between us, but I push both out of the way— barely taking notice of the black and white uniforms they wear. Several of my teammates surround me, the familiar gold and black jersey colors visible, but my vision is too blurred by anger to be able to tell which ones finally drag me away from the bloodied Berglund on the ice.

"Jesus, Bash, what the fuck did you do?" Mac stands above and behind me, one arm wrapped around my chest to hold me back.

I glance back at him, and the world around me that had been so distorted by my anger finally starts to clear. Red still fills it though. I shake my head and squeeze my eyes shut. The roar of the crowd, usually such a positive, driving force, suddenly stings my ears.

"Bash? Are you okay?" The concern heavy in Mac's question has me reopening my eyes to take in the scene before me.

The Whales medical staff huddles around Berglund down on the ice. Blood stains the area around him—a lot of blood. A vision of what I did to Miller in the game that got me traded here flashes at the forefront of my brain. My teammates struggle to push back the other Whales, to keep them from getting to me where I'm still being restrained by Mac.

I finally notice the sharp sting in my hands, and I stare down at the broken skin and blood over my knuckles. Bile fills my throat, and I swallow it down while examining the aftermath of my rampage.

Oh shit. What the fuck did I just do?

My gaze slowly drifts over to our bench. Hard green eyes glare back at me with so much wrath it hits me harder than any other player ever has.

I thought I was angry to have been able to do this, but what lives in Coach's stare right now is ten times worse.

Fuck. I just royally fucked this up.

7

BASH

The heavy door slams shut behind me, and I shove past Mac into our hotel room. He watches me warily from where he stands near the bathroom but wisely doesn't say anything.

Any conversation he might try to engage me in would only go nowhere. The last thing I want to do is talk after a game like that. And the fact that we're stuck in this hotel another night instead of flying back to Vegas like we planned because of a freak ice storm shutting down the airport is just adding salt to the open wound.

Even a walk in the freezing rain didn't help, and the cold eventually forced me back in here, like a caged fucking animal.

I drop onto my back on the bed and rest my forearm over my eyes. A huge sigh slips from between my lips. Even with my eyes squeezed shut, I can feel Mac looming over me, staring down, but he doesn't say a word.

What is his fucking problem?

I lift my arm and peer up at him with one eye. "What?"

He crosses his arms over his chest and raises a brow. "You know what. What the fuck happened back there? I've never seen you like that, and that's saying a lot considering you're Bash fucking Fury."

None of the guys *dared* speak to me in the locker room after that. They knew better than to approach me in that condition, but Mac knows me too well. We've been friends for too long for him to drop it.

I lower my arm back down across my face. Mac isn't owed an explanation for my behavior, and regardless, I don't want to repeat what was said about Greer. She doesn't deserve that. Those words should never be spoken by anyone, let alone by a colleague who knows what it means for her to be in this position and that she's more than qualified.

The simple answer will have to do. "He was being an asshole. He deserved it."

"That's all you're gonna say? He deserved it?"

"Yeah"—I shift up onto my elbows—"that's all I'm gonna say."

Mac scoffs and shakes his head. "You think that will be a good enough explanation for Coach? She was pretty damn pissed."

Don't I know it...

The fact that she wasn't waiting for me outside the locker room after the game to tear me a new asshole says a hell of a lot more than if she had reamed me out.

She's so angry, she couldn't even talk to me about it.

Shit. Shit. Shit.

Normally, I wouldn't give a flying fuck what one of my coaches thought about something like what went down tonight, but ever since I saw the hurt and anger in her eyes seeing what I'd done, I haven't been able to shake the queasiness in my stomach.

I need to explain myself. She needs to know I wasn't just being a dick.

This time, anyway.

It's insane. And it's definitely never happened before. But for some inexplicable reason, I actually give a fuck what Coach thinks about me as a person, not just as a player.

I shove off the bed and rub at the back of my neck as I try to move around him.

Mac takes a step back. "Where the hell are you going with that determined look on your face?"

"None of your fucking business."

He grabs my arm. "It is my business if you're gonna go do something stupid, Bash."

I growl at him, and he releases my arm.

Probably a wise move on his part. We played together long enough in Chicago for him to understand that this isn't the time to push me.

I stride to the door and yank it open. "Don't worry. I promise it's not anything stupid."

"Oh, yeah, that's really reassuring coming from you."

I roll my eyes and let the door slam shut behind me. The sound echoes down the ghostly silent hallway.

Going to my coach's room in the middle of the night is probably not a great idea, but there's no way I'm getting any sleep tonight knowing how pissed off she is when she doesn't know the whole story.

Everything is deserted as I make my way toward her room at the opposite end of the building. I blow past all the rooms on either side of the hall, where my teammates are probably sleeping soundly. The only reason Mac was even still awake was because he was waiting for me to show up after I went for a walk to cool down and think.

I stop outside her door and glance at my watch. It's almost one. She might already be asleep. This should probably wait until tomorrow. I can tell her when we're on the plane rather than disrupt her when she might already be asleep.

That's the rational decision.

The one I should make.

I turn to walk away, but the anger tightening my chest forces me to spin back.

No. I can't let Greer go to bed, thinking I'm some fucking asshole who just beats people up for the hell of it.

And I refuse to consider why it matters so much what she thinks of me, but it does. Something about that look in her eyes...the disappointment there...it's just eating away at me from the inside. The same way it always did when Mom looked at me that way. With Dad, it wasn't about disappointment. It was always anger. Even his fists never hurt as much as Mom giving me that same look Greer did.

I rap my knuckles against the door and wait. She would be wise not to answer—for both of us. But the chain slides, a deadbolt turns, and she pulls open the door.

The same hard eyes that glared at me from the bench meet mine. She crosses her arms over her chest. The thin white T-shirt and yoga pants she's wearing leave very little to the imagination.

Christ, she's stunning.

Toned and firm in all the right places. Hips big enough to grab onto. And her breasts...

She's probably crossing her arms over her chest because she's not wearing a bra. The shirt is practically see-through, and I can't find any telltale signs of straps.

And I absolutely should *not* be ogling my coach—now or *ever*.

I swallow through my suddenly dry throat. "Can I come in?"

She narrows her hard gaze on me and then glances back

into her room. Her bare foot taps, drawing my attention to the bright-red polish on her toes.

Why is that so damn hot?

"My eyes are up here, Bash."

I jerk my head up to find a flash of annoyance in her stare.

Shit. Called out with my own line.

We stare each other down a moment, neither of us willing to look away or back down, both of us intent on proving *something* in this moment. It would be easy to walk away, to tell her we can talk tomorrow, to let her cool off and allow myself to do the same, but I don't move.

I'm held in place by the pain and disappointment in her gaze.

Eventually, she nudges open the door farther and lets me brush past her. The crisp scent of soap mingles with something flowery and sweet that's all Greer. I inhale deeply and try to shake the image of what she looks like under those very flimsy, comfortable clothes.

Even though she likely thinks so, I'm not a complete dog. I know it's all kinds of wrong to be attracted to the woman who is—for all intents and purposes—my boss, but I'm also a human male who has eyes and a body that reacts to things despite my best attempt not to.

And right now, with her pale-blond hair piled high on the top of her head in some sort of bun, face free of makeup, and her lip pulled between her teeth, she looks far too young to be coaching grown men.

God, even with no makeup on and in these clothes, she's freaking beautiful.

She pauses at the door a minute, staring out at the hall where I just stood, as if she's contemplating sending me right back out there instead of coming to join me in the room. I open my mouth to say something, but I bite it

67

back as she lets the door close and follows me into the room.

I watch her steady, deliberate approach, that acid in my stomach churning and working its way up my throat.

She stops well back from me, and anger twists her lips into a frown. "What the hell do you want, Bash?"

———

GREER

It can't get any more inappropriate than having a player in my hotel room in the middle of the night.

I should never have let this man in. I should've told him to go back to his room and to bed. He's the last person I should be talking to right now considering how fucking pissed I am at him.

One thing Dad always told me was to never lash out when I'm angry. And I've already failed miserably at that since Sebastian Fury arrived. I had planned to talk to Bash later. To give myself a day or two to calm down so that I wouldn't say or do anything I may regret. Like kick him off the damn team and have to deal with the fallout from Bob that could affect my own career.

But he looks so genuinely distressed—dark-blond hair disheveled, brow furrowed, and eyes darkened—by something I can't quite place.

I hate to see somebody so upset even if that someone is on my shit list. If there's something he needs to get off his chest about what happened in tonight's game, I'll let him. Then, I'll kick him out so I can get to bed before we have to get up early tomorrow to fly home for our next game.

Arriving half a day late is going to mess with our entire

schedule, but in addition to not being able to control Bash Fury, I also apparently can't control the weather.

The man who's the current focus of my ire and has occupied far too many of my thoughts since he arrived moves to the corner of the room by the small table near the window and runs his hand through his hair. Stress tenses his shoulders, and he fists his hands at his sides.

"What are you doing here, Bash? What's so important that this can't wait until we get back to Vegas to discuss?"

He shakes his head and rubs his jaw. "I need to explain what happened today."

"No, you don't. It's pretty fucking clear what happened." At least, it was to me. "You completely ignored everything we talked about because you're Bash Fury, and Bash Fury doesn't follow the rules. Bash Fury does whatever the hell he wants."

He recoils slightly at the harsh words I hurl at him like daggers. "Is that really what you think? That I'm *inherently* a bad guy?"

If he had flat out asked me the same question a few days ago, I probably would have said no. I likely would have told him I believe no one is *inherently* bad and everyone has something good deep inside them. It's the very thing Jill warned me I would look for, the thing I thought I saw during that brief moment in my office.

But what he did tonight has me questioning that belief. Maybe it's naïve to think there's good in people. Maybe some human beings are just born bad, through no fault of their own. With volatile tempers, lack of conscience, and general apathy toward other humans.

This isn't the first time he's beaten the shit out of someone for no apparent reason other than a foul that happens every night on dozens of rinks. The same thing *he* has done hundreds of times to someone else during his career. It didn't warrant his response. Not in any way, shape, or form. And Bash *knows* it.

That's the most frustrating part of it all. He's clearly intelligent and understands why I feel the way I do, yet he just can't break the cycle—even in a new city with a new team.

My conversation with Dad has been running through my head since I watched Bash decimate Berglund on the ice in a blind rage only hours ago.

"Trust your gut."

"What if I don't know what my gut is telling me?"

"Then, you wait 'til you do know."

I know now. After seeing that, it's clear this man is completely out of control. It's not safe for anyone for him to be out on the ice, and he will only drag the team down.

Despite the distress on his face, I have to answer him honestly. "You've done absolutely nothing to prove otherwise, Bash. In fact, what happened tonight just proves my point. You're out of control, and out of control is dangerous in this game."

He clenches his teeth—probably to keep from retorting with something he shouldn't say to his coach—and a muscle tics along his perfectly chiseled jaw. His chest heaves as he sucks in deep breaths, the fabric of his t-shirt tightening against his pecs and abs.

My words seem to have genuinely upset him.

Why the hell does he care what I think?

He certainly doesn't act like he cares what anyone thinks when he's out on the ice.

"Bash, you really hurt him tonight. He has a severe concussion. He lost four teeth, and you busted one of his orbital sockets."

Bash scrubs his hands over his face. "Shit."

"You did all *that* today for no reason. You don't have any

control. You're going to get suspended for what happened —*again*. When your suspension is up, there's no room on the Scorpions for a player like you."

That muscle in his jaw jumps, and the air between us thickens. His fists open and close at his sides. He's fuming mad. It's the same look he got on the ice—like a bull ready to charge.

I shouldn't say anything more other than "get out," but I can't keep myself from pushing more. "I thought..." I suck in a sharp breath, crossing my arms over my chest. "I really thought tonight that things had changed. That maybe you had *somehow* taken my concerns to heart and wanted to try to make your time here work." Shaking my head, I stare up at the white, textured ceiling, trying to blink away the threat of tears I absolutely shouldn't be crying over this situation. I return my gaze to him. "I thought there might be a chance. But you shattered that in one fucking second with your damn temper."

He flinches as if I've struck him and takes a half step toward me, opening his mouth to reply, but he bites back whatever it is he was going to say in favor of storming past me and jerking open the door.

Just like when he left my office, he pauses for a split second, as if he wants to turn back and say something, but then he shakes his head and it slams shut behind him, sending a deep vibration through my chest.

I drop onto the bed with my hands over my face and my entire body shaking. Every confrontation I have with Bash leaves me more and more dazed, and it's not just because of how angry I am at him.

It's the tension between us that's far more than professional.

Every argument feels like foreplay. Like we're building up to something that I know can never happen between us

71

and never will. Even if I weren't his coach, even if he weren't a player, I can't be with somebody who shows such utter disregard for other people.

It just can't happen.

And Bash can't stay a Scorpion.

8

GREER

We finally pull into the gate, and the engines on the plane wind down. Everyone starts gathering their belongings and preparing to deplane now that we're home.

Bash hasn't even looked my direction the entire flight. I can't say I blame him. He knows how angry I am and that any conversation we would be having wouldn't be one that should occur in front of the rest of the team, or in a confined space with no means of escape for either of us.

He's kept to himself somewhere behind me, toward the rear of the plane, the entire flight, and that's for the best. The tension hanging in the air seems to have affected everyone, only low murmurs of conversation reaching me the entire time here.

I reach down to grab my bag from under the seat in front of me and toss it onto the empty one next to me. My lower back protests the move after tossing and turning in a hotel bed all night.

God, I can't wait for a long, hot bath.

Traveling and flights always mess with my body and leave my muscles achy and sore afterward. Even the short one is enough to leave me begging for relief. And I'll continue to blame my sleeplessness on the shitty mattress and pillows and not on the fact that I could still smell Bash with every breath I took in that room last night.

I glance over my shoulder toward the back of the plane. Bash shoulders his way past anyone in his path in the central aisle. He never so much as glances my way as he passes and stalks off the plane, his small bag slung over his shoulder.

Yep, he's still pissed, too.

Though I don't understand why. He's the one who fucked up last night. Not me. I'm not the bad guy here.

Maybe what I said was harsh, but it's the reality of the situation *he* has put himself in. I don't deserve to shoulder the blame for him feeling shitty about the consequences of his own actions.

I just hope he doesn't drive like an asshole and hurt himself or someone else just because he's mad at me. It's already going to be bad enough having to meet with Bob and discuss this entire situation without wondering if Bash is out doing something stupid off the ice, too.

The guys all file off the plane one by one, but I stay in my seat. Instead of sleeping, I took the time on the flight back to Vegas to figure out how to handle the Bash situation.

It's time for me to man-up and draw a line in the sand, but I hate having to do this. I've been dreading this conversation with Bob. I hate being at such odds with the man who gave me every opportunity in this sport, the man who taught me how to coach, but he's also the person who brought Bash into my life, knowing it was the last thing I wanted. It makes me love Bob and hate him at the same time.

That peculiar mix of feelings isn't one I want to experience any longer.

I sigh and grab my bag from the empty seat next to me, prepared to be the last one off the plane.

Lebedev steps in front of me and holds up his hand. "Wait for a second, Coach."

"Dimitri, what's going on?" It's highly unusual for one of the players to want to discuss anything in this setting. Everyone's exhausted and ready to head home for a while before tomorrow night's game, me included. The late return today means no practice and extra time with their families—and me with my bathtub once I've sorted things with Bob.

Dimitri glances around to make sure no one else can hear us, but the cabin is empty, and the flight attendants and crew are busy with their post-flight checklists.

A tiny chill rolls through my spine.

What the hell could he have to say that no one else can hear?

He gives one final look around us before focusing his attention on me. "We need to talk about Bash."

I sigh and set my bag back down on the seat next to me. "Bash isn't going to be a problem anymore. I'm going to talk to Bob."

There's no way I'm going into any details with Lebedev, but I don't think anyone on the team doesn't know Bash is going to get raked over the coals.

"Fuck." He runs a hand over his stubbled jaw. "I can't believe I'm gonna say this. Because you know how I feel about that asshole. He walked on this team like he owned it and took my spot. So, you know he's not my favorite person in the world. That's why saying this hurts even more."

"Saying what?"

What the hell is he getting at?

He sighs and leans forward to rest his arm on the back of

the seat in front of me. "We all saw what went down last night during the game. But you don't know the whole story."

"What do you mean *the whole story*?"

"What I mean is, you don't know why Bash went after Berglund."

I snort and roll my eyes. "Bash goes after whoever he wants, whenever he wants."

Lebedev chuckles and nods. "That's true. Most of the time. But, there was actually a reason this time. One I think might change how you feel about the situation."

I scoff. "I highly doubt that."

If there were, Bash would have told me himself last night in my room, but I certainly can't tell Lebedev that.

He crosses his arms over his chest. "You need to give Bash a little more credit."

Strong words coming from the man who's essentially his biggest enemy on the team.

"Why? He sure as hell hasn't earned it."

"You want to know why Bash went after Berglund?"

I push up to my feet. "Of course, I do, if there is one." Not that it's going to change how I feel about the entire situation, but it might shed a little light on what was happening in Bash's head.

"Because that *fucker* said something to Bash about how hard he banged you the night before the game."

I jerk back and search his face for any signs of humor. "You're shitting me."

He shakes his head, and his lips twist into a scowl. "I wish I could say I was. I'm sorry I even have to repeat it to you, but I thought you needed to know. He said it to Bash, but I was only a few feet away and heard it, too. Bash didn't go after Berglund for no reason or because he was pissed about that hit. He went after the douchebag because he was defending *you*."

Well, shit.

That definitely does put what happened in a different light and makes me look like a real fucking asshole.

BASH

All I want to do is lie on this bed, eating room service, and drinking the bottle of scotch Caleb sent over. Nothing else exists as far as I'm concerned. The ten voicemail messages I received since the game last night can go not listened to forever, for all I care.

I don't need to hear everyone in my life tearing into me about what happened. I don't need everyone trying to make me feel like shit when they have no idea what really went down. It was bad enough having to hear Greer say those words last night...

Rachel...Caleb...

Hell, even Jameson has tried to get in contact with me.

No doubt to weigh in on a situation they have no clue about.

I'm determined to just lie here and drink and wait for word on my suspension.

It's a position I'm more than familiar with, one I really thought I could avoid until Berglund had to open his stupid fucking mouth.

The Department of Player Safety should hand down a decision today. And after the agonizing telephone hearing today after getting off that plane, I just want it to be over with.

For some reason, Bob stood behind me with the panel, even without knowing the real reason behind what happened, but it won't be enough to avoid a massive suspension. Not with my record. If they knew why it happened, it wouldn't have changed anything, anyway. But I never plan to repeat what was said to anyone.

Given my history, it's likely going to cost me six games, maybe more.

Two more fucking weeks lost...

At the worst possible time for the Scorpions.

I pour a glass of Lagavulin and down it in two swallows. The smoky burn down my throat is a welcome break from the fire of anger over what Greer said.

She really does think I'm a piece of shit on her otherwise pristine shoes. That woman doesn't believe it's possible for me to have acted for a reason she would deem justifiable. All she sees is the man the press presents me as. She sees "Bash" Fury and doesn't want to listen or take the time to find out the truth about Sebastian.

Well, she's not worth my fucking time.

No doubt Greer will be telling Bob she's benching me the rest of the season since we're past the trade deadline. And as soon as this season is over, I'll ask Bob to trade me somewhere far the fuck away from the Scorpions. I may end up somewhere shitty, but it will be worth it to go somewhere I can play on a team with a coach who trusts me and *wants* me on the ice.

Something I'll *never* find here.

A knock at the door sends my empty glass tumbling to the bed.

Shit. I'm jumpy.

It's probably my food.

Thank God.

I'm fucking starving.

I crashed hard when I got back from the airport and slept straight through lunch and dinner. Maybe I'll feel better once I get something else in my stomach besides expensive booze.

Unlikely.

But I push to my feet and make my way to the door. Pulling it open, my breath catches. This is definitely *not* room service.

A familiar set of haunting green eyes look back at me.

It takes me a moment to form words. "Um, Coach. What are you doing here?"

She looks almost scared as she stares up at me from under long, heavy black lashes, and she shifts nervously on her feet. "Hey, Bash. Can we...um...talk?"

Holy déjà vu of my visit to her room.

Only now, she's the one who looks completely off-kilter.

But why?

I was expecting never to see her again after all that talk about being banished for the rest this season. All signs pointed toward her bending over backward to see that I was benched, but instead, Coach is standing here, looking at me in a whole new way.

Like I'm a human being.

What the hell is going on?

Standing here staring at her isn't going to give me an answer, so I sweep my arm back, inviting her into my room. I may be pissed, but I'm not going to slam the door in her face. Mother taught me better manners than that. Plus, I want to know what could have possibly driven her to come here tonight.

She steps through the door hesitantly, her eyes scanning the suite. "Well, they sure put you up in a nice place."

I shrug and let the door close. "Better than most of the places I've stayed. I should be looking for a permanent place to live, but honestly, I may just stay here. Room service and maids. It's better than doing it all on my own in a house or condo."

Coach twists her hands in front of her and avoids making eye-contact.

She's nervous? That's a first.

"What can I do for you, Coach? You come tell me about my suspension?"

It would be unusual not to hear from the GM or someone from the department, but maybe this is an unusual circumstance. Maybe she asked to be the one to deliver the shitty news because it would give her some sort of vindication.

She sighs and walks over to the row of windows that overlook the Strip. "No." Her shoulders rise and fall as she sucks in a deep breath. "I came to apologize."

I freeze and shake my head. The scotch must be fogging my brain. She didn't just say that.

Did she?

Her soft, green eyes glance over at me like she's waiting for a response.

Hell. Maybe she did say that.

I lean against the wall and try to figure out what her angle is here. Greer doesn't seem to be the type of person to admit she's wrong easily, and as far as I know, she has no reason to believe she *was* wrong in anything she's done or said since I arrived. "Apologize for what?"

A long silence draws out after my question, and she stares off out the windows, the bright lights illuminating her in various colors and flashes. "For what I said last night. I didn't know…"

She trails off.

Bile climbs my throat, and I swallow it back, unease creeping over my skin suddenly.

"Didn't know what, Coach?"

There's no way she could know what happened on the ice last night.

Her shoulders rise and fall. "I didn't know what I know now. About what Berglund said."

Shit.

Someone told her.

I didn't think anyone else was close enough to hear it. I had *hoped* no one else had so it wouldn't get spread around.

Apparently, I was wrong.

Greer has been around this world for most of her life. She knows what goes on and what gets said between guys, and she surely understands that she is going to get a lot of flak for being a female coach. But that doesn't make the sting in my chest from knowing she now heard what was said dissipate.

"I never wanted you to know what that ass said."

She shrugs again and finally turns to face me, resignation written all over her soft face and slump in her shoulders. "It isn't wholly unexpected."

"Doesn't make it right." And now that she *does* know, I can't help but wonder what that does to Coach's opinion of me. "Does it make you hate me a little bit less?"

I want her to admit it. Greer never caves on anything, yet, she's *here,* and she's apologizing. Which means she knows I'm not a bad guy.

The tiniest of grins tilts her lips despite her obviously trying to fight it. "A little bit. But seriously, Bash, while I appreciate your defending my honor, it's completely unnecessary."

I shake my head. "No way, Coach. You have a hard-enough job being a woman in this world without assholes like that making comments. I can't just let shit like that slide."

She nods and bites her bottom lip. "The truth is, things

like that are going to get said about me. A lot. This is a male-dominated sport. Some of your peers are macho assholes who never want to see a woman coach because they think we're inferior. It's just the way it is. I accepted it would happen when I decided to get into coaching male teams and knew it was inevitable when I reached the NHL."

"You against the world? All alone?" I shake my head, push off the wall, and step toward her. "That's hardly fair. You should let people help you."

If Rachel were in Greer's shoes, I sure as hell hope someone would defend her if I couldn't. The thought of her being alone with an asshole like Berglund without anyone to stand up for her would be a big brother's worst nightmare. That protective instinct I've had since childhood for the women in my life seems to flare to life around Greer. She may not be getting beaten by my asshole father, but she doesn't need to be beaten down by misogynistic douchebags with nothing better to do than pick on someone trying to do something great.

Greer sighs. "I have to stand on my own two feet, Bash. People are waiting for me to fail." Her gaze hardens. "And it doesn't help when my star player refuses to listen to me."

I raise an eyebrow at her. "Your *star* player?"

"Shit." She drops her face into her hands and shakes her head. "I hadn't meant to say that out loud."

No shit.

Greer admitting I'm her star player is like my admitting someone else is a better forward than me. Never. Going. To. Happen.

I smirk at her. "That one hurt, didn't it, Coach?".

She chuckles and nods, averting her gaze slightly. "But seriously, Bash. You don't need to defend my honor. I can take care of myself. And that includes standing up to douchebags like Berglund."

"And douchebags like me?" I raise an eyebrow and wait for her to respond.

Given the way she's been tearing into me since the moment I landed in Vegas, I would expect her to say yes. But her entire vibe is different now. There's no hostility radiating off her in violent waves. Instead, there's an acceptance.

Of what...I'm not entirely sure.

She considers me for a second and shakes her head. "You're going to make me say it. Aren't you?"

"Come on, Coach. You know you want to."

She sighs and throws her hands up in surrender. "Fine. I don't think you're a douchebag."

I grin at her and shrug. "See? That wasn't so hard, was it?"

9

GREER

H e has no idea. It's not in my nature to admit I'm wrong. Saying you're wrong shows weakness, and you can't be weak when you're in this world. It's something I learned at a very young age while I was the only girl playing with the boys.

None of them wanted me there. All of them thought they were better than me, and I had to prove my worth over and over again, every time I moved up in an age bracket.

Dad always told me never to let them see me break. Never let them see that they could get to me. And I've done a really good job of doing just that for the vast majority of my life.

But here I am at thirty-two...head coach of an NHL team. Something a woman couldn't even consider achieving until I did it. And yet, I'm standing in front of Bash Fury, with his hard, naked chest and those goddamn gray sweatpants hanging perfectly off his trim hips, and I might as well be a horny teenage girl standing in front of her crush.

My heart races as he closes the distance between us.

"It's okay to admit that you're wrong, Coach. It's okay to say I might actually be a decent guy. It's all right to confess you misjudged me. No one will think any less of you."

No, but they would think less of me if they knew how damn attracted to you I am.

Bash isn't just hot. He's the kind of stupid hot that has women stripping off their clothes at games and throwing themselves at him. Even if he weren't a star player making millions of dollars a year, he would still have women climbing all over him.

But I can't be one of those women.

It's completely inappropriate given our positions.

He inches closer to me.

"What are you doing, Bash?"

"What does it look like I'm doing, Coach?" He pauses a few feet from me, close enough that he could reach out and touch me without any effort at all.

I inch backward slowly. "It looks like you're getting way too close to me and into my personal space."

He moves with me, until he's barely a foot away, so close I can smell the soap he used in the shower mingled with that scent that's all Bash.

His head dips down until he's eye-level with me. He holds my gaze without blinking. "You want me to back away, Coach?"

Christ.

Even the way he calls me "Coach" has me clenching my legs together. All the players call me that, but coming from *his* lips, the way *he* says it, it's like he's making love to the word, making love to *me*.

So, do I? Do I really want Bash to back away from me right now?

The way my heart thunders against my rib cage and my body tenses in anticipation, I don't think I do. Not really.

Even though the man is making it impossible for me to just apologize. Even though he's ripping me wide open and making me show weakness. Even though he's forcing me to admit the feelings I've been shoving deep down inside and hoping to keep buried...I still want him to touch me.

I want him to touch me in a way that is oh so wrong. "We can't do this, Bash."

His dark eyebrows rise playfully. "Why not, Coach?"

"Because of *that*." I hold my hand up and press it against his hard, bare chest, forcing him to stay back.

The warmth of his skin radiates into my palm. He flexes under my hand, and I choke back a moan. It would be totally unprofessional for anything to happen.

He's your player.

And even if he didn't play, Bash is exactly the type of guy I know I should stay far away from. One who will break my heart.

It would be fun for a few weeks or even a few months, but eventually, he'll be gone, and I'll be left picking up the pieces again, only I'll have to do it while seeing him every day during the season and maintaining the illusion nothing ever happened between us.

Bash steps closer to me, until only a few inches separate me from the heat rolling off him. I flex my hand on his chest. It's the only thing preventing him from taking this last bit of space between us and obliterating it.

But despite my best efforts, I find myself leaning toward him when I know I should be moving away.

He places a hand on the wall of windows behind me. "Coach..."

I lick my lips, and my focus narrows on his.

"...I'm going to kiss you. If you want me to stop, I suggest you leave now."

Oh, my God.

Yes.

I should leave now.

Good idea.

The best idea.

The one I should've had before I ever got in this position with Bash. Because now that we're this close, now that I'm practically drowning in his scent, I can't seem to find the words to tell him to stop.

I can't seem to find *any* words.

Stringing syllables together to make words and words together to make sentences is suddenly too much for my brain to handle.

Instead, I stand frozen in place with the gorgeous man who has been driving me absolutely insane since the day he skated onto my ice, staring at me like he wants to eat me alive.

And God, do I want him to.

I want him to make me forget all the bullshit that's going on between us. Forget the fact that I'm basically his boss, and this is something that can get me fired. I want it all to go away until all that's left is Bash and me standing together like this and the attraction buzzing between us.

That's all...

The corner of his mouth tics up when I don't say anything, and he grasps my wrist and pulls it down to my side as he shifts forward, until the tiny space that had separated us no longer exists.

His warm chest presses against mine. His heart thuds in time with my own, and his free hand comes up and cups my cheek. He brushes his thumb over my quivering lip and leans in until only millimeters separate our mouths.

"I gave you an out here, Coach. You didn't take it. You have no idea what's in store for you."

BASH

I pounce on her like a starving wolf descending on its quivering prey. My lips meet hers with the same ferocity with which I crash into other players on the ice—full-on, brutally, and with everything I have.

It's a release of all the tension building between us. A collision of bodies that have been hurtling toward each other since the moment we met. It's everything I thought it would be, have fantasized it could be, and so much more.

She moans and shifts against me, pressing her tight body to my own and crushing my aching cock between us. The hand I'm holding down at her side presses against my thigh, and her nails dig into the skin there. The sharp sting only serves as a fuel for the fire burning between us. I wrap my arm around her and drag her entire body to mine as she responds to my kiss earnestly, her tongue sliding between my lips and begging for entrance.

Fuck yes!

Greer has finally let down that icy façade she keeps up, allowed it to melt away, even if only for a moment. And I don't plan on letting it slip away.

I use one hand to angle her head while the fingers of the other dig into her hip, holding her in place because if she keeps grinding against my cock, this is going to go a lot further than I think either of us is prepared to handle at the moment.

God knows, I sure as shit am not ready for any of this.

Greer has crashed into my life in a way I never could have anticipated and managed to use her strength to attack the walls around my heart designed to keep anyone out who might make me care. Anyone who might make me want more. Anyone who might hurt me. Everything she does that should push me away has only driven me closer and made me want her more. I want to prove who and what I am. That I'm not just what I am on the ice and how I appear in the fucking media. That all of this is just...Bash...but Sebastian is so much more.

I'm a fucking idiot for giving into this attraction.

It's a mistake I'm sure I'll pay for later. But right now, I can't worry about it. I can't let the reality of our situation seep into my thoughts. Not with her soft, willing body pressed to mine and her moans falling into my mouth. Not with her groping hands and desperate gasps.

I groan and shift her until her back hits the glass, pinning her against the cool surface. The neon lights of the Strip flash behind her, illuminating her in an almost ethereal glow.

This is stupid.

She's my coach, and I'm already on thin ice with Bob and the league. The last thing I should be doing is breaking the rules like this—breaking *this* rule. But there's just something about Greer Waterson that drives me mad. In so many ways.

Arguing with her is the best foreplay I've ever experienced. And we've been building to this since the moment we met. Every snide comment. Every witty retort. Every wisecrack. They've all been nothing more than a sexual dance designed to get us to this point.

This woman is wicked smart and funny, and she's willing to stand up to me and the other players, some who are even more hostile—like the fucker who made the comment that got her here tonight.

I can see how hard she tries to keep it all together, to carry the weight of her position with her head held high and pretending nothing affects her. But it does, and she can't keep going it alone.

She's one of the strongest and most frustrating women I ever met, and that's like a shot of heroin into my bloodstream. It's something I've never had. Something I didn't know I wanted or needed. Something so deadly and dangerous, I never would have even considered it a possibility.

And now that I've had a taste, I want it *all*.

I want to explore every inch of her. Experience all that drive, all that passion directed at me in a positive way instead of through hostility. I want Greer under me and over me, giving all that she has to me, the same way I give all that I have on the ice.

I want Greer in my bed.

Right.

Fucking.

Now.

I force myself to pull back from her sweet lips and stare down into her lust-soaked, evergreen eyes. Our chests heave against each other, both of us struggling for air from the kiss that just threw my entire world off its axis.

Greer shakes her head slightly, and her vision seems to clear. She presses her hands against my chest and pushes.

I take a step back. Then another.

She squeezes her eyes shut. One of her shaking hands shifts back through her disheveled hair and tugs at it. "What the hell are we doing?"

The moment is gone.

Lost to the reality of the position we're in.

I take another step back, and she slowly opens her eyes, as if doing it that way will somehow make what just happened disappear. As if I won't still be standing in front of her with a raging hard-on and desire coursing through my veins.

Her gaze that only moments ago was filled with lust is now glazed with panic. "No. No. No." She squeezes her eyes shut again and sucks in a deep breath. "Shit." When she opens her eyes, there's a renewed purpose there. A determination that wasn't present only a second ago. She presses her hand over her quivering lips and then drops it to her side. "I'm sorry, Bash. I can't."

Shit.

I rub my eyes and open my mouth with no idea what to say for maybe the first time in my entire life, but she brushes past me and bolts out of the door before I have a chance to utter a single word.

Not that I know what I would've said. Because...she's right. She should leave.

This is stupid and dangerous. This is the kind of thing that will get her fired, even though both of us made the decision to let this happen.

Christ...

I reach down and adjust my hard cock in my sweatpants. It felt so fucking good to have her pressed against me. Like it was exactly where I needed to be. I lick my lips. Her taste still lingers there—a sweet combination of mint and something sugary, like she just brushed her teeth then ate a piece of butterscotch candy.

My dick throbs and twitches. There will be no sleeping tonight. Not now that this memory lives and breathes in my brain.

I need to take care of this.

And only one woman will be on my mind as I stroke myself—Greer fucking Waterson.

10

GREER

E ven being out alone on the ice this morning can't cool the heat coming from my body, remembering last night with Bash. I send another puck sailing toward the goal. It ricochets off the pipe and to the right.

Shit.

Everything feels off today, like there's a fog over the world. One I can't manage to shake no matter how many shots I take or laps I skate.

Maybe it's because I didn't sleep more than ten minutes last night. It was impossible when all I could think about was Bash and the way his lips felt against mine. How the heat of his body radiated into me. The squeeze of his hands on my hips. The way my knees quivered and buckled when he kissed me. His masculine scent wrapping around me and enveloping me. I could still smell it with every breath I took and taste him on my tongue hours later.

As embarrassing as it is, Bash Fury has become the man of my literal dreams, who also haunts me during my waking hours. My clit throbs at the memory of touching myself last night, at coming undone while thinking of Bash doing the same to me.

Shit.

If he was that good at kissing, God only knows what he'd be like in bed. Those talented hands...

Shit. Shit. Shit.

I shake my head, grit my teeth, and fire off another slap-shot. It whips across the ice and straight into the net. Clapping from behind me has me jerking up and whirling around on my skates.

All the air rushes from my lungs.

Bash.

He leans against the opening in the boards that leads to the tunnel to the locker room. His dark T-shirt stretches taut over his chest, and his biceps bulge against the sleeves. My eyes drift down to his muscular thighs and crotch encased in his jeans without even thinking about it.

God, his hard cock pressed against me last night felt so damn good.

I haven't felt more like a horny teenager since I actually was one. It would be comical if it wasn't so damn wrong and inconvenient when I'm struggling to remain professional.

"Nice shot, Coach, but my eyes are up here."

Shit.

His lips tip up in a grin, and he nods toward the net then steps onto the ice. I whirl away from him and fire off another shot to avoid facing the embarrassment of being busted.

What the hell is he doing here?

Morning skate doesn't start for another hour, and he won't be able to participate anyway once the decision on his suspension comes through, which should be at any moment. The whole reason I came early was to avoid having to see anyone and to work out a little of my frustration.

Having the damn cause of it show up looking all sexy and arrogant in no way helps my situation.

I really must've done something to piss off karma.

He moves across the ice carefully and stops a few feet from me. Crossing his arms over his chest, he watches me fire off another shot.

Maybe if I don't look at him, if I don't stare into those warm bourbon eyes, I can keep some semblance of control. I can pretend my little slip last night didn't happen. I can go back to just being his coach.

"You have a master touch, Coach."

I turn toward him and lean against my stick. "What's that supposed to mean?"

Was that some sort of innuendo about what happened last night?

Bash raises an eyebrow. "I mean, you always did have a good shot. And you haven't lost your touch."

Heat creeps along my neck and over my cheeks.

Shit. I read way too much into that, and now, I'm the one who turned it sexual. Fucking perfect.

He watched me play. Even though he mentioned my history in my office the other day, I never imagined he paid *that* close attention. Why would he have? At the time I was playing in the Olympics, Bash would have been playing juniors and dreaming of his career in the NHL, not concentrating on women's hockey.

"I didn't think you would have had the time to watch much back then."

Bash grins at me. "I make time for things that are important."

"And watching women's Olympic hockey was important to you?"

He nods slowly. "Don't look so shocked, Coach. I loved watching it. I liked the purity of it. Without a women's NHL, all the Olympic players were doing it for the love of the game. They weren't doing it for fame or fortune or hopes that they might get picked up by a pro team afterward. It's like the difference between watching college basketball and the NBA. In college, players still play as a team, but once they get to the NBA, it becomes a one-man show."

I never thought about it that way, but he's kind of right. It's a pure sport, one where my teammates and I played for the love the game and our country. I was never in it to get famous or a big contract. I just love the ice.

He slowly steps closer to me, like he's afraid I'm going to bolt. "How did you get involved in playing hockey in the first place?"

I shift my stick in my hands, aim, and fire off another shot before I turn back to him. "Why do you want to know?"

He moves over to me until he's too close for comfort or professionalism. "Why is it so hard for you to believe that I just want to know more about you?"

I shrug and lean against my stick. "Most men have ulterior motives for everything they do."

His eyes widen. "Wow." He chuckles and shakes his head. "You sure are cagey. You ever let anyone in through that ice surrounding your heart?"

I scowl at him. "I don't have ice around my heart."

Humor tugs at his lips and dances in his heated gaze. His eyes drop down to my chest, then back up playfully. "You don't?"

"No." I shake my head and square my shoulders. I'm not some ice queen. "I don't."

He leans forward until his lips are mere inches from my ear. His warm breath flutters against my skin, sending a shiver down my spine that has nothing to do with being on the ice. "Then why did you run last night?"

BASH

It's a simple question. One that's been bouncing around my head since the moment she fled from my hotel room last night. I saw the fear in her eyes. The way she was over-analyzing the situation and was thinking of everything all at once.

But I hadn't expected her to bolt like that, without a word, without even a look back at me after the moment we shared. I stood there frozen for several minutes before I was finally able to process what had happened. Before I dragged myself to the bed and jerked off with that kiss replaying in my head—the feel of her nails on my skin. The taste of her flooding my mouth.

Each release only made me want more—of *her.* Of *us.*

Greer seems like the kind of woman who faces anything that stands in her way and beats it back until it lets her pass, so her decision to run instead of dealing with the attraction between us surprised the hell out of me. Even as I tried to fall asleep, I couldn't get her actions out of my mind.

This isn't going to just go away. These feelings won't just disappear overnight. If anything, they're only stronger this morning, now that I've gotten a taste of what being with Greer would be like. So, if I can assume anything based on my own feelings, Greer is reeling, too.

Though she's definitely trying to fight it.

She presses her pale-pink lips together in a firm, hard line. "I didn't run."

The incredulous note in her voice has me barking out a laugh. "Oh, you didn't?"

She shakes her head, her blond hair spilling around her.

"No, I..."—she considers her answer for second—"...walked fast."

My laugh booms so loudly through the rink that Greer glances around to make sure we're alone. "Oh"—I press my hand over my chest—"I'm sorry. Why did you 'walk fast' away from me last night?"

Her lips droop into a frown. "I needed my sleep before the game tonight."

A game I'm not sure I'll be playing in. I usually get a decision from the Department of Player Safety within twenty-four hours. The delay has unease creeping up my spine, but it could just be because they're reviewing my very long list of prior offenses.

Until I know for sure, though, I'm going to have some fun messing with Greer. I step closer to her until she's within arm's reach and that damn flowery scent of hers wraps around me and makes my cock twitch. I wave my arms and point at the rink. "It's a good thing you left early... with all this strenuous work you're doing."

She scowls at me, and I can't bite back the laugh. It's a dick move to find such humor in this situation, but Greer's attempted denial of the attraction between us is just that...*laughable*.

It's like denying that the Earth revolves around the sun.

"Come on, Greer. Why are you pretending there's nothing going on between us?"

Her eyes harden, and she leans in toward me. "Because nothing can happen between us, Bash. If it did, I would lose my job. My career."

I take another step closer to her and wrap my hand around her waist. She stiffens in my arms but doesn't pull away. I tug her toward me until her body is pressed against mine and the hockey stick is positioned directly between us. "Then, we don't get caught."

She shudders in my arms, and I grin. If she's picturing the same thing I am, then I understand her reaction. I spent last night fantasizing about all the things I could do to her while I made myself come over and over again.

I reach up and run my thumb across her bottom lip. "If we let ourselves go, this could be something really spectacular."

A huge release of breath flutters the hair off her forehead. "That's just it, Bash. We can't just let ourselves go. This job is too important to me to do that."

It should be.

She's worked her way into a position that most hockey players can only dream of. And she did it with a set of tits instead of a cock. Though Greer definitely has balls. She stands up to me, and not many people do that.

It makes her different, so fucking different from all the other women I've ever been with. And that makes her irresistible.

I lean in and feather my lips over hers gently. She sighs and sags against me.

"Then tell me you want me to stop, Greer." Another brush of my lips. "Tell me to walk away."

Seconds tick by with nothing but the warm press of her body and the cool air around us. Her soft-green eyes never leave mine. And she doesn't utter a word.

I capture her mouth in a demanding kiss, one intended to show her that all her fears and reservations may very well be warranted, but they aren't worth giving up this or ignoring the combustible attraction between us. We don't need to throw this all away just because we're scared of what others will think.

She moans into my mouth and returns the kiss. That same sweet flavor that's all Greer floods my mouth as she slips her tongue along my lips. Her stick clatters to the ice, and she wraps her arms around my neck, her cool fingers tangling in the hair at my nape.

Exactly what I wanted. For her to just let go.

And fuck does it feel good.

A door slams somewhere down the tunnel, and she jerks away from me and shifts back on the ice, putting several feet between us. Her chest rises and falls rapidly. Even though the temperature down here should have her shivering, her pale skin is rosy pink. Her eyes never leave mine, as if she's searching for something, but I'm not sure what.

An apology? A promise? Both?

Footsteps echo up toward the rink, and Bob appears at the entrance to the ice. He glances between us with a stern set to his mouth and points at me. "Don't bother suiting up, Bash. Just got word from the league. You're suspended for eight games."

Well, shit.

11

GREER

My hands shake as I press the button in the elevator. Bash's parting words before he left the ice this morning float through my head.

"Take a risk, Greer. I promise you won't be disappointed."

What happened between Bash and me at the arena couldn't have been more wrong and stupid, especially when we could have been caught at any moment.

Maybe that's part of the appeal, though.

The rush of the forbidden. Something we absolutely shouldn't be doing, giving into base needs while risking what's most important to both of us—our careers.

Or maybe I'm just a big ol' Bash slut, incapable of fighting the attraction.

Whatever the reason...I'm here. The elevator doors slide open, and I step out onto the fiftieth floor of the Prestige and turn toward Bash's door.

Again.

The same walk I made last night, the same route I fled after our kiss, only in reverse. And this time, I don't want to run. Except maybe *to* the man I should be fleeing away from.

I *should* leave, but after our loss tonight, after watching my team crumble in the third period and play like a damn geriatric club league team, my first inclination was to come here.

Of all the places in the world.

If Bash hadn't been defending my honor, he would have been out on the ice tonight. Maybe it wouldn't have made a difference. Maybe we still would have fallen apart faster than a piece of IKEA furniture, but he might have been just what we needed to nail them.

We'll never know.

But what I do know is I got into my car and drove straight here without hesitation once I left the arena.

Self-preservation says I should turn around and hightail it back to my place, but nothing has felt as good as being in Bash's arms in a long fucking time.

I stop outside his door and knock. A few seconds pass before the door swings open.

Bash leans against the jamb with that cocky grin of his plastered on his lips. "I was hoping I'd see you tonight."

All I manage is a nod because words seem to be too complicated for me...again.

Why do I turn into a quivering mess whenever I'm around this man?

It's everything I'm not. Everything I've always told myself I would never be. The kind of woman who makes bad decisions because of dick.

Hopefully, it's just something I need to get out of my system. The alternative is unthinkable.

He steps back and ushers me into his room. "Tough loss tonight."

No shit.

It was painful to watch from the bench. Even worse for the guys on the ice. Slow skating. Slower hands. Bad passes. Bad penalties. You name it, it happened in the third period. It was a hot mess.

Bash follows me into his suite, and I stand awkwardly in the center of the living room area.

I don't know how to do this.

It's been a long time since I had a date with someone, let alone someone like Bash. Plus, I don't even know what this is.

Is it even a date?

I force myself to take a breath and turn to face him.

That stupidly sexy grin is plastered on his face, and he crosses his arms over his chest, causing the dark-blue fabric of his crisp button-down shirt to pull over his biceps. "Don't look so nervous, Coach. I don't bite...much."

He winks at me, and my heart does this embarrassing little yo-yo thing I haven't felt since Kirk McNamara kissed me in sixth grade.

"Take a seat." The man who has the uncanny ability to undo years of hardening myself with a simple look motions toward the couch and grabs the phone from the small end table. "I assume you haven't eaten yet?"

I shake my head and settle onto the couch. "I came straight here from the game."

"I'll order us room service."

"You don't have to do that."

He waves me off. "Hi. Yes, can I get two Wagyu ribeyes medium rare with fries and a bottle of Sea Smoke Ten? Thanks."

Uh...what?

I glare at him as he sets the phone down.

He raises an eyebrow at me. "What's that look for?"

"Did you just order for me?"

A smile plays at his lips as he stalks over to the couch. He leans down and rests his hands on the back, so he has me caged in. "I did. Are you going to complain about me ordering you a hundred-dollar steak?"

Truth be told, a steak sounds amazing, but admitting that to him would make him think it's okay for him to decide what I'm going to eat and how I like my meat cooked. Dad taught me better than to let a man make decisions for me about anything. It's a policy that's served me well over the last thirty-plus years.

"It's pretty fucking presumptuous."

He dips his head lower, shifting his hands on the back of the couch until the heat from his arms warms my shoulders and his hot breath flutters over me. "Can't you just let me do something nice for you, Coach?"

I bite back my retort. I've spent so many years fighting against men who thought I didn't belong in this world that I can't even see that Bash may be trying to do something nice for me instead of just exerting control.

Then again...it's Bash. Mixed motives are definitely possible.

Probable even.

He may not even know he's doing it and might not be capable of turning it off. This is just who he is—bossy, arrogant, and so fucking hot.

With his hard, lean body only inches from mine, his arms caging me in and preventing me from moving away, it's like being trapped in the direct path of a tornado and being unable to find shelter.

He inches closer until his lips brush against mine. It's unexpectedly sweet compared to the other kisses I've experienced from him. This one is slow. Light. Almost toying.

Butterflies dance in my stomach, the kind that are beautiful and could be very, very dangerous.

He pulls back and grins.

He knows.

Sebastian Fury knows *exactly* what he's doing to me, and he loves it. He loves playing with me, knowing I can't stay away. He wants me to beg and thinks he's so damn cute keeping me off-balance. And he is. Because what's going on between us is overpowering the looming risk of whatever this is being discovered.

This is where I want to be.

Which is absolutely terrifying.

He pushes away from the couch and makes his way to the bar set up across the room. "Do you want anything to drink while we wait for the food?"

I eye the bottle of scotch sitting in the corner. Hard liquor around Bash might be a bad idea, but I need something to calm my nerves. This is worse than my pre-Olympic jitters. And I despise the fact that it's Bash doing it to me.

Only a few weeks ago, I despised him. Wanted nothing to do with him and was intent on keeping him hundreds of miles away from me and my team. Yet, here I am...

He follows my line of vision and nods toward the bottle. "You want some? A good friend of mine sent this over."

"I guess, if you're having some."

It sounds better than begging for alcohol in order to form some control over myself.

His strong, deft hands pull the cork, and he pours the amber liquid into two tumblers. "I don't meet very many women who drink Islay scotch."

I try to relax back on the couch. "My mom died when I was very young. I was raised by my dad. He never had any sons, so I ended up doing a lot of father-son things with him."

One of his sandy eyebrows wings up. "You drank with your father?"

I laugh as he hands me the glass. "Sort of. When I was old enough, he would let me take a sip of his drink, probably because he thought the burn would deter me. But it kind of backfired on him. I actually liked it."

"A woman who can play hockey, coach it, and drinks scotch?" He presses his free hand over his heart and settles into the couch next to me. "My dream woman in the flesh."

A hot flush spreads across my cheeks, and I take a sip to hide it. Alcohol does the same thing, and I'd much rather Bash think it's because of the booze instead of the compliment. But he saw it, and even if he hadn't, he knows how women react to him. How *I* react.

He's used his looks and charm to get into the pants of many women over the years. I have no doubt. That probably makes me stupid for being here and thinking this is any different. But it *feels* different with Bash. It has since the first time he winked at me and grabbed his crotch.

My anger morphed into something else, and the way he looks at me suggests it has for him, too.

I take a sip of my drink. His friend has great taste. "You know this is dangerous."

He raises an eyebrow at me and takes a sip of his drink. "What is? Having scotch?"

Smartass.

"This." I wave between the two of us.

"I thought we were past all that. If we aren't, then why are you here?"

I clasp the glass between my hands and squeeze. "I don't know what's happening here."

He leans forward and sets his glass on the coffee table in front of us then shifts on the cushion to face me. "Yes, you do. You're here because you feel the same thing I do. There's something here. Something between us pulling us together. Something more than our heated tempers."

I shake my head. "I'm not saying there isn't, Bash. I just want to know if I'm risking my career just to be another notch on your hockey stick."

He frowns and opens his mouth, but a knock at the door interrupts him. It may have saved him from saying something I don't want to hear, something I may *need* to hear.

I should go.

The longer I stay, the more the temptation to act on this attraction is going to grow. It's inevitable. The only way to escape it is to leave and stay far, far away from Bash Fury. I need space. Somewhere I can think. Somewhere I can't be influenced by his panty-melting grin.

But I don't want to leave. Not really. Not when I consider what I'd be doing if I were at home.

Thinking about Bash Fury.

I've had time since our first kiss to consider what it means, what it *will* mean if things go further. And I keep coming to the same conclusion—I can't avoid my attraction to Bash. Even if I tried to keep things professional between us, this kind of pull would continue until we collide with potentially catastrophic consequences.

He shoves to his feet. "Time to eat."

I release a shaky breath.

Thank God for the momentary reprieve.

But it *is* only momentary.

He and I are going to have to come to some sort of understanding—one way or the other.

———

BASH

Who would've thought watching somebody eat could be an erotic experience?

Certainly not me. But with every bite Greer has taken, my dick has twitched and grown so much, my pants now feel like they're three sizes too small.

I reach down and surreptitiously adjust my semi.

Hopefully, that gives me a little relief.

This has been almost forty-five minutes of a giant cock tease. Every single thing this woman does is hot, and after seeing her out on the ice, nailing shot after shot this morning, I was already prepared to dive into her. And I was wholly unprepared for *this*.

Thank God her plate is almost empty.

If I had to sit and see her wrap her lips around that fork one more time, then issue that low little pleased hum of approval, I might knock everything off this table and fuck her right here and now.

It would be hard and fast and reckless.

That wouldn't be very gentlemanly of me.

It would be very Bash, though.

And I've never worried about that before. I've had sex in dozens of public and random places, not even counting the women I've brought back to hotel rooms and my place for more private romps.

But this is *Coach*.

She's not the type of woman who does things spontaneously, without meticulous planning and thinking ten steps ahead. She's not the kind of woman you fuck in an alley outside a bar or the back seat of the car because you can't wait long enough to get back to your place.

This woman has a kind of class the puck bunnies can't possess. She's busted her ass and held her head high through a gauntlet of media scrutiny.

She deserves something different. Something more than a quick fuck on the closest flat surface. At least, for our first time together. After that, all bets will be off. I can already tell I will want to have her everywhere and anywhere and won't be able to keep my hands off her once she allows me in.

But in this moment, I need to maintain my control, which is easier said than done with her sitting across this small table from me, making those damn sounds with her wet, pink lips wrapped around the damn fork again.

I lean back in my chair and watch her. She grabs her wine glass and brings it to her lips. Her eyes drift closed as she swallows. Watching her throat work has me biting back a groan.

I've spent the last few days imagining what it would be like to have her doing that to my cock. And now she's here in my hotel room, and given what she said before dinner, it seems she might be willing to accept that this might *actually* be something to explore between us.

It would be an epic mark for the win column—one I haven't had many of when it comes to Greer since I arrived.

She's a fighter, through and through, and I have a feeling she'll continue to fight me any way she can for as long as whatever this is continues. Getting her to let down her guard and let me in will truly be a feat, but I'm known for pulling off miracles.

Those might be on the ice, but even off it, I have game.

And I love to win.

It's what drives me forward on the ice, what makes me push myself harder and the only thing I have ever really wanted...until I met Greer.

Almost as if she can feel me watching her, her eyes fly open and meet mine, and that beautiful blush materializes. She averts her gaze, sets down her glass, and presses her fingers to her mouth. "Uh, it was a wonderful dinner and wine. Thank you."

It sure as hell was.

Fighting a smirk, I shift in my chair slightly. "So, I did a good job ordering for us, then?"

That adorable little twist to her lips returns. "Don't have to be so smug about it."

"Yes, I do."

And the fact that she's still here tells me she's either accepted that about me or is willing to ignore it in favor of giving in to the sexual attraction and her base needs. Maybe it turns her on more than she wants to admit. It would certainly make things a lot easier for me if that were true.

I lean forward and rest my elbows on the table. "What is it you're so afraid of, Greer?"

Her brow furrows, and her shoulders tense. "What do you mean?"

Without waiting for my answer, she pushes away from the table and wanders over to the windows overlooking the Strip, arms wrapped protectively around herself. She turns back to face me, but her lip disappears between her teeth, her worry stiffening her stance.

I spread out my hands. "I mean...are you afraid to get involved with *anyone,* or...are you just afraid to get involved with *me*?"

She scowls and points at me with a shaky finger. "See, that, that right there is exactly what I'm talking about."

"What is?"

I'm actually *not* trying to be a smartass—maybe for the first time ever. I genuinely have no idea what she's talking about right now.

"*Involved with.*" She does air quotes and rolls her eyes toward the high ceiling. "What does that even mean?"

Oh, God.

We're going there...

I push to my feet and move toward her cautiously because she already looks like a deer frozen in the headlights of an on-coming semi and I don't need to agitate her more. "I don't know what you want, Greer. I've been very upfront with you about who I am. I've never made you any promises or done anything that wasn't completely in my character. You know me about as well as I know you. Promises at this point would be meaningless. And *you* know that."

One thing I have *never* done is lie to a woman to get her into my bed, and I sure as *hell* wouldn't do that to Greer. I won't promise her a relationship I don't want or any sort of future, and even if I did, she would know it's a fucking lie at this point.

She watches me suspiciously as I approach, worrying her bottom lip between her teeth.

Christ, that's hot.

It makes me picture my aching cock pressed between those lips. The harsh scrape of her teeth along my hard length. A little moan slipping out as she swallows me back...

I pause a few feet from her. Spooking her by getting too close now would undo any progress I've made in even getting her here tonight. It felt like a huge win, but she's already contemplating bolting again. The only thing I can do is keep being brutally honest with her and hope it's enough to get through to her.

"We are two consenting adults who are attracted to each other, Greer. There's absolutely nothing wrong with us acting on that."

She releases her lip with a heavy sigh, shoulders slumping. "The NHL and Bob might see things differently."

Fucking hell.

"I don't give a fuck what the NHL or Bob think. All I care about is what *you* want."

The words come out harsher than I intend, but her waffling is worse than the weather swings in Michigan in the summer. I shove a hand through my hair and tug at the ends. I don't want to say this, but I need to.

"You know where the door is, Greer. You left out of it before. And I'm not keeping you here now." I step closer. "But I would really love for you to stay for dessert."

She raises a pale eyebrow at me and glances at the table behind us. "Dessert? I didn't hear you order any dessert?"

I bark out a laugh and shake my head as I step forward and take her face between my hands to tilt it up toward me. "I wasn't talking about food, Coach."

Her mouth forms the perfect little *O* of surprise, and I lean forward and kiss her before she can recover. That soft little mewl comes from her throat, and I push my lips harder against hers, willing her to give in. Begging her to let me in and to throw away all the thoughts and worries weighing down on her and holding her back.

She wanted clarity, an explanation from me for what *this* is, but I don't have a fucking clue where this goes after tonight. Neither does she. To pretend otherwise wouldn't be fair to either of us.

But with this kiss, there can be no doubt what I have in mind for *right fucking now*.

12

GREER

The man can kiss.

Oh, good God...can he kiss.

My entire body vibrates with anticipation with every lick of his tongue and press of his lips. I want more. I *crave* more, but I can't turn off that tiny voice inside my head telling me to hold back.

This is wrong.

So fucking wrong.

But if feels so right. My entire body lit from the inside out with the flutter of his mouth over mine.

Bash tears away from my lips and kisses his way up my neck to my ear. His hot breath tickles over the sensitive skin there, and I practically melt into his arms. The only thing keeping me upright is his firm hand on my hip and his knee wedged between my legs.

"When was the last time you were well and truly fucked, Coach?"

Oh, God.

Fucked? Two years ago.

Well and truly?

I can't even think back that far.

And something tells me that what Bash considers "well and truly fucked" is completely different from what I have in mind, so far above and beyond anything I've ever experienced. If his *real* game is anywhere near his dirty-talking game and his arrogance matches his skills in the bedroom, I'm in big fucking trouble.

I shudder against him, and he reaches down and cups me between my legs.

Christ, can he feel how wet I am through my pants?

At this point, I don't even have the ability to be embarrassed anymore. I'm like putty to Bash's expert touch. The way those hands know how to handle a hockey stick, I can only imagine what they'll do with me if given a chance.

He sucks the lobe of my ear between his teeth and bites down gently. The jolt of pain mixed with pleasure ricochets through my body, and I tighten my grip on his neck to keep from falling over on weak legs.

His hand curls against my pussy. "You didn't answer me, Coach. How long has it been?"

All I manage is a whimper.

"What do you say, Coach?" He nips at my ear again. "Are you going to stay for dessert?"

God, yes!

"Yes."

My response comes out more harsh rush of held breath than speech, but it seems it's enough for him to hear me because he issues a low satisfied growl that vibrates in his chest and through mine.

He lifts me into his arms easily. I wrap my legs around his waist, but instead of walking us backward to the bed on the other side of the room, he presses me against the cool glass of the floor-to-ceiling windows.

The world spins around me as he kisses his way across my collarbone. A hazy fog descends with every press of his lips to my heated skin.

He pauses with his mouth at the corner of mine, his hands tighten on my ass, and he pulls back. "You sure this is what you want, Coach?"

With a million reasons to say otherwise, only one word sits on the tip of my tongue.

"Yes."

He stares at me for a moment, searching for any signs I'll back out, but when I roll my hips against his hard cock pressed between us, he groans and releases his hold on me so I can lower my feet to the floor.

What's he doing?

His hand slides down my side to the waistband of my pants, and he drags them down my legs slowly, letting his fingertips linger on my warm skin. I shiver at the light touch, and he pulls them off and tosses them across the room toward where I kicked off my shoes before dinner.

Liquid-whiskey eyes flare with heat as his gaze centers on the black lace between my legs. He licks his lips and reaches forward to stroke his thumb along the fabric, right below my clit. "Already wet for me, huh, Coach?"

I bite my lip and clamp my thighs around his hand.

He grins and flicks my clit with his finger, making me jerk. "Have you been thinking about my cock, Coach?"

"Bash!"

"Don't look so shocked, Coach." He shifts his hand to rub his fingers along my wet slit. "You know it's true."

It is.

As much as I'd love to brag that I'm immune to Bash

Fury's charms, ever since he walked into my office in nothing but that towel, my imagination has run wild. Even though I was pissed at him. Even though I wanted him *gone*. I also wanted to see what was beneath that soft, fluffy fabric.

The man just oozes the kind of energy that says he will give you the dirtiest and most satisfying sex of your life.

And God, could I use that right now.

He slips a finger under the fabric of my thong and drags it through the wetness there. I groan and shift against him, urging him to slide inside me and tightening my grip on his shoulders. Instead, he pulls it away, and I jerk my head up and watch him.

"You're not coming on my hand, Coach." He pushes down his sweatpants slowly, taunting me with the leisurely exposure of his smooth, hard skin until his huge cock springs free between his muscled thighs.

Good God.

He wraps his hand around the base of the shaft and strokes slowly. "I want you coming in my mouth and then on my cock."

Sweet Lord above.

I could come just from the words tumbling from this man's mouth, but after seeing what he's packing, I can't even bring myself to look him in the eye. I can't drag my focus off his cock.

He releases his dick long enough to tug his shirt up and off and kick off his pants.

Bash Fury...in all his natural glory.

Hard, rippling muscles. Blazes of vibrant ink across his legs, chest, and ribs. I want to explore those, learn all their curves and lines. Trace every word with my tongue. My mouth waters just thinking about it. I lick my lips and shift against the window.

He steps forward and grasps the hem of my shirt. Fingertips play at my belly, making me suck in a sharp breath. He grins and pulls it over my head, then unhooks my bra and lazily drags the straps down my arms in the same torturous way he did my pants.

Goose bumps pebble in the wake of his touch, and he leans down and presses a slow, languid kiss to my lips as he lets my bra fall to the floor. His fingers brush along the sensitive skin just above my thong, then he slips them in and pulls it down my legs and off.

Naked with Bash Fury.

I'm NAKED with Bash Fury.

But instead of bringing me to the bed, he drops to the floor.

"Bash, what are you—"

His hot breath flutters over my wet pussy, and I squirm, knowing he's assessing every exposed inch of my body. One of his large hands flattens across my stomach, and the other slides under my ass and squeezes before he drags it over his shoulder.

"Every bite of food I took tonight, I thought about what you would taste like." He leans forward and drags his tongue through my wetness.

"Oh, God!" I rock forward, angling myself open to give him better access.

"Fucking incredible, Coach." He flicks my clit with the tip of his tongue, sending my hips bucking up. His hand presses me back against the glass and holds me steady while he proceeds to explore every inch between my legs.

And when I say explore...I mean a fucking expedition.

He covers every single centimeter, licking at me with his talented tongue that usually only says things that piss me off and now drives me insane in a completely new way.

Because he doesn't give me what I really want. What I really need to come.

I dig my fingers into his shoulders. "Please, Bash."

His eyes lift to meet mine, and he shakes his head, determination filling his heated gaze.

"Come on, Bash"—my words come out breathy and heavy with need—"now you're just playing dirty."

He pulls back and flashes a grin, my arousal glistening on his lips. "Baby, I always play dirty, and you haven't seen anything yet."

———

BASH

I would love nothing more than to toy with her all night. To bring her to the brink of orgasm over and over again only to back her down again and make her beg for release.

But my aching cock isn't going to let me wait long enough to do that.

Not when I've been fantasizing about this since our first confrontation. Not now that her arousal coats my tongue, and I know how goddamn sweet she is everywhere.

I want to see her come undone. I want to see that second of true and utter bliss when she hangs on the precipice and then falls and shatters. I can't remember wanting anything else more in my life than I want that this exact moment.

Greer stares down at me with hooded, lust-soaked eyes while the lights of the Strip flash and spin behind her through the glass.

She's so fucking beautiful—her pale skin pink and flushed and her perfect high, round breasts heaving.

I won't make her wait.

Not tonight.

I may be a dick, but I'm a selfish one, and my cock needs to be inside of her more than I need to play with her now.

There will be plenty of time to play later. Once we're both satisfied.

I press a trail of kisses from her navel down her left thigh, then switch and move up her right one and back to the center of her body. Her legs shake, and her nails dig into my shoulders as I plunge my tongue into her hot cunt again.

She groans, and one of her hands shifts up onto my head to push me tighter against her. "Please, Bash."

It's the last time I'll make her beg. At least tonight. At least this round.

I suck her clit between my lips and slide three fingers inside her, spreading her wide and curling them into her G-spot. She gasps and shudders as I quickly work her to the point of no return.

"Oh, fuck! I'm gonna come."

"Damn right, you are." I flick her clit. "Come for me, Coach." Another flick. "I want to taste all of you."

She moans and rolls her hips against my face in time with my sucking lips and thrusting fingers. A moment later, her body stiffens, and she cries out. Her mouth drops open, and her head falls back against the glass. She squeezes her eyes shut and gasps as she comes.

Her body twitches and trembles, and her pussy clamps around my fingers in a spastic rhythm that almost has my cock exploding. I suck down her release, relishing every single drop of it, knowing I was the one giving it to her.

With a satisfied moan, her body stills, and she sags against the glass and me. I pull back and rise to my feet with an arm around her waist to keep her from falling.

This is what I wanted Greer satiated and wrung out on pleasure.

But it isn't nearly enough.

I claim her lips, and she groans and tangles her tongue around mine. It doesn't even seem to bother her that her release still fills my mouth. If anything, it only seems to animate her more.

Nails score the back of my neck, and she mewls and presses her lush body against mine almost frantically.

So fucking hot.

My cock twitches between us, and I slide my hand down and stroke it slowly.

If it were anyone else, I'd be reaching for a condom right now. I don't do unprotected sex, but this isn't just some random girl. I know Greer, and I want to experience all of her.

I need to feel her hot cunt tightening around me with nothing between us.

"I'm clear, Greer. I was tested right before the trade."

Her small hand snakes down and wraps around the head of my cock, and she glides her thumb across it, spreading my pre-cum over the hyper-sensitive flesh. "I am, too, and I'm on the pill." She kisses me hard, her hand tightening around me as she strokes. "And I trust you, Bash."

Damn.

Those words shouldn't affect me so much. They shouldn't make warmth bloom in the center of my chest.

But not so long ago, she hated me and couldn't stand to be in the same room. Now, she's begging me for sex and letting me fuck her bareback because she *trusts* me.

Good God.

I grasp her hips and lift her to wrap her legs around my waist. My cock brushes against her soaked pussy, and I grit my teeth and suck in a breath through my nose.

That felt too fucking good.

Only a mere precursor to how incredible it will feel to be buried balls-deep inside her.

I pin her against the window with my chest and shift my hips back to grasp my cock and align it with her wet heat. She locks her gaze with mine, the green there flooded with a frantic need I share, and I shove into her, impaling her fully in one hard thrust.

Her mouth falls open. "Oh, God."

I grit my teeth. "Fuck."

She clenches around my cock and rocks her hips, shifting the angle to take me even deeper than I knew possible.

"Sweet *fuck*, Greer." I drag my hips back and plunge into her again, driving her back against the window. "I could get lost in your fucking cunt forever and die happy."

Her nails score along my nape, and her heels dig into my back, urging me on and clinging to me while I hammer into her. I squeeze her ass hard enough that it will probably leave bruises and thrust even deeper, bottoming out and letting the head of my cock drag against her G-spot on each withdrawal.

Greer's head drops against the glass, exposing the long, smooth column of her neck to me. It's too much to resist. I kiss my way along it, from her elegant collarbone up to her ear.

"You feel so fucking incredible, Coach. This pussy might be heaven."

She groans and rolls her hips even harder to meet my rhythm. Sweat slickens our heated skin. Our breaths come fast. Both of us chasing something we never wanted to admit we needed.

I kiss my way across her cheek and retake her mouth with the same ferocity as her pussy. This isn't slow and sweet. I *never* do slow and sweet. But Greer knew what she was getting. She knew the kind of lover I would be, and she wanted it anyway.

Wanted me.

Wanted *this*.

And thank fuck she did because *this* is truly spectacular.

We move together like rolling waves, arching, meeting each other in a perfect dance of two bodies becoming one. Her breath hitches, and a low mewl starts deep in her chest.

She's going to come again, and I'm going to come with her while I watch her fall apart.

I kiss her harshly and shift one hand from her ass to slide it between our bodies. My thumb finds her clit just above where our bodies are connected, and I grind against it with every thrust.

"Yes, like that. Fuck." Her head shakes, and she pulls her lip between her teeth before her mouth drops open in a silent scream.

This orgasm doesn't wash over her, it collides with her like a runaway train. She bucks wildly, pinned between my body and the window. Her pussy ripples and clasps at my cock, and the warm tingle of my impending release starts.

"Fuck, I love watching you come." I grunt out the words between thrusts, and when she finally comes down from her high, I pull my hand from between us to grip her chin. "Look at me, Greer."

Her eyes fly open, cloudy and unfocused, but with a roll and snap of my hips, they widen, and she moans.

"I'm going to come inside you, Greer. I'm going to give you every fucking thing I have."

I push into her half a dozen times and then fulfill that promise. My orgasm hits me like a tsunami, flooding my system with ecstasy, and I empty myself into her until I finally sag against her quivering body, the window the only thing still holding us up.

Fucking hell.

I press a light kiss to her collarbone, then pull back. A tiny smile tugs at her lips, but her half-lidded eyes look heavy, like she's about to pass out.

"You better not fall asleep on me, Coach. We're just getting started."

13

GREER

Jill gasps. "You did *what?*"

I lie back on my bed with my phone pressed to my ear and sigh. "I slept with Bash."

And then ran the hell out of there like I was a sinner in church while he was passed out, so I could avoid staring at the proof of what we did. *After* I stared at his naked body for what felt like an hour and finally read his tattoos...

Jill squeals. "Oh, my God. I told you that man would be like crack to you. You weren't going to be able to stay away."

"More like poison than crack." The kind that seeps into your veins and the air you breathe. The kind you feel with every breath and every beat of your heart. "And...you are right."

Staying away is going to be damn near impossible. Even if I didn't have to see him almost every day, I'd be lying if I said I wouldn't find another reason to end up in the same room as him. Preferably alone. So we could have a repeat of last night.

Jill laughs. "I know. I just like hearing those three little words out of your mouth."

I chuckle and lower my face into my palm. "Ugh. I am in such deep shit, Jill." Like the pile of triceratops shit they had to dig into in *Jurassic Park* kind of size. Maybe even bigger. "I'm drowning in it."

"Why? No one needs to know what happened. Or that it's going to continue to happen."

"I don't know if it is." The words come out even though they're a blatant lie.

It will.

Probably over and over again.

And there will be lots of screaming and orgasms. So. Many. Orgasms.

Jill scoffs. "Bullshit. A man like that is not someone you go to bed with once and then he's out of your system. It doesn't work that way."

That's exactly what I'm afraid of.

But Jill has never met Bash. She can't possibly understand what it's like to be in his orbit. To be the focus of his attention and charm. "How the hell would you know?"

"Because I know his *type*. And so do you."

"I do."

Too good-looking.

Charming.

Amazing in bed.

Total alpha.

My pussy clenches just thinking about what he did to me last night—multiple times.

"Sooo..." Jill draws out the word, "when are you going to see him again?"

I sit up and shake my head. "Actually, I'm not sure. He got suspended for what happened in the Whales game. So, he can't practice or come to the games."

"For how long?"

"Eight games. He won't be back until the middle of our road trip in two weeks. Right before the Stingrays."

Which feels like an eternity...

"Well, that's good. They're your biggest rivals, aren't they?"

"One of them, and they're right behind us in the division, so we need to beat them."

We need to be as many games ahead as possible going into these last few weeks of the regular season to ensure we secure a playoff spot.

"Well"—Jill pauses like she's considering something —"if he's not playing for the next couple weeks, maybe *you* can find another way to occupy his time."

I bark out a laugh and push to my feet. "You're supposed to be talking me out of this, not encouraging me."

She scoffs. "If you wanted somebody to talk you out of this, you called the wrong girl. This is exactly what you need to loosen the hell up."

"But—"

"But what?"

I pinch the bridge of my nose and try to figure out a way to explain this to her. There are a lot of reasons this is an awful idea, but I just keep coming back to one. "What if it turns into something more?"

"What do you mean? Are you developing feelings for this guy?"

"I don't know."

And that's the honest answer.

Bash is nothing but contradictions. An amazing player but out of control. Annoying but entertaining. Charming but also a dick at times. He's not the type of guy you get involved with if you're looking for *I love yous* and happily ever afters.

I sigh and pace. "Bash is a player in every sense of the word. He's the guy you go to for a good time."

"Isn't that all you're looking for? A good time? I mean, you're not looking for marriage and babies, are you?"

"Right now? No. It would be really shitty timing to even think about that. Not with my career where it is. But I'm already thirty-two. If I put it off too much longer, all my eggs are going to be shriveled up and crusty."

Her laughter floats over the line. "I just got a really uncomfortable visual of your fallopian tubes."

"Gee, thanks."

"Hey, you brought it up."

I wander over to the window that overlooks my backyard. Instead of the lush green lawn and trees I grew up with, I'm stuck staring at rocks and palm trees. The desert will take getting used to. Even after over six months living here, I still long for the scent of rain and the changing fall colors.

Or maybe I only want to go home because it's my safe place. Where I can get a hug from Dad and forget what's happening with Bash and the stress of the approaching playoffs.

"I don't know what I want, Jill, but it just seems like I'm risking a hell of a lot for this guy if it's just a fling. I could find someone to have meaningless sex with pretty much anywhere. Do you know what I mean?"

"I do, hon, but you also need to live a little bit. You've been so focused on your career for the last fifteen years that you haven't done much living outside hockey."

"What about Sean?"

"Sean was a douche. You were with that guy way too long, and I never liked him."

Something she informed me of many times during the years I was with him. I thought they just didn't mesh, but she saw something beneath the surface I couldn't. She sensed he was no good when all I saw were hearts and roses...and his warm, dark eyes and sexy grin.

Shit.

I pinch the bridge of my nose. "You know who Sean reminds me an awful lot of."

"Let me guess. Bash?"

"Yep."

How could I not have seen it?

Sure, Bash plays hockey while Sean was an accountant, but they are so much alike in so many ways. I definitely have a type. Jill called me on that before, and she was absolutely spot-on with her assessment.

"Greer, you're wrong. Sean was the guy who should've been stable. The kind of guy you spend the rest of your life with. The fact that he turned out to be a total player had nothing to do with the type of guys you're attracted to. He was the polar opposite of Bash. Just because they might look a little alike doesn't mean you should be pushing your feelings about Sean on him."

"I'm not. It's just hard not to compare the two when he was my last serious relationship."

My only one, in all honesty. There were other guys in high school and college, but with constant practices and traveling, maintaining any sort of relationship was nearly impossible.

Until Sean.

He seemed to get it. He understood why my career was so important. Or so I thought. Turned out, he just liked my being gone from town all the time because it meant he could fuck around more easily.

"Seriously, Greer. You're overthinking this. You need to just have some fun. See where it goes."

"Or I need to leave it in the rearview mirror and get back to just being his coach."

"As if you can really do that…I gotta go. I'll talk to you later."

The line goes dead, and I toss my phone onto the bed.

Jill made a few good points. Maybe I am overthinking this thing with Bash, but it's hard not to when the stakes are so high. If I let myself actually develop feelings for him, it's only going to get worse.

So, don't get a case of the feels for the guy.

It sounds easy. Maybe if I concentrate on reminding myself of the things about him that I *don't* like, it will be easier to discount the things that I do.

Yeah. I can do that.

But if I'm going to go down this path with Bash, there have to be some ground rules.

One—no public displays.

Two—no feelings.

If he can live with that, so can I.

———

BASH

"Dude, you just love to get yourself deep in the shit, don't you?"

I take a bite of my burger and glare at Caleb across the table. "You know, when I came down here to Phoenix to see you during this forced vacation, it wasn't to have you be a total jackass."

He grins and takes a sip of his beer. "I'm just telling it like I see it. I mean, to be fair, you're only here because you're suspended for beating the shit out of someone."

I growl and shove a handful of fries into my mouth.

And here I thought an eight-game suspension would be a decent time to go see Caleb and Tara. I, apparently incorrectly, believed seeing my best friend would help kill the downtime and also give me a chance to sort out my feelings about what's going on with Greer. Now Caleb's kind of being a dick, and I wish I was back in Vegas, preferably with Greer underneath me again.

Caleb sets his beer down and leans across the table toward me with a glance at the people around us. "Bash, come on, you slept with your *coach*. That's ten times worse than anything else you've ever done."

I shrug. "That people know about." I flash him a grin and down the rest of my beer. "There are things even *you* don't know, my friend."

He chuckles and relaxes back in his chair. The loud and raucous crowd around us cheers for the game on the TV, and I glance up.

We're up by three. I kept my eyes on the screen, hoping for a glimpse of her, but they've only shown her once. She's so intense. So focused on the game.

I wonder if she's even thought about me once since she snuck out of my hotel room while I was still passed out the other day.

"Maybe sleeping with my coach wasn't the best decision I've ever made." My cock twitches, remembering how incredible it felt to be inside her. "But, man, it was so worth it."

"You're such a dog." He tips his beer toward me. "Do you realize how complicated you just made your working relationship with her?"

I offer him another shrug. "Can't be any more complicated than it already was. I mean, we basically argued every time we saw each other."

"You argued because she asked you to act more like a human being and you refused."

I scowl at him. "What's your point?"

He scoffs and takes a long pull on his beer. "My point, Bash, is that, at some point in time, you're going to have to grow up and realize that your actions have consequences. Whether it be a suspension"—he waves his hand toward me—"or worse. What's going to happen when you go back in a few days?"

"What do you mean?"

"Between you and Greer. What's going to happen?"

I know what I *want* to happen. I want to be with her again. I don't want this to just be a one-time thing. Though *why* I want that, and where I want it to go are still dark, gloomy, indecipherable questions floating around in my head.

Greer is incredible, but I've been with *a lot* of incredible women in my life.

Incredibly beautiful ones—supermodels galore. Incredibly smart ones—it's always surprising who comes to games and throws themselves at me, even people with doctorates in subjects I can't even pronounce. Incredibly talented ones—rock stars, actresses, authors, and television hosts. Incredibly *sexy* ones—women who are practically professionals at sex.

But over the last couple of days, I haven't been able to think of a single one who has it all—except Greer.

I grab a fry and swipe it through the ranch dressing on my plate. I'll have to pay later for eating this fried crap, but I'm on "vacation." I chew slowly and watch Caleb. "How did you know that you wanted more from Tara than just a booty call?"

He sighs and crosses his arms over his chest. "When I couldn't stop thinking about her and worrying when we were apart, wondering if she was okay. When I realized the time I *had* spent with her was the most satisfying and happiest I could remember."

It makes sense. Caleb has never looked so deliriously happy. Tara and the kids have totally changed how he views the world and his life. He's a playboy no longer, and even though part of me mourns the loss of my wingman and the carefree lifestyle he used to lead, I have to admit there's a tiny bit of jealousy there, too.

"I never thought that would be something I want—to settle down and have kids and give up the sport."

His eyebrows fly up. "You would give it up?"

"I would have to...if I ever wanted that. You know what it was like growing up the way we did. I wouldn't do that to a woman I was in love with or to a kid."

He nods sympathetically. "It certainly wasn't easy on any of you."

That's an understatement, but I know he understands. He saw Jameson and Rach struggling to get Dad's attention when he was home. Caleb saw Mom and me struggling to hide from them how bad things really were between them. He helped me distract them from the fact that Dad cared more about the sport than he did us.

"No. It wasn't. And the whole marriage and kids thing sure as hell isn't anything I want anytime *soon*. Maybe not ever. I'm at the height of my career. Giving that up is out of the question. And even when I'm done...I don't know..." I shake my head. "I don't think I'm cut out for that life. I don't have a clue how to be a good husband or father."

Caleb offers a sympathetic look. "So, where does that leave things with you and Greer, then?"

I pop another couple of fries in my mouth as I consider his question. "I don't know. Do I really have to put a name on it or decide what it means right now?"

Can't we just do what feels good until it stops feeling good?
It seems so simple.

So easy.

He laughs. "For someone who gets laid so much, you sure don't know very much about women."

I grin at him. "I think those women I've been with would beg to differ."

"You may know something about a woman's body, but in terms of what they're thinking and feeling, you're pretty clueless, brother."

"Maybe I am." I shrug and sip my beer. "But I think Greer and I are on the same page."

He scoffs and gives me an incredulous look. "What makes you think that?"

I was upfront about who and what I am with Greer from day one. She knows I'm not a relationship guy. I'm not the white knight or prince. I'm not the one to look for if she wants some whirlwind, long-term romance.

"She never gave any indication she was looking for anything more than just a good time."

Caleb shakes his head and downs the rest of his beer. "You are in so much trouble, Bash."

I want to believe he's wrong and I can just keep things casual without it getting complicated. But something in my gut tells me he's right.

Greer isn't the type of girl a guy can sleep with without there being more.

That does leave me in quite the predicament because I don't think it's possible to stay away from that woman.

14

GREER

Sixty exhausting minutes of play have worn me the fuck out, and I wasn't even on the ice. I flop down onto the hotel room bed and release a groan as I kick off my heels.

Who thought it was a good idea to wear heels to every game?

I could probably get away with wearing flats to be more comfortable, but I feel like it looks more professional to be heeled. Even though no one can really see them. It's just become a habit. My coaches always made their players dress up game days, and they were always in suits and dress shoes. My being a woman shouldn't change that. Nor should the fact that I'm the coach now.

No sneakers for me.

Just really sore feet.

Between the late flight here from San Diego after the loss there, and the brutal game tonight, I'm just mentally and physically *done.*

It was like for every step forward we took, they took four. And it was even harder because we're still missing Bash. We managed to win the first couple games of his suspension, but then, it was like we fell apart. Everything we did looked sloppy and slow. Like we were a completely different team overnight.

And Bash's suspension isn't technically over until after tonight's game.

Which means he'll be arriving here in L.A. tomorrow in time for practice so we can use him against the Stingrays.

Thank fuck because we need him.

There are only a handful of games left before the end of the season, and with tonight's win in *their* game and *our* loss, they're only two points back. We can't let them gain any more ground. Having Bash back will help—a lot.

As long as he can keep himself under control.

And while I don't condone the actions that got him suspended, I can at least understand why he did it. He was defending me, in his own completely inappropriate way. I fought tooth and nail against having Bash Fury on this team, but now, I can't wait to have him back—at least, on the ice.

On the personal front, I have no clue how to deal with the awkwardness of seeing him for the first time since we slept together. I thought a couple weeks would be enough time to figure out what I want to tell him, what I want to say and how to even begin to address this awkwardness our romp has created, but it all still feels like nothing more than a jumbled mass of confusing emotions.

My body and my head are warring worse than the Flyers and Penguins.

All I want right now is to have a drink and take a long, hot shower to relax away the tension in my back and shoulders. But that would mean moving from the bed, which I definitely don't want to do even if I *could* drag myself up.

A loud knock at the door has me jerking up, and I glance around the room.

Where did that come from?

The knock comes again.

That wasn't the hallway door.

It's the door that leads to the adjoining room.

What the hell?

I slide off the bed and make my way over to the door on aching feet. This is like the start of a horror movie where the stupid girl opens the door to a serial-killer stalker in the room next to her.

Really dumb, Greer.

Don't answer it.

My hand curls around the lamp on the dresser running along the wall next to the door. At least if someone tries to murder me, I have some sort of a weapon to defend myself.

I stare at the door.

The second knock makes me jump again. I swallow thickly and take a step closer. "Who is it?"

A familiar deep chuckle comes under the crack in the door. "It's me, Coach."

My heart flips in my chest. "Bash?"

I twist the lock on the door and pull it open. The devil himself leans against the jamb in the adjoining room, a grin occupying his lips and a glimmer of that arrogance in his eyes.

Damn. He looks good.

The time off didn't change a thing or weaken my reaction to him. Heat flares in my belly, and a dull ache forms between my legs. The same one that's haunted me since our night together.

I am so not ready for this.

Here I thought I had more time to consider this entire

situation, that I wouldn't have to see him face to face until he rejoined the team tomorrow.

I need another day!

I'm not mentally prepared to have this discussion, but he's standing only two feet in front of me. It's not like I can slam the door in his smug face, even if part of me may want to. "What are you doing here?"

He raises an eyebrow. "My suspension is over. I'm back tomorrow."

I sigh and wave my hand. "Yeah, yeah, I know that. I meant what are you doing *here*." I point to his room. "You weren't supposed to arrive until morning."

Bash takes a step toward me, his whiskey eyes raking over me in a way that suddenly makes me feel naked, even though I'm still wearing a blouse and my suit skirt.

"I decided to come early. And, when I checked in, I asked for an adjoining room."

My mouth drops open. "And they just *gave it* to you? What if you had been some kind of stalker or pervert?"

He grins and takes another step toward me, the move menacing and demanding. I step back until my knees hit the bed behind me. There isn't anywhere left to run from this man, and he knows it.

"I'm not a stalker, Coach, but I'm definitely a pervert." His tongue snakes out and over his lips like he's remembering the taste of something he really enjoyed. He winks at me. "But you already knew that."

God, why is that so hot?

I should *hate* this—his swagger, his attitude, his big fucking ego that can barely fit in this room, yet heat floods every limb, and my legs begin to shake.

"I've missed you, Coach."

Fuck.

The way my stomach flips with his words also makes me wince.

Does he mean it?

Is this just a game?

I haven't said a damn word, and I can't retreat any farther or leave—the bed is behind me and Bash directly in front—I'm caged in. Nowhere to go. Nowhere to run. Nowhere to hide from this man who has already broken me down and gotten under my skin in a way I never knew anyone ever could.

His assessing gaze scans me from head to toe.

Say something, Greer!

"Oh"—I clear my throat—"you did?"

He nods, and his focus zeroes in on my lips. "Sure did."

Then why didn't you call or text?

The question hangs on the tip of my tongue, but I bite it back because I don't want to look like *that* girl, the one who needs a man to call her the morning after. Especially when I'm the one who bolted from his room while he was asleep.

That was sheer panic, but I need to make it seem like I was just trying to keep things light.

I can do casual. I can do casual with Bash.

I think.

He closes the distance between us and wraps one arm around my back while the other cups my cheek. "I was trying to give you a little time and space, Coach. To think about what happened and to figure out how you felt about the situation."

"Oh." My response comes out breathy and needy, not at all the strong, confident woman I had hoped I would sound like when I finally came to face to face with him again.

"Oh?" He raises a brow at me and grazes his thumb over my bottom lip. "That's the only response I get? *Oh*?"

I suck in a sharp breath and shrug. "I'm not sure how else to answer that."

He leans in until his lips are a mere hairsbreadth from mine. "How about you tell me you've been thinking about me, too? That you've been fantasizing every waking moment about what it felt like to be with me. What it felt like when my cock was pounding into you. How it felt when my tongue was deep in your pussy."

Christ.

My clit throbs. My legs tremble. I wobble, but his strong arm around my waist holds me steady.

His lips barely feather across mine. "Why don't you tell me that, Coach?"

"I...I can't."

Long, strong fingers tighten on my hip. "Why not?"

Because admitting that would give him all the power.

I can't do that. Power is like gold to a man like Bash. And he already has far too much over me. I've somehow let him take charge of this situation, and that could be lethal for everything I've worked so damn hard to achieve.

Another gentle brush of his lips sends a rolling shudder through me.

"Come on, Coach. Do it. You'll feel so much better after you do."

His hand drops from my back down to my ass and squeezes firmly. His fingers slowly inch their way around until they find the hem of my skirt.

I bite my lip to prevent the moan threatening to work its way up my throat from slipping out and giving me away.

Heroin.

Bash Fury isn't crack. He's ten times worse. He's heroin. One hit is all you need to become addicted. And I sure as hell am.

To his touch.

To his kiss.

To everything about him, even his damn arrogant grin.

BASH

She's like putty in my hands.

Her soft, warm body sags against mine.

Her legs shake.

Her fingers tighten at my sides.

Her lips move greedily against my own.

The way she's responding to me tells me everything I need to know even though she won't say the words.

Greer may be fighting a battle between her attraction to me and what a good girl would do, but she's losing against that little voice in her head telling her to stop.

She's spent the last two weeks thinking about me just as much as I've been thinking about her. Reliving every moment we spent together that night. Reliving every touch, every kiss, and every orgasm. Touching herself thinking about it the same way I've been stroking my rock hard cock each time even a flicker of memory floats through my head.

And the longer I kiss her, the more I know I'm making the right decision.

Not to walk away.

Because I can't. Not when she occupies every waking thought and fills every dream when I finally rest my head on my pillow at night.

Caleb asked me where this was going, and I didn't have a fucking clue. Even after thinking about it for two weeks, I had no idea what would happen between us when I got back.

If I'd listened to my head, nothing would have

happened. We would have gone back to coach and player, hopefully with some of the tension between us relieved so we could remain professional. But fuck if I can remember the last time I listened to my head.

The longer I was away, the more I realized that this thing with Greer didn't need to be one-time only. We both know what's happening here, and if we want to use each other to scratch an itch and offer relief during a very stressful time, why the hell wouldn't we?

Especially after having experienced how extraordinary we are together.

I need a repeat.

We can let this runs its course, have fun for as long as it stays that way. And I want nothing more than to sink into her welcoming heat right now. But I can see she's utterly exhausted. She doesn't need another marathon of sex tonight.

What she needs is to be taken care of. Adored. Worshipped.

It's not something I can claim to be very good at, but I can damn well try.

I reluctantly drag my mouth away from hers, and her head follows me up, trying to keep her lips pressed to mine.

Her eyes fly open, and her clouded green gaze screams in confusion. "What?"

I chuckle and press another quick kiss to her lips while squeezing her tightly to me so she can feel my very eager cock pressed between us and doesn't think I'm not just as interested as she is. "Hold that thought." I lower her down to the bed, and she sits there staring at me with her mouth open. I lean over her and drop my palms on the mattress, boxing her in with my arms. "You're exhausted, Coach. It's been a long road trip for you, and we have a game tomorrow. You need to relax. I'm going to go draw you a bath. We're making use of the massive whirlpool tub in this suite tonight."

Her eyebrows fly up. "Are you serious?"

I grin and stand. "As a heart attack. Don't look so shocked, Coach. I'm not giving up on what we just started, only delaying it a little." The disappointed look on her face makes me chuckle again. I wink at her. "I promise, I won't leave you hanging, Coach."

She blushes a beautiful shade of pink, and I make my way to her bathroom and crank on the faucet while adjusting my erection away from the painful press of my zipper.

Down boy.

At least for a while, this is one hundred percent about her. She deserves that. She needs that. And even though I don't have any fucking clue how to take care of someone, I can fucking try.

I run my hand through the water until it hits the right temperature, then plug the drain. The level rises in the tub, and I trail my fingers through the warmth, a sudden flash of how a naked Greer will look under it filling my head.

She appears in the doorway and leans against it, watching me. "We're really going to take a bath together?"

I push to my feet and pull my shirt up and over my head, letting it fall to the floor. "Yep, we are." I pop the button on my fly and lower the zipper. Her eyes follow the movement, and I cough. "My eyes are up here, Coach."

She grins at me and it morphs into a carefree, genuine smile that doesn't hold any of the apprehension or reluctance it once did. What happened before I left town broke open the dam of animosity that had been holding back our attraction for each other. That had been keeping us from exploring whatever the hell this is. It shattered that heavy barrier and even two weeks away hasn't been enough time to build it back up.

I shove down my pants, and my still-hard cock springs free. She eyes it and licks her lips, shifting slightly on her feet.

"If you want to taste it that badly, Coach, all you need to do is ask."

Her eyes widened as they shoot up to meet mine, and her jaw drops. That pink flush turns bright red. "I wasn't..." She buries her face in her hands. "Shit."

A light, tinkling laughter floats through the small bathroom and lifts away any remaining doubts that I'm doing the right thing.

I kick off my shoes and pants and stalk over to pull her into my arms. Her hands still cover her face, and I tug at them until she lowers them. I tilt her chin up to make her look at me. "There's nothing to be embarrassed about, Coach. I fucking love the way you taste, and if you want to find out if you feel the same way, I'm more than willing to let you do some exploring in that regard. Watching my cock disappear between these plump, beautiful lips would be fucking ecstasy."

In fact, that would be one of the many fantasies that's been running through my head over the last few weeks. My dick deep down her throat. Coach staring up at me and sucking me hard. Little moans of approval and pleasure rippling across my cock.

Fuck.

I grind my hips against hers, pressing my hardness against her. She reaches down and grabs my shaft, wrapping her palm around it tightly. I lean forward to kiss her deeply. Instead of the harsh, aggressive kiss I gave her earlier, this one is languid, lingering, exploring, and tasting. It's unhurried and sexier than any kiss I've had in my entire life.

Shit.

I hadn't planned for anything to happen in that tub other than maybe give her a nice shoulder massage to release some of the tension there, but I don't know any man in the world who would turn down a blow job from a woman like Greer Waterson.

"But," I whisper the word against her lips, "I get to take care of you first."

The way her pink, kiss-swollen lips turn up into a smile has my cock twitching in her grip.

It's such a simple gesture. One I'm sure she does a hundred times a day when we aren't playing, but not at the arena. Not with the team. Greer is all business there. She doesn't let her hard exterior crack around the guys.

It's a self-preservation technique, one that has probably been necessary her entire life. That's both sad and infuriating. I don't think anyone has ever accused me of being a feminist, probably about as far from it as is humanly possible, but Greer shouldn't have to hide her joy or amusement just to appease some guys who think their balls are bigger than her résumé.

"You should do that more often, Coach."

Her brow furrows. "Do what?"

"Smile." And if I have any say in it, I'm going to ensure there's one plastered to her face as long as I have access to her stunning body. "Now, let's get you naked and into that tub."

I have plans...

15

GREER

"**W**here are you taking me?"

Bash flashes a grin from the driver seat and then returns his focus to the road in front of us. The road that *isn't* going toward the Prestige.

I twist in my seat to watch him and try to get a read on what he's doing. A playful smirk curls his lips, and I heave out a sigh. "This is definitely not the way to your hotel."

And I don't have the energy to go anywhere else.

The game tonight was particularly brutal, as the final games of the season always are—a full sixty minutes of a drag-down, knockout fight, and then we still ended up in overtime and a shootout.

We got the win—one we badly needed to maintain our position in third in the conference going into our final game two days from now—but the guys are beat up, and we're all utterly exhausted. The last two weeks since Bash got off his suspension have been nothing short of all-out war in the Pacific Division.

When Bash suggested relaxing tonight, I *thought* we'd be

going back to his hotel, maybe taking a long, hot shower or bath together again, but this is the opposite direction, and the playful look he has means he's up to something.

One thing I've learned very quickly about Bash since we started our—*what? affair? relationship? fling?*—whatever, is that he loves to play—literally and figuratively. Whether it be on the ice, in the bedroom, or in life, he's always making moves.

"Trust me, Coach. We're going somewhere you'll be able to unwind and have a good time."

"Bash, I'm not up for anything you consider '*a good time.*'" I use air quotes for emphasis. "I'm tired."

A good time with him, more often than not, leaves me more exhausted than I was before it.

He barks out a laugh and reaches over to squeeze my thigh. "Coach, you canceled practice for tomorrow. That means tonight is a rare night I can take you somewhere without us worrying about getting up at the ass crack of dawn. So, just trust me."

Trust Bash Fury?

Strangely, I do. The more time alone I spend with him, the more I come to realize that he isn't just the persona he puts out in the media and on the ice. There are layers to Bash—ones I'm just beginning to peel back and unravel. Ones I'm not so sure anyone else has ever seen—save for maybe his closest friends and family.

Bash does his best to never show any cracks in his façade, but when we're alone, when we're *together*, that entire mask crumbles. He's still cocky and arrogant and infuriating but in the *best* way possible. The way that leaves me panting and utterly spent almost every night. He *deserves* to be cocky about his skills in the bedroom, but when it's just the two of us, I see the real person with real feelings and worries under all the bravado.

I sigh and rest my head back on the seat as I watch the Strip disappear behind us. "And you're not going to tell me where we're going?"

He stops at a red light and winks at me. "That would ruin the surprise, Coach."

"I don't know that I'm up for any surprises."

But the little gifts Bash has been leaving for me are very sweet...and totally unexpected. Just another sign that he's so much more than anyone gives him credit for.

I've never had anyone do anything like this for me before—little surprises on my desk every morning...

First, it was the cupcake with the Scorpions logo in icing —adorable, thoughtful, *and* delicious—along with the note that read:

Not as sweet as you. - S

Then came the gold puck-shaped keychain with the word "COACH" engraved on it and a card that said:

You are this team. - S

But the one that *really* got to me, the one that had me wondering if Bash could actually be the exact *opposite* of everything everyone believes, was the flower. A single red rose.

No note.

One wasn't needed.

Given what happened the night before, it was clear what it meant.

It had been magical—unlike anything I've experienced with anyone else in my entire life.

Slow. Passionate. It was a connection—two bodies becoming one. No words were said because none were necessary. And the rose was the perfect acknowledgment of that.

If I didn't know Bash and his reputation, if we hadn't agreed this was just going to be fun until it stopped being that, I might even say he had made love to me. So, maybe I should give him the benefit of the doubt that where he's taking me tonight will be exactly what I need.

"I'm trusting you, Bash, but I'm telling you right now, I don't want to be out late tonight. The entire point of canceling practice tomorrow was for everyone to relax and recover from the game, to recharge."

"I promise you'll enjoy this, Coach, and it will be incredibly relaxing."

Somehow, I doubt that.

Although, the long, hot bath and shoulder massage Bash gave me last week when he surprised me at the hotel in LA *was* relaxing. At least until he put his quick, talented hands to work on something other than my tense shoulders.

He is just so much...*everything* that it's hard to keep a clear mind when he's in the vicinity.

He's just so...Bash.

We turn onto Highland Drive, and my unease grows. I stare out the window at the industrial buildings and dirty clubs lining the street. This area is part of the seedy underbelly of Vegas. There isn't any good reason to come down here, at least not for me.

He turns us into a parking lot, and I glance up at the neon sign on the building.

I look over at him. "You have to be kidding me."

He pulls up to the valet, throws it into park, and grins at me.

I scowl at him. "Bash, I am not going into a strip club with you."

He barks out a laugh and shakes his head before he

leans over and presses a quick kiss to my lips. "Spearmint Rhino is a fantastic place, Coach. Give it a chance."

Hell no.

I cross my arms over my chest and shake my head. "No, Bash. What the hell are you thinking? We can't be seen together, especially in a place like this."

He brushes his lips against my ear. "Already thought of that, Coach, and called ahead. We're going in the private VIP entrance and will have our own room."

Our own room? What the hell does that mean?

It makes it sound even seedier.

There's a reason I've always avoided places like this—definitely not my scene—but I shouldn't be surprised it's where Bash would bring me. This place is very...*Bash.*

He grabs my hand and squeezes as a valet comes to my door. "Half an hour. If you're not having fun, we'll go. I promise."

His bourbon eyes sparkle with humor, and I can't help the smile that pulls at the corner of my mouth.

"Fine. Thirty minutes."

Bash jumps out of the car, leaving the keys in the ignition.

The valet opens my door and offers me a hand. "Good evening, ma'am."

So formal for a smut show.

I feel like I should be bowing or something. "Good evening."

A large man in a black suit steps forward and holds out an arm, indicating we should head down the side of the building instead of to the front door. "Right this way."

Bash wraps his arm around my shoulder as we follow the man through a side door and down a dimly lit hallway. Deep bass from the music in the main club vibrates the walls, the ceiling, and even the floor beneath us.

The man motions into the room. "Your VIP suite."

Suite? What the hell is Bash up to?

This all seems very elaborate for a "relaxing" night, even for Bash.

Bash nods at the man and presses his hand against my lower back to usher me in.

Wow.

I don't know what I was expecting the inside of this place to look like, but it wasn't this. Plush, luxurious leather couches line the walls, and a small stage with a pole stands in the center of the room. Bash closes the door behind him and directs me to take a seat.

He settles in next to me and presses a kiss to my temple. "Don't look so angry, Coach. Just relax, and you'll have a great time."

"I'm not so sure about that." I scan the room to ensure we're alone. "This isn't exactly my scene, Bash..."

He grins at me, the same cocky one that I used to hate so much that now stirs something low and warm in my belly. "No shit, Coach. I never would've guessed."

I swat his shoulder. "Ha, ha. Very funny."

"Is this your first time at a strip club?"

"Of course, it is, Bash. Come on."

He shakes his head and reclines back. "It's a valid question, Coach. A lot of women come to strip clubs."

"'A lot.'" I use air quotes. "Maybe the women *you* associate with."

His eyes widen, and he presses his hands over his chest. "Ouch, Coach. That one stung a little bit."

I roll my eyes at him. "You know what I mean, Bash."

"No." He shakes his head, and something that looks an awful lot like actual hurt crosses his face. That vulnerability I've caught glimpses of during our intimate time together. "I don't. Explain it to me—"

A knock at the door stops what would have undoubtedly turned into a very uncomfortable situation or even an argument like the ones we've managed to avoid lately, and a beautiful redhead with tits bigger than my head enters with a tray stacked high with bottles of water and what looks like mixers.

Bash holds up a hand to me. "I know what you're going to say, Coach, and no worries. No alcohol tonight."

"Good. You are really starting to worry me..."

He frowns and leans in. "You worry too much." He kisses me again as the woman sets down her tray. "Relax is the word of the day. Just let go."

A beautiful blonde waltzes in wearing sky-high heels and basically nothing else. The tiny G-string covering her pussy can't really be called clothing. Her perfectly high, round breasts have me crossing my arms over my own chest.

Bash glances at me and chuckles low.

The waitress disappears and shuts the door behind her, and the blonde moves over to us and leans forward, dangling her breasts practically in my face. "I'm Lila. What's your name?"

I can't get the words out.

Should I even be using my real name?

Sweat breaks out on my palms, and I brush them against my leggings.

Bash wraps his arm around me and squeezes. "You can call her 'Coach.'"

My mouth falls open, and I elbow him in the chest, but he just laughs.

Lila grins and runs her long-nailed finger slowly down my arm. "Well, Coach, is this your first time here?"

I nod.

Do I look like someone who frequents trashy strip clubs?

Bash leans forward and waggles his eyebrows. "It's her first time *ever* at a strip club."

Lila's blue eyes widen, and a slow smile spreads across her too-red lips. "Ooh...a virgin."

Bash barks out a laugh and shakes his head. "Exactly."

The beautiful stripper winks. "Well, we'll just have to make sure she has an amazing time, then."

Oh God...what have I gotten myself into?

———

BASH

I shouldn't enjoy seeing Greer so uncomfortable, but this is the *good* kind of uncomfortable. The same kind of uncomfortable she felt when we argued in her office and I had on nothing more than a towel. The same kind of uncomfortable when we were alone in my hotel room and I kissed her for the first time and made her admit I wasn't so bad. The same kind of uncomfortable as when she saw my cock and then couldn't look me in the eye. The same kind of uncomfortable as when I made her come for the first time and when I showed her what being "well and truly fucked" really meant.

This is the kind that leads to good things—for both of us.

And she needs it.

With the playoffs so close and our position in third so rocky, she's been wound so tightly that I've thought she might actually explode lately. Even climbing into my bed every night and letting me work her over and leave her boneless and quivering hasn't been enough to release that tension from her shoulders.

But I knew Greer would like it here, and that it would be

a challenge for her to admit it. She might not be there yet, might not be ready to say she's having a good time, but the way she watches Lila move to the music right in front of her, the way her cheeks redden as Lila rubs her bare ass all over Greer's thighs, the way Greer's body stiffens and her tongue darts out to lick her lips...

Christ, watching Coach get turned on is the biggest fucking turn-on for me.

My cock swells and pushes uncomfortably against the zipper of my jeans. I reach down and adjust away from the offending metal as I watch Greer, unable and unwilling to look away from her.

I don't give a shit about Lila.

This was never about coming to watch some random woman shake her ass and tits. It was about watching *this*. Seeing Greer's reaction. Feeling it. Watching her let go of all the pressure she crushes herself under all the time.

A pink flush spreads over her chest, up her neck, and across her cheeks. It's one I recognize all too well. One that spells success.

I lean in and move Greer's hair to the side, exposing her neck and ear, but her focus remains on the woman directly in front of her, swaying and grinding to the sensual music. I gently brush my lips against Greer's ear. "I told you that you'd have fun, Coach."

She flinches ever so slightly at my words, and I slide a hand across her thigh, only a few inches from where Lila twirls her hips and gyrates her toned, perfect body.

"Does this turn you on, Coach? Watching a beautiful, naked woman in front of you, brushing up against you?"

She shivers and squeezes her eyes closed for a second. When she reopens them, she glances down at my crotch, then at my eyes, with something dark flickering deep in her green gaze. "Does it turn *you* on?"

Jealousy.

That wasn't truly a question. It was an *accusation.* She thinks I'm hard because of this blonde in front of us, but it couldn't be further from the truth.

I grin at her.

Greer jealous is so fucking hot.

Her lips twist into a frown, and she waits for me to answer her question.

Instead of responding with words, I kiss her hard, sliding my tongue between her lips and demanding entrance until she relents and opens for me, tangling her tongue with mine. I slide my hand up to the waistband of her leggings and the other behind her back to hold her hip. I squeeze her there and pull back until my eyes meet hers.

"No, Coach." I feather my lips just behind her ear. "*You* turn me on. Seeing how worked up you're getting watching Lila is what has me hard as a fucking rock right now."

Her breath hitches.

I glide my tongue along the shell of her ear. "I bet if I reached inside your panties right now, your cunt would be wet and ready for me."

A tiny little whimper slips from her lips. She'll never admit it, but when I talk dirty to her, it really ramps her up just as much as it does me.

Greer has spent too much of her life fighting—against expectations, against limitations, against everyone wanting her to fail. And even though she's given in to this *thing* between us, she's still holding back. Still wound too tightly.

If she keeps living like this, she's going to break in a way that she won't be able to put herself back together again.

Lila moves from the lap dance up onto the small stage in front of us with a sultry grin, and I shift my hand to slide it into the thin fabric of Greer's leggings and down between her thighs.

"Open up for me, Coach." Instead of following my command, she clamps her legs around my hand, trying to stop the intrusion, and I chuckle against her ear. "Don't be embarrassed, Greer. Lila doesn't care that I'm touching you. I bet she likes watching..."

I nip at her ear, and it has the desired effect. She gasps and opens her legs for me on a little needy moan and digs her fingernails into my forearm sticking out from her pants.

Lila wraps herself around the pole, dangling in my peripheral vision. Greer's gaze stays locked on her but mine is focused solely on the woman who is my fantasy come to life.

I slip my fingers beneath her thong.

Fuck.

Just as I suspected...wet and ready. My cock twitches in my jeans, straining against the restrictive fabric.

Christ, I wish I were inside her right now.

If we were anywhere but here, I would be.

I slide my middle finger through Greer's arousal. She groans and arches into my hand. Lila peers over at us with a grin as she continues to dance. I glide up and around Greer's clit, applying light pressure, just enough to leave her needing more. She mewls and rocks against my palm while she watches Lila wrap herself around the pole like she's fucking it the way Greer is trying to my hand.

The sexy bass-heavy music pumping around us sets my pace, and I work Greer up, slowly and methodically, until she's practically vibrating in my arms. Slipping a finger in. Dragging it out. Glancing over her clit. Probing and retreating. All of it designed to bring her to the brink of insanity.

She fidgets on the leather seat, trying to direct me to where she wants me to get the friction she needs. I tighten my hand on her hip to keep her from shifting and slip two fingers inside her. She moans, and her eyes roll back. Her cunt tightens around my fingers, and I adjust my hand to roll her clit with my thumb while I thrust into her.

Her hips buck and move in time with the music and my hand while Lila gyrates on the stage, her breasts swaying and her ass gleaming in the overhead lighting.

There's no denying that Lila is a beautiful woman, but she's nowhere near as beautiful as Greer is right now on the cusp of coming undone in my hands. I press my lips to her neck and kiss my way up to that spot behind her ear. I lick and suck there then pull her earlobe between my teeth.

She whimpers and shakes. "I'm gonna come."

"Good. Come for me, Coach. I want to feel your cunt strangling my fingers."

It only takes a few more seconds before she explodes, squeezing around them so tightly that it feels like she might break them while she bucks against my hand.

"Oh, God...Bash!"

My name falling from her lips on the wave of her orgasm almost has me blowing my load in my pants. Only years of practiced restraint keeps me from doing just that.

Who would have thought the woman who hated me so much only a few weeks ago would let me finger-fuck her in a strip club?

Or that it would matter to me so damn much that she's happy?

Because it does.

More than I ever thought possible.

Greer Waterson has ruined my ability to remain ambivalent. She's stripped away the things I thought I had established. The rules I've followed about keeping people at arm's length.

Now, I crave having her close. I long for her when she's away. I despise having to pretend there's nothing but animosity between us when we're with the team and in public. It precisely the kind of thing I've avoided my entire life. The kind of emotions that ultimately lead to all sorts of heartbreak.

This was never meant to be anything more than a release of tension, a way to allow us to continue to work together without tearing out each other's throats. A way to make our professional relationship easier. But it's become so much more than that so fucking fast.

The brilliant blond coming on my hand brings out so many conflicting emotions.

Anger. Lust. Fear. Desire.

And there are so many reasons to question this and push it away.

But in this moment...none of it matters.

The only thing that does is her.

16

BASH

Greer sighs and presses her temple to the window. "I kind of feel like this is déjà vu."

I glance over at her then back to the road. Even getting her in the car this morning was difficult.

She's so damn stubborn.

The woman never wants to just *trust* me. Maybe that's my fault for giving myself this well-deserved reputation. I'd be lying if I said it didn't hurt a little bit that she can't see past it all the time, but after last night, I would've thought I earned some more faith from her.

We had a great time at the club. An even greater one when we got back to my hotel. Yet, she's sitting with her jaw clenched and her shoulders tensed as I drive this morning.

I reach over squeeze her hand. "You gotta trust me, Coach."

It feels like a fucking broken record playing.

"I do." She says it, but I don't know that she totally believes it. "I hope you're not taking me to another den of debauchery."

Den of debauchery?

Spearmint Rhino should use that in their ad campaigns.

I bark out a laugh and shake my head. "I guess you'll have to wait and see."

But not for too long. Two blocks later, I turn into our destination.

She leans forward and stares up at the building with wide eyes. "An ice rink?" She turns and narrows her gaze on me. "What the hell are we doing here, Bash?"

"You'll see."

"You know your contract says you can't play anywhere else, even a pickup game, right? I gave you and the rest of the guys the day off, so you'd all relax."

I roll my eyes and park the car. "Stop asking so many questions and making so many assumptions, Coach."

Most women don't give me so much attitude—except Rach, but she doesn't count. That's kind of a little sister's job.

Maybe that's why this thing with Greer feels so different. She doesn't make anything easy. I do love a good challenge, but I generally avoid anything that's going to make my life more complicated.

This certainly isn't *uncomplicating* my life, which probably means I should be looking long and hard at it. But I don't have the balls to do that and risk losing *her*. Whatever this is between us, I *like* it. Probably too much.

She sighs and steps from the car. "You know we shouldn't be seen in public together."

It never ends.

I slam my door shut and rest my arms on the roof. "There you go again, Coach. Stop worrying so much. People won't even think twice about us walking in here together."

No trust.

I'm not stupid, and the fact that Greer seems to think I am is starting to grate on me the tiniest bit. If I didn't understand where she's coming from—the need and desire to protect both our careers—it might be offensive enough to really question continuing this. Because it's only fun if she doesn't *really* hate me and think I'm a fucking idiot.

But as it stands now, it's somewhat entertaining to watch her fret over something she's going to feel *really* silly about in a few minutes.

She scowls at me over the top of the car. I push away from it, grab my bag from the trunk, and let her follow me inside the building, past the reception desk, and through the doors to the actual rink.

At least twenty kids between the ages of six and ten fill the space, some still pulling on their skates, others already out sloshing around on the ice with their tiny hockey sticks.

Greer's eyes widen. "A youth league?"

I grin at her, and she follows me toward where Nancy and Russell wait, examining a clipboard.

Nancy glances up and waves at me. "Bash, you made it."

I give her a hug and a quick peck on the cheek and shake Russell's hand.

He grips my hand tightly. "Glad you could come, Bash. The kids are really going to love this."

I offer him a reassuring smile. "Anytime I'm available, I'll try to be here."

Typically, these types of things are too hard to manage in my schedule, but with practice canceled, I didn't want to miss the opportunity to come help.

Greer's gaze darts around the kids and back to Nancy and Russell. They both smile at her and wait for an introduction.

I usher her forward. "You both know Coach Waterson."

Nancy claps excitedly and bounces up and down. "I can't believe you got her to come."

I flash my best innocent smile at Greer. "It didn't take much convincing."

She tosses me a dirty look and reaches out to shake Russell and Nancy's hands. "I'm happy to be here. What do you need us to do?"

That's so Greer...getting right down to business. She didn't skip a beat, and this sort of thing is right up her alley. I knew once she saw the kids, she'd be on board one hundred percent.

Knowing her, she probably sees this as a way to cleanse herself of the filth from last night.

I chuckle to myself, and Greer turns to me with a raised eyebrow.

Nancy saves me. "This is so great. I'd like to introduce you guys to the kids and let them ask a couple questions, and then maybe you guys can give them a few pointers."

"I'd be happy to." I glance out across the sea of kids. "Anything you guys need."

Greer watches me with something I'm not sure I've ever seen in her eyes before. I've definitely shocked her in the past, but this almost looks like adoration. Maybe she's finally realizing I'm a decent guy underneath it all and good for more than incredible sex and scoring goals.

Or maybe that's wishing for the impossible.

Russell motions toward the front desk. "You need skates?"

I hold up my bag. "I have mine."

Greer takes a seat on one of the benches. "I need an eight, please."

Russell runs off to get her skates, and Nancy turns her attention to helping one of the kids. They crowd together in little groups on the ice, and one small boy who can't be more than seven skates toward the goal and makes a perfect slapshot straight into the net.

A grin pulls at my lips, and I turn back to find Greer examining the rink.

She glances up at me. "Do you do this a lot?"

I shrug and shove my hands in my pockets. "I used to help with one of the youth leagues in Chicago. I always had a good time when I could manage to get there, so when I moved out here, I got in contact with a few of them. Nancy and Russell asked me to come out a few times."

"Well..." She shakes her head and holds up her hands. "I never would've expected this from you."

Of course, she wouldn't. Because she still sees Bash Fury as nothing more than who he is in a jersey.

Even after all the time we've spent together, she can't get past that.

I squat down in front of her and fight the urge to reach out and touch her. I can't be doing shit like that in public. "You know, Coach, I told you before, and I'll tell you again, as many times as it takes, I'm not a bad guy."

She recoils slightly. "I don't think you're a bad guy."

"Oh no?"

Her blond hair flutters around her as she shakes her head. "No, I think you're a decent guy who does bad things sometimes."

How is that any different?

Russell heads toward us with the skates, and I chuckle and push to my feet.

"Here you go." He hands them to Greer and moves over next to Nancy.

I drop next to Greer on the bench, open my bag, and tug on my skates. Greer probably would have preferred to use her own, but that would have given away where we were going. And I like seeing genuine reactions from her.

Greer does her damnedest to hide her feelings, but she's

a shitty liar, especially when she isn't anticipating something. Like last night...and today.

We lace up and follow Nancy and Russell onto the ice with the gaggle of kids. Russell ushers them together and whistles to get their attention. It takes a few minutes for everyone to gather and settle down, like herding cats.

We stand in front of them, staring down into innocent, wide-eyed faces.

Nancy holds up her hands. "Okay, everyone, we have two very special guests today. How many of you know who the Scorpions are?"

I fight a grin as two-dozen little hands shoot into the air.

Eager group. And so adorable.

"Hockey team," one little boy calls with a proud smile.

Russell nods. "That's right. They're the professional hockey team here in town, and we have the coach of the team, Coach Waterson, and one of their players, Sebastian Fury, here today."

The kids all "ooh" and clap.

Nancy motions toward Greer, who stands somewhat awestruck. "Coach Waterson played in the Olympics. Does anyone know what the Olympics are?"

One little boy raises his hand. "It's when teams from all over the world play against each other."

Russell nods and smiles at the eager kid. "That's right, Kenny, and Coach Waterson has a bunch of medals."

I glance at Greer out of the corner of my eye and find her grinning from ear to ear.

And to think she didn't trust me.

Even she enjoys having her ego stroked.

———

GREER

Who would have thought that the laughter of children could bring so much damn joy?

And it's not just me feeling the warmth of their delight at being out here.

Bash looks...different.

That grin that's been plastered on his face since we got onto the ice isn't the same one he gives me or the one he flashes after he smashes an opponent during a game. It isn't full of swagger and self-satisfaction.

This one is pure. More genuine. One brought from seeing these innocent children experiencing the love of the game *he* loves so much through untainted, pure eyes only someone their age can.

It's like I'm seeing the *real* him he hides underneath all the arrogance and attitude. Glimpses have broken through before...when we're alone. When he's sure no one else is going to see it. But this is the first time he seems to have completely dropped his guard, surrounded by dozens of kids and the various volunteers.

Warmth blooms in my chest watching him interact with them despite the chill in the air. He bends over behind a small boy and helps him adjust his grip on his stick. The boy looks up at Bash with such adoration, it makes my heart ache. This kid probably doesn't know who Bash is. He hasn't been to Scorpions games and watched him play. He hasn't memorized his stats and followed his career since he was drafted into the league. He doesn't know Bash is the son of NHL royalty. He doesn't care about *any* of that.

And in this moment, Bash doesn't either.

He's capable of being so *real*. Of being so *selfless*.

It's the kind of realization that's so fucking dangerous. It means I can't continue to ignore the fact that Bash has the ability to be the kind of man who is more than just a plea-surable way to unload my stress going into the playoffs.

Bash says something to the kid, and the little one draws back and shoots the puck at the net. It goes wide right, but Bash repositions him and helps him this time. The next puck flies straight into the center of the net, and the little boy erupts into a cheer.

A wide smile splits Bash's face, matching his young charge's, and they high-five before the little boy skates off to talk to one of his friends.

"He's great with the kids, isn't he?" Nancy practically swoons next to me.

I nod and watch him move on to another kid. "He really is."

Nancy laughs and fans herself comically. "Who would have thought? Makes him even sexier, if you ask me."

Did I ask you?

The question almost comes out, but I bite my tongue to keep it back.

Damn. When did I become such a jealous bitch?

Bash obviously doesn't bring out the best in me. But it's hard not to be jealous when I'm staring at a man like *that* and see the way women react to him. Especially when I have no idea where we stand and don't have the heart or the balls to ask.

The confusing man who has managed to tie my heart up into knots makes his way over to me. His eyes dance with humor. "You having a good time?"

"Yeah, I actually am." I glance around the rink at the smiling faces of all the kids. "They're so...happy. They really love it."

When was the last time I played hockey just for the joy of it?

For as long as I can remember, I had one goal in mind—being the best. I busted my ass and worked instead of playing with my friends so I could make the Olympic team at eighteen. Then, it was about staying at the top and playing as long as I could. Then it became about working my way into a coaching position that might open doors to something even bigger—like where I am now.

But this, these kids, they just *love* the sport. It's completely pure.

How different would my life have been if the game had been just that—a game instead of a career?

I glance over at Bash, where he leans against the boards and watches the kids with a permanent smile. Growing up with Mike Fury as a father, there were probably a lot of mornings like these, where he was on the ice with his dad, learning from one of the stars of the sport. Bash is like me— driven to be the best, and no doubt his father helped push him there and teach him everything that made him an All-Star over and over again.

"Did your dad ever bring you to things like this or help out with your youth teams growing up?"

Bash stiffens next me, and the carefree look he's been wearing all day slips from his face in an instant. Dark, hard eyes meet mine. "I don't want to talk about him, Greer."

Shit.

No witty banter. No calling me "Coach" in that sexy, playful way. A hard, don't push it edge to his voice.

He's pissed. Though, I have absolutely no idea why.

He got a little testy with me when I brought up his dad during our first argument, too, but he has yet to offer me any reason for his disdain for the man. He's never talked about him at all, now that I think about it. He's never opened up about *anything*, really. A fact I've ignored during our time together because he's kept me in a haze of orgasms, food, wine, and strippers.

The least he can do is answer one simple, innocent question without the attitude. "Why are you so pissed when I bring up your father?"

His jaw clenches, and a vein in his neck throbs. He glances around to make sure no one is close to us, then steps closer to me and drops his head. "Leave it alone, Greer."

The warning is growled low, so no one else could possibly hear it, but with enough force that it makes me recoil from him. For the first time since he joined my team, I can *see* that danger he usually only presents on the ice directed at *me*.

Anger and confusion mix into a volatile concoction in my blood.

"Fuck you, Bash." I shake my head and check for young ears that might be listening. "You can drag me to a strip club and then do unspeakably nasty things to me, but I can't ask you a personal question?"

He shoves his hands through his hair and stares at the ceiling for a minute. "You can ask, but it doesn't mean I'm going to answer." His normally warm bourbon eyes meet mine, now iced over with a *don't fucking push me* warning. "Some things are better left in the past, Greer, and my *relationship* with my father is one of those things."

The true anguish in his reply slams into me, rocking me back slightly. This isn't about him being angry at me; whatever this is goes a lot deeper and stems from something traumatic that happened a long time ago. Something with his father.

"Was it really that bad?"

His eyes answer my question even though he doesn't offer a verbal response.

Yes.

Jesus. What could his father have possibly done that was so awful?

"Please, Greer, just leave it alone. You don't want to know

the truth. No one wants to hear what growing up with Mike Fury was really like."

I shift closer to him, probably closer than we should be to continue to maintain the illusion that we're nothing more than player and coach. "I do, Bash. I *do* want to know. Because it *means* something to you. Because your relationship with your father shaped who you are today, on and off the ice. I can see how upset you are, and I want to understand."

He closes his eyes and inhales a deep breath. When he opens them again, determination lies in their depths. "I can't, Greer. I'm sorry."

Bash pushes off the boards.

"I am, too."

But he doesn't hear it.

He skates away from me without a look back, beelines for the gate in the boards, and stalks off the ice, leaving me with two questions.

What the hell just happened?

And how the fuck am I supposed to get home?

The little boy Bash was just working with skates over to me and tugs on my arm. "Where did Mr. Fury go?"

I force a smile and fight the tears pooling in my eyes. "He had to go prepare for our game."

A grin spreads across his face, his blue eyes lighting up. "That's so cool. I can't wait to watch."

Normally, I would agree with him.

Watching Bash play since he returned from his suspension has been truly awe-inspiring. He's playing differently. With a renewed vigor and purpose. And *without* spending half the damn game in the penalty box.

Something changed, and part of me thought that something might have been me. But he just proved how fucking wrong I am about that.

17

GREER

Excited chatter and the clinking of glasses and bottles surround me. The din might as well not even exist, though. Everyone moves around me like I'm in a dream, a light ethereal fog surrounding everything.

Somebody pinch me.

Is this for real?

It still hasn't sunk in...

We're going to the Stanley Cup Playoffs.

Ten years ago, if someone had told me I'd be standing here celebrating with *my* team, I would've told them they were insane and it wasn't even funny to joke about something like that. It was so far out of the realm of any possibility.

But here I am, dumbstruck at the bar with a glass of champagne in my hand while the guys celebrate around me.

Thankfully, we have the entire space to ourselves. It's just one of the perks of your GM owning the restaurant. And considering how loud and obnoxious the guys are, I'm glad we're the only ones here.

They *deserve* to celebrate, though. They've earned it. It's been a long, hard season fighting not only the other teams but all the naysayers who didn't believe we could do it.

Leaning back against the bar, I examine each one of them, considering their roles in getting us here. They played their fucking asses off. On the road, first line a man down half the time because Bash couldn't stay out of the penalty box, yet they came through.

We pulled it off, and I still can't believe it.

If only I could fully enjoy this, but I can't. It's impossible when things are so messy and unresolved with Bash.

I look down at my shaking hand, bring the cut glass to my lips, and sip at the cool, crisp bubbly liquid. Coupled with a deep breath, it helps calm my nerves slightly. But no matter how hard I try, I can't shake this dark cloud of fear from over my head.

It shouldn't be there. I should have faith. This team can play. *Really* play. Somehow, this mismatched band of misfits has pulled off the impossible. We have a *real* shot at winning. If we can just keep it together.

If *Bash* can keep it together.

While he's been on his best behavior the last few games, I don't know if it's because he knows what it would mean for the team if he fucked up again or if it's because he knows what it would mean with me.

Of course, I want to believe it's both, but with him, I never really know.

Not when he's constantly flipping between being sweet, sexy, thoughtful Bash and brute, barbaric, out-of-control Bash. It's giving me a horrible case of whiplash.

The other day at the rink with the kids was a prime example. Bash's flip-out when I mentioned his father came so far out of left field, it's left a strange rift and tension between us.

Even Jill couldn't help me figure out what went wrong. After she picked me up and I attempted to drown my sorrows in carbs at one of the local buffets, I gave her the entire rundown of the conversation, and her only insight was that Bash was "a man," and I should expect this kind of shit.

Real fucking helpful.

And while I think I've managed to keep the awkwardness between us out of our professional interactions, it's still left me with an ache deep in my soul I can't seem to shake.

Why can't he just fucking talk to me?

I rub at my neck with my free hand, and the man in question flicks his gaze over to me from across the room. The corner of his mouth turns up in that sexy lopsided smile, like all this bullshit between us can instantly be wiped away with it.

I wish it were that easy.

But Bash is two people.

The incredibly caring, generous lover who always ensures my pleasure before his own. And the volatile, angry man who goes off in an instant for some reason I can never figure out.

Yet even now, when things are so weird and unsettled between us, when we've been dancing around each other and avoiding discussing what happened the other day, he still manages to unravel me with one look.

My pussy clenches, remembering what he did to me that night at the club and after. The last time those large, talented hands touched me before our blow up.

Maybe it's best if we leave it that way.

What we're doing is so stupid. If we ever get caught, it means the end of my career. Letting that argument be the end of it is probably the smartest thing I can do, but I can't tear my eyes away from the man who has me so tied up in knots.

"Greer? Did you hear me?"

"What?" I turn toward Steve next to me at the bar, surprised to find him looking at me expectantly.

Shit. Was he talking to me?

"Sorry, Steve. I was lost in thought." I force a smile at our equipment manager. "What did you say?"

He smiles and leans closer, so I'll hear him over the noise. "I asked if you were all right. You looked a little distressed."

I force a return smile. "I'm fine. Just thinking about what's coming."

For the team and for this thing with Bash.

The man himself catches my eye again, his gaze narrowing on Steve and me, and he says something to Mac, smacks him on the shoulder, and makes his way across the room toward us. Every step he takes ratchets my heart rate up until it's thundering against my rib cage and throbbing in my ears.

My entire body heats at his assessing gaze raking over me. He's undressing me with his eyes; there's no question about it. And he's seen me enough naked now that I know he's visualizing every single inch of me—every single inch that he knows so goddamn well.

Bash handles me and plays my body the way a musician would a guitar, the way a hockey player handles the stick. He's so damn good at it, and he knows it. The smug smirk that accompanies every time our eyes meet assures me he doesn't need to be told.

I hate to stroke his ego—I wouldn't want his head exploding—but there's no denying it...Bash fucking Fury is a god in bed and on the ice.

Damn him.

He finally reaches us and glances at Steve. "Hey, buddy. Can I get a word with Coach quick?"

Steve shifts back and nods. "No problem, Bash."

Bash slams him on the shoulder, and we both watch Steve disappear into the crowd before Bash turns back to me and tilts his pint glass toward mine. "Congratulations, Coach. You got us here."

I shrug and take a sip of my champagne. "The team did it. It wasn't just me."

He shakes his head and turns to lean back against the bar next to me. His forearm brushes against mine, and a little electric jolt shoots through me and straight to the place I crave him the most. I press my thighs together and shift to relieve some of the ache there.

Does he have any idea what he does to me?

Of course, he does. I'm talking about Bash here.

He inclines his head toward me. "Don't downplay your role here, Greer. I played for one of the best teams in the league for the last half-decade, and you're as good as any coach I've ever had. Maybe better."

I twist my head to face him. "You don't mean that."

Given what he said to me during that heated argument we had in my office—or "the towel incident" as I like to remember it—this is a new development. *If* he does really mean it and isn't just blowing smoke up my ass to get in my good graces after how he acted the other day.

Maybe this is just his version of an apology because something tells me Bash Fury doesn't say "I'm sorry" very much or very easily.

He grins at me. "Why do you say that?"

I press my lips together and search his gaze for the lie. The warm amber depths hold a lot of things, but I don't see deception there.

He leans in closer until his lips practically brush my ear. "I'm not just saying it to get in your pants, Coach. We've already established I can do that whenever I want."

I jerk my head back, my mouth agape. Glancing around the room, I check for any eyes on us, but no one seems to be paying us any attention. "Bash...You can't say something like that to me."

"Why not?" He shrugs slightly as his eyes scan the room, too. "Nobody's paying attention. No one gives a shit, and no one heard me. Besides"—he takes a sip of his beer—"it's true."

There is that lack of tact and arrogance I love to hate so much.

It's infuriating...because he's right.

It *is* true.

And right here, right now, even in this room with all these people who could expose us and ruin my career, and even though he hasn't apologized for being such a dick the other day, if Bash pressed his hard cock up against me and told me to bend over, I would do it.

Because my body craves him.

I've become addicted to the way he kisses me, the way he touches me, the release I get from his skill in the bedroom.

It would be the *best* way to celebrate this win and our advance to the playoffs.

One of his hands drops and presses into my lower back, then drifts down. He squeezes my ass and pulls his hand away. "You coming home with me tonight, Coach?"

I keep my eyes on the room, watching for anyone who may be paying attention to us.

Biting my lip, I try to remember that I'm still mad about what happened at the youth league. But I want to go home with him. I want to so badly.

Yet the longer this goes on, the harder it's going to be to hide it.

The way he looks at me.

The way he smirks.

It's written all over his face that he *owns* me.

Only by some miracle has no one sensed something going on. And now he's getting reckless in front of everyone —leaning in close, whispering, touching me...

I shake my head. "I really shouldn't, Bash. We really shouldn't."

"Whether we should or shouldn't is irrelevant, Coach." His bourbon gaze meets mine, his intent clear in the darkening orbs. "Just tell me if you're coming or not."

I close my eyes and suck in a deep breath. The war I've been fighting since the day Bash winked at me and skated out onto that ice has never let up, but one side is almost completely defeated.

Every moment I spend with him decimates the remaining troops and practically hands the win over to the side willing to give him everything.

"You know I am."

———

BASH

It's exactly what I had hoped she would say.

Nothing is sweeter than hearing *yes* from this woman.

Because the more time I spend around Greer, the more time I *want* to spend with her. She's intoxicating. A complex mix of sweet and sassy. Hard and soft. Reserved and reckless.

And the constant push and pull for control between us is the ultimate aphrodisiac.

Even now, she's fighting it, trying to deny what she feels pulling us together. And I get it. She's mad about how I acted the other day, and she probably has every right to be.

I didn't mean to snap at her. The pain in her gaze in that moment matched the one I felt when she started asking questions about Dad. It's something I never wanted to see in her eyes, never wanted to put there, but some things are just off-limits for me.

I've been willing to break some of those rules for her. She's the first woman I've spent this much time with in my entire life. Usually, I enjoy a night or two, sometimes even a week, with a beautiful woman then send her on her way to get back to focusing on my job. It's the way I like it—keeping up a wall that doesn't allow anyone close enough to ever hurt me. But Greer finds cracks in that wall. She somehow slips through those tiny little fissures and fills the gaping holes in my life that I wasn't even aware were there.

But when it comes to Dad, some things should stay buried.

No matter how close I might let her get, that part of my past needs to remain there, tucked safely away so it can't haunt me anymore.

Still, I never meant to hurt her with my response, and the strange tension that's existed between us since then—neither of us bringing up our argument or broaching the subject of *us*—has been eating away at me.

And now, we're in front of the whole team here, and I'm doing everything in my power to encourage her to forgive me because in an hour, we won't be surrounded by all our colleagues, and I'll be able to do what I've been thinking about since we last left my bed.

It's the only way I know to show her how sorry I am for the way I acted. All I'm capable of when it comes to expressing that type of emotion. It's warped and fucked up, not being able to say the words, but Greer knew what she was getting into when she chose not to walk away again that night. She knew I wasn't a hearts and flowers, happily ever after kind of guy. I'm the guy who makes her come unraveled and find ecstasy for a while, until things get too complicated and it isn't fun anymore.

We're dangerously on the line of that after our argument, but I'm not ready to let go of this or her yet.

Not yet.

Her voice comes from behind me rather than at my side, and I turn and glance at the television above the bar and see her face there. The post-game interview from our final game plays on the screen, and I twist back and motion to the bartender. "Turn that up."

Greer looks over her shoulder and rolls her eyes. "You don't need to watch my post-game interview."

"I think I do." I grin at her. It's so cute when she's embarrassed.

"And Coach, what can you tell me about Bash Fury? It seems you've managed to rein him in a little. Do you think he'll continue this trend of staying out of the penalty box during the playoffs or are you going to end up on the permanent penalty kill?"

The Greer on the screen laughs at the commentator and shakes her head. *"Nobody can rein in Bash Fury."*

I nudge her with my shoulder as we lean our elbows on the bar and watch. "Is that what you want, Coach?" I raise an eyebrow at her. "You want to rein me in? Do you want control?"

Fuck.

The thought of her taking control and dominating me in the bedroom has never crossed my mind before, but it sure as hell has my cock rising with interest now. She shudders next to me, and I brush my hand across her lower back as I lean into her and press my lips against her ear.

"Maybe I'll let you have it once."

She jerks away, her eyes wide and heated with desire. Her wet pink lips part. "Bash—"

"Well, don't you two look cozy."

Shit.

The hand around my beer tightens, while I jerk my other away from Greer to adjust my semi-hard cock so it won't be so damn obvious how much this woman turns me on.

I turn back toward Lebedev standing behind us. "Coach and I were just discussing her post-game interview from the last game." I tilt my head toward the television and flash a grin. "Care to join us?"

Lebedev scowls at us and crosses his arms over his chest, not even glancing up at the television where Greer still talks with the commentator. "Sure, you are. And *no.*"

"What do you want, Dimitri?"

Besides being a fucking asshat and cock-block me.

He holds up his hands. "Just came over to check on Coach and my favorite teammate."

My free hand curls into a fist. This jerkoff has been up my ass and on my case since the day I got here. I get that he thinks I took his position, because I did. But it's not like he doesn't play. He gets almost as much ice time as me, and things have been going well with rotating him into the line.

There isn't any reason for the continued animosity. It will only hurt us going into the playoffs if we can't all get along off the ice. He needs to pull on his big boy pants and grow the fuck up.

I force a fake smile, one so saccharine sweet, he's sure to see right through it. "Why don't you go check in on someone else?"

Someone who isn't likely to strike out and belt him in the fucking jaw.

He glares at me as if he's considering pushing me, then seems to think better of it and turns and disappears with a dirty look over his shoulder at us.

Greer releases a deep sigh. "Shit. You don't think he saw us?" Her entire body tenses with her question. "You don't think he knows?"

Fuck.

I chug my beer and scan the crowd again for watchful eyes. Lebedev isn't the only one we need to be worried about.

"I think he's just fucking around, Coach. Trying to start shit when there's nothing to start."

She raises an eyebrow at me. "Is there nothing to start?"

Shit.

Maybe that wasn't the right thing to say. "That's not what I meant."

At least, not in the way she thinks.

It would be *impossible* to deny what's happening between us, but it can't go beyond what we have. We started something that has an end date, one that looms over us like a dark cloud. And reminding her of that has apparently ruined my chances of having her in my arms tonight.

She holds her hand out to stop me from continuing to try to explain myself. "I'm going home, Bash. I'm exhausted. We need to get prepared for the Wolverines. I'll see you at practice tomorrow."

That's it?

It isn't like her not to push.

I wish she would.

Having Greer tear into me and argue would be preferred to this cold shoulder she's giving me.

She downs the rest of her drink and pushes away from the bar before I can say anything to stop her. Though the way she's acting, I doubt anything I could say *would* have prevented her from walked away.

I won't be doing all those things I fantasized about tonight, unless it's in my dreams with my own hand wrapped around my dick.

Fucking hell.

Lebedev watches her cross the bar and leave, then his eyes sweep back to meet mine. He sneers at me, his shoulders tense and arms crossed over his chest. The asshole thinks he knows something, but we've been careful.

At least, I think we have.

Maybe I walked a little too close to the line tonight. Maybe the risk of being caught only made me want to do it more. But even if that weren't the case, I couldn't have stayed away.

Greer looked so fucking beautiful and happy. I didn't just want to be next to her; I needed to be touching her, smelling her, feeling her pressed against me.

It was selfish and stupid.

Two things I'm very familiar with.

But this place is loud and out of control. Leaning in to talk to someone isn't suspicious. Neither is a player having a conversation with his coach. Anyone who saw us together wouldn't have seen anything unusual to throw up red flags. And even if they did, it's none of their fucking business, anyway. It doesn't affect them. It doesn't affect the team. Greer and I are professionals and will continue to be no matter what happens between us.

We're both adult enough to separate our personal feelings from what needs to happen to succeed on the ice. So Lebedev can leer at us all he wants. He doesn't know anything that can hurt us.

Hayes sidles up next to me and smacks me on the shoulder. "How you doing?" He flashes me a grin. "Dimitri giving you shit again?"

I nod and down the last of my beer. "What do you think?"

He chuckles and glances toward Lebedev. "I think he's a little bitch who needs to understand this is a game, and sometimes, someone plays it better than you."

"I couldn't have said it better myself." I set my empty glass on the bar and nod to the bartender for another. "He needs to get over his personal issues with me to ensure it doesn't affect the game."

This team just pulled off the impossible, and Lebedev is still being a douche because he resents my coming on board. He can't just enjoy the feeling of going to the playoffs without his ego getting in the way.

As long as it doesn't get in the way of my playing or my thing with Greer, I don't give a fuck.

But he already cock-blocked me tonight.

Fucking douche.

He better not try anything else though; otherwise, the "old" Bash might need to make an appearance and have a chat with him.

18

BASH

The practice facility door swings shut behind me, I scrub my hands over my face and back through my hair to keep it off my face. After a restless night of non-sleep thinking about Greer, it's hard to concentrate on what's ahead for the day. Especially knowing I'm going to see her and have to pretend she's just my coach.

Maybe suiting up and getting on the ice will help me push my concerns about what's happening with her to the back of my mind, but I have a stop to make first.

I make my way toward Bob's office and practically collide with Greer just in front of his door as she comes from the opposite direction. She skids to a stop and stares up at me, her eyes widening.

Her gaze darts to the closed door, then back to me.

I narrow my eyes on her. "What the hell is going on?"

Why is she at Bob's office?

She hisses *shhh* at me from between her teeth and frantically motions for me to follow her around the corner. A few steps down the hallway, she spins to face me. "I don't know. Bob just asked me to come meet him in his office."

"Shit." I run a shaky hand through my hair and check behind me toward where our GM apparently waits for both of us. "He asked me to come in, too." Acid crawls up my throat, and I swallow it down. "You don't think he knows..."

A very unflattering shade of green overtakes her face, and she looks like she's about to throw-up. "Oh, God."

I place a hand on her shoulder, then quickly jerk it back and glance down the hallway both directions. Everyone will be coming in soon. I'm only here this early because Bob called to ask me to talk before practice. But anyone could come around the corner, and someone catching Greer and me in a compromising position in the hallway outside the GM's office isn't going to help whatever is about to happen.

And honestly, this could be about *anything*.

Returning my focus to Greer, I try to sound confident when my stomach is tied in knots. "Let's not assume the worst. Take a deep breath."

She closes her eyes, sucks in a breath, and releases it slowly. Her eyes flutter open, and she pushes away from the wall she's leaning on. "I'll go in first. You wait a couple minutes before you come in."

Good call.

Arriving together might look suspicious, especially if he's already called us here with certain information in his head.

Is it possible he knows?

It was stupid to touch Greer last night. To get so close. To be so fucking reckless in the way I spoke to her and looked at her.

Anyone with half a brain could have figured out what was going on between us, and despite what many members of the public might think, hockey players aren't stupid.

Far from it.

We have to be observant of everything that happens on the ice—and that translates off it, too. Anyone could have seen something as simple as a heated look and read into it something they felt Bob needed to know.

This meeting could be the thing we've dreaded this whole time.

Greer disappears around the corner to Bob's office, and I drop my forehead against the wall.

Shit. Shit. Shit.

What if Lebedev said something to Bob last night about what he saw...or what he *thinks* he saw. I was *touching* her.

Idiot.

This could be bad fucking news. I've been terrified of what Greer has been doing to *me* without really considering the consequences in the greater scheme of things. I've ignored her concerns, encouraged her to forget them and push them away in favor of exploring our attraction.

And it could have catastrophic consequences.

But I have to take my own advice.

Don't freak out until we know what's going on.

Panic never helped anyone in any situation. It doesn't when we're on a 3-5 penalty kill or when we're down one with thirty seconds left in a game. It won't here, either.

This could have absolutely nothing to do with me banging Coach, and I have to walk in there as if it doesn't.

I drag my head away from the wall and follow after Greer around the corner and into Bob's office through the door she left open.

Greer sits in one of the chairs facing Bob's desk, twisting her hands on her lap, unable to control her nervous energy any other way.

Our GM and the man who has been Greer's biggest advocate and role model her whole career looks up and smiles. "Oh, Bash. Good. Can you close the door behind you?"

Why do we need the door closed?

Because he's about to ream us out?

I nod and shut the door before slowly lowering myself into the seat next Greer. She glances at me with fear darkening the green of her wide eyes. Not so long ago, she told me she sucked at concealing her emotions, and it seems I'm seeing that in full force right now. If she doesn't calm down, Bob will *certainly* know something is wrong if he doesn't already.

Bob leans forward in his chair and rests his elbows on his desk. He watches us, gaze darting from Greer to me, then making the sweep again.

Ten seconds pass.

Then another ten.

I shift in my seat under his silent assessment.

Another ten.

Greer crosses and uncrosses her legs, still twisting her fingers nervously in her lap.

Another ten.

Bob reclines in his chair and steeples his hands in front of his mouth, his eyes never leaving us.

What the hell is he doing?

I shift again.

Should I ask him why we're here?

Shit.

No way.

I'm already getting the feeling I'm not going to like what he has to say. There's no need to move things along and make the inevitable come any sooner.

Finally, after a goddamn eternity of uncomfortable silence, Bob leans forward again. "I wanted to talk to the two of you in private. About what's been happening in the last few weeks."

Shit.

Greer tenses next to me, and my entire body goes rigid.

He knows.

Bob shoves up from his seat and walks around to sit on the edge of his desk directly in front of us. "I think the three of us need to have a frank discussion."

Greer clears her throat nervously. "About what, Bob?"

He raises his bushy gray eyebrows and glances between us. "About the two of you."

We're fucked.

Everything Greer and I have worked so hard for our entire lives is going down the drain. All the color drains from Greer's face. She opens her mouth to speak, but I hold up a hand.

If anyone should take the blame here, it's me. I'm the one who pursued her, who pressured her into giving in and turning against her morals and what she thought was right. I'm the one who already has the shitty reputation. This is expected from someone like me. "Bob, you have to understand—"

He holds up his hand to stop me. "I'm just so thrilled to see you two finally getting along."

What?

I jerk my head to the side to look at Greer, and her wide, confused eyes meet mine. We both turn back to Bob.

Greer clears her throat. "What do you mean?"

Bob claps his hands together. "I've noticed there hasn't been any of that tension between you two when he's out on the ice since he came back from his suspension. You finally trust him. And it shows. He's playing better, and you don't look like you're about ready to have a heart attack every time he jumps off the bench."

Chuckling, I release a shaky breath at the way we just averted a death sentence. "You're right, Bob, we *have* been getting along amazingly the last few weeks."

I catch Greer's scowl out of the corner of my eye, but Bob seems to have missed the innuendo in my comment.

He just grins at us. "I saw you two at the party last night, chatting. It looked very carefree and effortless. Not at all how you two were together when Bash first arrived. It's been a one-eighty."

No shit.

There was nothing but anger and pent-up hostility. Now, there's just this raging sexual tension that always seems to build between us when we're together that will snap if we don't release it again soon.

We could have worked it out last night if she had come home with me, but her refusal only led to a sleepless night and even more desire for her.

Greer's hand tightens on the arm of her chair until her knuckles whiten. "Yes, Bob, things have been going well. Bash and I have come to an...understanding."

Bob claps and rises to his feet. "I'm so happy to hear that. It seems we're in good shape heading into the playoffs. Our star player is finally getting along with the coach and hasn't had any major penalties in the last few games." He freezes and points at my chest. "That doesn't mean you're due for one, though."

I chuckle and hold up my hands, flashing my trademark grin at him. "I can't make any promises, Bob. You know how I play."

Hard.

Without reservation.

Holding *nothing* back.

Greer once called it *dirty.* And there are undoubtedly others who have the same assessment. But if anyone bothers to look past the hits and penalty minutes, they would see the beauty of my game and that I *never* act without a purpose.

He grins at me. "I don't want you to change that, Bash. It's why I brought you onto the Scorpions. But we can't afford any stupid penalties right now, either."

"I agree."

Greer nods. "I certainly agree, too. Nothing *stupid*."

It's obviously directed at me, and she's not just talking about potential penalties.

———

GREER

Bash needs to stop messing around.

The last thing we need is anyone, especially Bob, discovering our relationship. Or whatever the hell this is. And his little joke might have been only for me but it isn't impossible for someone else to pick up on it.

I glance at the man who is equally frustrating as he is irresistible.

What the hell is this, anyway?

The never-ending question.

My hands clench so tightly on the arms of my chair, my knuckles actually ache. I shake them out and rest them on my lap.

Try not to look so worried. Bob will know something's up.

Especially if this jackass next to me keeps making sexual innuendos.

Bob is not an idiot. If Bash continues with his cocky flaunting of this in front of him, I'm going to end up fired. We both know that's what would happen. They're not going to boot Bash and potentially take a hit on his contract when they could get rid of me much cheaper and replace me with somebody who is probably more qualified, anyway.

I was a gamble. One that has paid off...

For now.

But who knows what's going to happen in the playoffs? Who knows where I'm going to be able to take this team?

Unless we win the goddamn cup, there will be people calling for my replacement.

It doesn't matter what I've accomplished. And if word of Bash and me hits the media, I'll be a fucking laughingstock. I'll never get a head coaching position again. Maybe not even an assistant coach job. I'll end up coaching college or hell, maybe some kids at a local ice rink back home.

My hands start shaking on my lap, and I clasp them together and force a smile at Bob.

He grins. "So, I can expect more of the same in the coming games?"

I nod. "We don't need any more dirty play." I glance at Bash, and his mischievous eyes connect with mine. Any concern about what Bob was going to say has dissipated and been replaced by his typical arrogance and playfulness. "And Bash has assured me he'll be on his best behavior during the playoffs."

He flashes me a grin—one that is always a precursor to very *not good* behavior. The kind of not good behavior that ends up with me naked and his cock buried inside me.

I clench my thighs together against the ache there. Even when I'm terrified of losing my job and sitting in front of my boss, Bash Fury still manages to turn my body into a quivering mess of need.

When did I become such a wanton slut? When did I let a man convince me to risk my future career just because he's good with his dick?

Bash winks at me. "I'll be on my best behavior, but even those who are best behaved get dirty sometimes."

Anger tightens my skin, and a warm flush spreads over my cheeks.

This asshat is going to get us caught.

Bob chuckles. "I'm so glad the two of you are getting along." He motions for us to rise. "Even joking around now. I love it."

If he only knew.

We both stand, though Bash seems a lot more secure than I do. My legs quiver under me, and I smooth down the front of my pants that don't need any smoothing just to wipe off the sweat that's forming on my palms.

Bob places a hand on each of our shoulders. "I knew you two would make a great team, if you gave it a chance."

Bash laughs and winks at me again. "I did, too."

Goddamn, that wink.

It makes me want to punch him in the fucking nuts and simultaneously jump on his cock. Truth be told, there's a lot about Bash that brings me to the brink of violence, but what Bob told me during our first meeting has rung true—Bash isn't a terrible guy at all. He's the type of guy who, if we had met anywhere but on the ice, I would've ended up falling into his arms.

It's just this situation...my position...it's all so wrong.

Bob claps both of us on the shoulder before ushering us out of his office. "You've got practice in a little while. Can't wait for tomorrow night."

The first game of the playoffs and we're facing the Wolverines. Number one in the division and the second-best record in the entire league. It's going to be a fight with them. It always is. And they're one of the teams that always manage to set off Bash the most. He just can't seem to keep his cool with them, so this will be a real test of his willpower and his desire not to push things with me.

Bash motions for me to exit Bob's office in front of him, and as I step through the door, he places his hand gently on my lower back. A familiar shudder runs through me, as does the memory of the last time his hands were all over me.

Was it only a few nights ago that we were in that hotel room and going at each other like wild animals? When he was kissing his way up my neck as he thrust into me with slow and long strokes...

Christ.

Heat floods through my body as I step out in the hall. The door clicks shut behind Bash, and I wheel around to face him.

His dark eyebrow rises in question. "What's that look for, Coach?"

"You know what it's for, Bash." I hiss the words through clenched teeth and stalk down the hallway toward my office on the other side of the complex.

One thing they did right when they designed this building was put me closer to the locker rooms and keep Bob somewhere where any high-profile visitors could be wined and dined in more luxury.

I'm going to need that distance when I go off on Bash for his behavior back there.

Bash's heavy steps follow me down the hall, and he tugs on my shoulder to force me to stop and look at him. "Greer. Stop."

I shrug off his hand and forge ahead. "I'm not stopping, Bash, because if I do, we're going to have a very public argument about a very private thing."

He glances around the hallway, and I pause before the final turn to my office.

His shoulders rise and fall. "I don't see anyone else here, Coach. Practice isn't for another hour."

"Bob is here." I jerk open the door to my office and step inside with him hot on my heels.

He slams the door behind us. "What is your problem?"

"What's my *problem*? My problem is that we just had a meeting with the fucking GM during which you couldn't even be adult enough to keep from making wisecrack innuendoes that he could've seen through in a second." I hold up a hand to stop him from interjecting the argument I'm sure is on the tip of his tongue. "Then, you winked at me in front of him. Actually fucking winked at me. *Twice!*"

He smirks and chuckles as he draws up his hands. "Coach, come on...Bob has no idea what's going on between us. No one does. I know that meeting scared you—"

"Scared me? Are you fucking kidding me right now?" I growl and stomp my foot. "Bash Fury, you make me so fucking angry."

And hot...which only makes me angrier.

He closes the distance between us so fast I don't have time to react or brace myself until he's pressed up against me and has my face between his hands. He jerks my head up, forcing my eyes to his. "I make you a lot more than angry, Coach. I can feel your heart racing against mine. That turned you on. Knowing what we've been doing and sitting there in front of him denying it. You loved it."

His thumb brushes across my quivering bottom lip.

Fucking lip. I can't even control that.

"Don't try to deny it, Greer, because I can see right through you, even if you think I can't."

"Oh, yeah? What is it you think you see?"

He moves a hand and wraps my hair around his wrist, tugging on it and forcing my head back even more. "You like it."

"No."

"You *love* it. Sneaking around. The possibility of being caught at any moment. The fact that this is forbidden. All of it turns you on."

His other hand leaves my cheek to drift across my waist and down between my legs. He cups me there, and I groan despite my best effort not to.

Pink lips hover over mine. "I bet you're wet right now, Greer. I bet the entire conversation we just had in Bob's office was one giant tease for you." His thumb centers over my throbbing clit, and he brushes it back and forth, pressing hard against the fabric of my pants. "I'm right. Aren't I, Coach?"

Christ. He's right, and I so don't want him to be.

He leans forward until his lips barely feather over mine. Every fiber of my being is screaming for him. For his touch. For his kiss. For his cock.

When did I become the girl who gets off on breaking the rules?

I've always been a rule follower. Even when I played...I played hard, and I played to win but never at the expense of anyone else. It's the reason Bash and everything he stands for has always pissed me off. But now, here in his arms, with his hot breath fluttering against my face and his skilled hand toying with my body, I can't deny the fact that *this* being against the rules is a fucking turn-on.

Something about it being wrong and forbidden when I've always followed the rules is like gasoline being thrown on an already out-of-control inferno.

He doesn't even wait for my answer. Probably because he already knows what it will be. He just presses his lips to mine and walks me backward until my ass hits the desk. His thumb swirls around my clit and presses against it hard.

I clench my thighs around his hand and tear my mouth from his. "No, Bash. We can't. Not *here*."

He pulls back and looks around my empty office. "There's no one here, Coach. Just you and me. And this will be hard and fast."

Oh, God. I am in so much trouble with this man.

Pushing him away isn't an option. Maybe it *never* was. I melt into his kiss and wrap my arms around his neck to drag him closer to me.

If I'm going to go down, I might as well go down in raging conflagration of flames.

19

GREER

Bash shifts his hand from between my legs and lifts me up to sit on the desk. He wastes no time removing my shoes and pulling off my pants and thong, and I drag him back to me, desperate to have his mouth and hands on me again.

It's only been a few days, but it feels like eons since we were last alone together, since I last felt his touch and felt...complete.

This is so wrong on so many levels, but he read me like an open book. Like a really smutty forbidden romance novel. The fact that anyone could walk in right now—Bob, Lebedev, any one of the staff or players—only makes this hotter. Only makes me want him and this even more.

I've thrown my morals out the window completely now. It was one thing to do this at his hotel, when we were traveling, even at my place, but here, in my office, in the place where the Scorpions practice is like throwing it in the face of the organization. It's the ultimate betrayal.

And I don't even care.

Not in this moment. I can't. Not when my gaze follows his hand as he unzips his pants and frees his hard cock. I wet my lips and watch him stroke himself—once, twice—before he moves back between my legs to kiss me again. He drags me to the edge of the desk and positions the head of his dick at my wet core.

Sweet fuck...

A shiver of anticipation moves through me, and I wrap my legs around him and dig my feet into his lower back, urging him to act. He grins at me with wicked intent, but he's not toying with me today. Not like this. He promised me fast and hard, and that's what I need. I won't settle for anything less.

I shift my hips forward, and he lets me take him in just a tiny bit, just enough to pull a groan from him. Such a sexy sound, one I can't hear enough of. It's Bash Fury barely on the edge of control. The thing that terrifies me when he's on the ice is kindling for the fire when we're together. Because there's nothing hotter than knowing I'm the cause, that I'm the reason he's about to unleash himself from the restraint he barely manages to keep a hand on.

It's a powerful position to be in, and one I crave more than I do air. I've achieved so much in my life, but doing this to Bash feels like the ultimate accomplishment. Like I should hang another medal on my wall for "First Place at Fucking Bash Fury and Driving Him Completely Insane."

His whiskey eyes beg and promise at the same time. I clench around the head of his cock, and he growls against my mouth and drives into me to the hilt.

"Fuck..." My hands curl around the edge of the desk to keep myself from sliding backward.

His fingers dig into my hips painfully, and he nips at my lip as he pulls back and plunges into me again.

"Oh, Christ." I drop my head back and squeeze my eyes shut.

"Fuck, Coach, you feel so fucking good."

Warm, wet lips move along the column of my neck and find my ear. He pulls the lobe between his teeth and sucks hard with the same rhythm as his thrusting hips.

This is the definition of a quick, hot fuck.

There's no romance here.

No long, lingering looks or slow, sensual touches.

This is two people who can't get enough of each other colliding for mutual satisfaction as quickly as possible.

The scare we just had with Bob only enhances everything about this—the sounds, the smells, the feel of Bash spreading me wide open and filling me completely. It's reaffirmation that all we're risking is worth it.

How am I ever going to let this go?

How will I ever say goodbye to him when this ultimately ends?

It's something I can't think about right now. Not when the tension in my body is coiling tighter and tighter. Not when Bash's lips move back down to meet mine. Not when the man is absolutely destroying me with the pounding of his cock while filling a void in my life I didn't even realize was there until he stormed into my arena.

Not when this is all I want.

It shouldn't be. God knows it shouldn't be, but it is all the same.

I really am going down in flames, and Bash is the one dragging me there just as he's dragging me closer and closer to a mind-bending orgasm.

With everything he has in him.

Bash doesn't do anything halfway. It's all or nothing every time he hits the ice and when he touches me. Whether he's in a game or we're alone and in his room at the Prestige or here in my office where anyone could walk in at any minute, he gives it his all.

I dig my nails into the flesh of the back of his neck. He tilts my hips to a new angle, allowing the head of his cock to drag in just the right spot inside me.

"Oh, God. Fuck! Right there."

He groans in satisfaction and redoubles his efforts. His hand tightens in my hair, jerking it back. Determination tightens his jaw and sweat beads on his brow. He's a man on a mission. One to ensure both of our pleasures.

And my building orgasm has overtaken my body and reached the boiling point. The pressure and heat low in my belly explode like a thousand fireworks detonating at the same time. My pussy clenches around his cock as he drives into me over and over, harder and deeper, racing to find his own bliss.

"Fuck, Coach." His hand tightens on my hip. His thrusts become erratic. He groans, stills, and then collapses against me as the little aftershocks of my orgasm twitch my body against his. His heavy breathing tickles the hair at the nape of my neck, sending a shiver through me. "Fuck."

He releases his grip on my hair and pushes his hand through his own as he pulls back from me. His darkened, hooded eyes find mine, and a knowing grin twitches his lips. He leans in and drops his forehead to my own and presses a flutter of a kiss to my lips. "Now, tell me again that what we're doing doesn't turn you on, Coach."

"Bash..." I shake my head and breathe him in. "What the hell *are* we doing?"

———

BASH

It's not the first time she's asked me this. The same question came from her lips the first time we kissed. It's no doubt circled in her head every moment we spent together since I got here.

And I've been asking myself the same thing.

Only I don't think she'll be satisfied with my answer. Most women wouldn't be.

Women want commitment. They want to know where things are going before they even take the first step, and Greer and I have never had that. All we've had is the hot and heavy need for each other and the tension between us that crackles with more energy than anything I've ever felt on the ice.

We've had the rush of an illicit affair. The clash of personalities that's combustible in the bedroom. But we've also developed something deeper, something I can't ignore or deny. The problem is...I still have no idea what that means.

I reluctantly drag my head back from hers and brush my thumb across her cheek. "Are we really going to have this conversation right now?"

It's kind of a buzzkill when we just had mind-blowing sex. I'd much rather bask in the afterglow of an explosive orgasm and enjoy the feeling of her hot pussy still wrapped around my cock.

Greer sighs and lets her hands drop from around my neck. I can feel her pulling away emotionally just as well as I can physically. She's shutting down. She's letting all the reasons this shouldn't have ever happened overpower the reasons it should.

"Don't overthink things, Coach." I pull my semi-hard cock from inside her and step back so I'm still standing between her spread legs but also keeping her from moving away from me. "Just don't."

If she walks away, I don't know if I can get her back. Not when my answer to her question is a very big, *I don't fucking know.*

I'm not emotionally equipped to deal with these types of feelings, and Greer should know that. She shouldn't expect me to be able to suddenly become someone I'm not.

She pushes at me, urging me back and slides off the desk to reach down and grab the rest of her clothes. "We need to address it at some point, don't we? Otherwise, what's the point?"

I shove my dick back into my pants and run a shaky hand through my hair. "What's the point? How about the fact that this"—I motion between us—"feels incredible? How about the fact that both of us have been enjoying ourselves far more than I think either of us ever anticipated? How about the fact that this makes you happy?"

And me happy.

Her head jerks up, and she pulls on her underwear and pants. "Happy is irrelevant."

I scoff and shift back another step. "Why would you say that?" Even to someone like me, that seems pretty fucking dismissive. "Shouldn't happiness be the *only* thing that matters?"

Whether it's for a few hours, a few weeks, or a few months...

It doesn't have to last, but while it does, we should relish in it.

She squeezes her eyes shut and shakes her head. "Not when it comes at a cost. You remember what I told you when you came to my office that day?"

There's no need to clarify which day she's talking about. That first major argument...the one that ignited my attraction to her. The one that started everything.

"I told you that winning wasn't worth it if it was at the expense of hurting others."

I raise an eyebrow at her. "Yeah...and?"

She sighs and runs her hands through her hair again as she walks around her desk and sits. "So, what's the expense of this?"

I don't get where she's going with this. "Greer...I don't understand why you're so upset right now."

What am I missing? I thought we were on the same page.

She drops her face into her hands. "Because there's an awful lot of expense here. *My* expense. If we get caught, *I'm* the one who's going down. The worst that can happen to you is you get traded and have another notch on your belt."

I recoil. "Is that really all that you think this is for me?"

A notch on my belt?

Before I came to Vegas, I played hard—on and off the ice —and there's no denying it. She knows who and what I was, but how could she think that's all *she* is to me?

She glances up. "Am I wrong?"

The words "of course" sit at the tip of my tongue, but I can't say them. Something is suddenly lodged in my throat, making it impossible to swallow or speak. It's the knowledge of what it means to utter those words. It means caring enough for someone that they can hurt you. They can shatter your entire world and flip it inside out.

Opening yourself to that kind of thing only leads to pain.

Greer shakes her head as she brushes a tear from the corner of her eye. "That's what I thought."

A knock cracks the tension in the room.

She glances away from me to the door. "Come in."

The door opens, and I swallow thickly and peek down to make sure none of my clothing is still awry.

Steve sticks his head in and glances between us. His dark

eyes narrow before he focuses his attention on Greer. "I wasn't sure if you guys were still here. Coach, Marty needs to talk to you before we hit the ice."

She nods and rises behind her desk. With our equipment manager standing right there, and with her assistant coach waiting for her, Greer has to pretend a bomb wasn't just dropped in the room.

Every step around her desk is laced with a heaviness I haven't seen in her before. This really is weighing down on her. It really is a career-ender if it goes badly, but I'm a selfish bastard, and I don't know that I'm ready to give her up just because there's a little at stake here. At the same time, is it fair to keep pushing her when I can't see beyond tomorrow?

Steve disappears back into the hallway, and Greer moves to walk past me, but I grab her arm, keeping her in place. She offers me a tight look and glances down at my hand on her.

I swallow and lean my head down to hers. "Don't walk away like this. We're not done talking."

One of her light eyebrows rises. "We're not? Seems to me that we are. I've got a lot to take care of before practice and before we leave town tonight."

Which apparently doesn't include figuring things out between us.

I release her arm, and she disappears out the door, leaving me alone with my confusion and a strange pain in my chest.

20

GREER

When I played, I used to love traveling. Getting to see new cities, meet new people, experience new countries and different cultures, it all was so thrilling. I never minded being away from home. I missed Dad, but I knew he could take care of himself. He took care of me alone just fine for a long time after Mom died.

But this road trip is different.

I can't pretend everything is all right. I can't pretend what happened between Bash and me isn't eating away at my insides, making my gut and my heart ache.

It's made concentrating on these upcoming playoff games almost impossible. The games, *this team* should be my *only* focus right now.

They have to be. It's what I'm paid for.

Everyone is expecting me to fail, and I have a duty to ensure that doesn't happen. So, everything that *is* in my control needs to be. That means the men on the ice take top priority. Not just the one *man* who happens to have worked his way into my heart from that chilly place.

I scan the keycard and open the door to my hotel room. Just another in a long list of hotel rooms that become temporary homes while on the road. All I want right now is to be at my real home curled up on the couch with a bottle of wine and Webflix and maybe Jill to listen to my troubles.

There are days that having this job really gets to me, and this is one of them. Between the stress of the game tomorrow and what's happening with Bash, I feel like things are about to reach the full-on breaking point. Where it's too late to go back or to salvage anything. Where everyone gets hurt in some way.

Especially me.

Frankly, I'm surprised it took this long. The first time I hooked up with Bash, I wasn't sure it would ever happen again. I wasn't sure it *should* ever happen again, even if I wanted it to, and now...all I can think about is that it never *will*.

And that reality has come harder and harsher than he did inside me in my office.

I drop onto the bed and pull out my phone, unable to stomach spending the night completely alone in here.

Jill answers on the second ring. "Hey! I thought you were on the road tonight."

I sigh and run a hand over my face. "Just got in. At the hotel now."

She giggles. "And is Bash in the adjoining room again?"

I cringe at her question and shake my head. "No. I specifically requested to have a suite with no *adjoining* room and told them not to reveal what room was mine to any of the players."

"Really?" Concern laces her voices. "Greer, what's going on? I thought things were good between you two."

"They are. Or...I guess they *were*."

I haven't had a chance to tell her about what happened

in my office. I've been dreading the possible rebuke I might get or, even worse, confirmation that I did the right thing by basically ending things. "Bash and I kind of had it out."

"What do you mean?"

I stare at the off-white wall of the room and replay everything that went down in my mind. "Well, Bob called us into his office, and I almost had a heart attack."

"Oh, shit. Does he know?"

I shake my head. "No, thank God. He just wanted to tell us how happy he was that we were getting along."

Her laughter trickles through the line. "I'd say you two are more than getting along."

"Very funny."

She and Bash share a fifth-grade sense of humor.

"Sorry, Greer, not trying to make a joke of the situation, but you sound so doom and gloom about it. He's a smoking-hot guy who you have smoking-hot sex with. I'm not seeing the problem."

"The problem is...I lose all semblance of control when I'm around him. After we walked out of the meeting with Bob, we had a quickie in my office."

She bursts out laughing. "Again, I'm not seeing the problem here, Greer."

I scoot back to sit against the headboard. "The problem is that anyone could've walked in on us and exposed what's been happening. It was stupid and reckless and not at all how I usually live my life."

"Maybe that's the problem."

"What do you mean?"

Jill releases a tiny sigh. "Maybe you need to live your life a little bit differently. I think Bash is good for you. You're carefree for the first time in a long time."

"I couldn't be further from carefree, Jill."

For someone who has known me for so damn long, she sure isn't reading the situation very well.

"I'm coaching a team in the Stanley Cup playoffs. If I get caught sleeping with a player, my career is over."

"Then don't get caught."

Wow. She really does think like Bash.

The same words he said to me ring in my ears.

"But that's my whole point, Jill. 'Don't get caught' is easier said than done."

Sneaking around may be hot, but eventually, we'll make a mistake. Everyone does. A slipped pet name. A shared look someone sees. A stolen touch that's noticed.

How long can we really sustain this? And to what end?

I pinch the bridge of my nose and squeeze my eyes shut. "I mean, how long can we really sustain this sneaking around? Even if no one sees us together, are we going to stay hidden forever?"

"Just until the end of his contract, I guess."

I bark out a sardonic laugh. "His contract is for three years and twenty-seven million dollars. Are we going to sneak around behind closed doors for *three years*? What about when he renews his contract? How can this possibly go anywhere? I asked him what we were doing, and he couldn't give me an answer because it's impossible to find one where this works. Or maybe"—I swallow thickly —"maybe he didn't answer because he doesn't want it to. This was never meant to be anything long term, and I think we both let this go on longer than we intended."

That silences her. Maybe she's finally seeing the real issue here. The issue is...this *can't* go anywhere—even if we *wanted* it to, which I'm pretty sure he doesn't.

We both know it. We're both too afraid to say it out loud.

Jill sighs. "Maybe you need to decide what's more important—your career or Bash."

"Is that a serious question? This is Bash we're talking about. He's likely slept with enough women to make up an entire hockey team, and that's probably just this year alone." A fact that makes my stomach churn and chest ache in a way I don't even want to examine. "And I couldn't even stand to be in the same room as the man only a few months ago. I'm not giving up my career opportunity so I can keep sleeping with him."

"Then it sounds like you've already made your choice."

Have I?

It sure doesn't feel like it. In fact, I'm more confused than ever. And I know I won't be getting much sleep tonight. Which means the game tomorrow is going to be agonizing —in more ways than one.

The man who is slowly destroying my life will be out on that ice with my career and my heart in his hands.

———

BASH

I flip the puck in the air and catch it as I stare out the hotel room window at the city lights of Portland in front of me.

It has to have been at least an hour that I've been standing over here, watching cars whizz by and people stroll on the riverwalk, but I can't shake the weight of the conversation I had with Greer before we left.

"Dude, what's your problem?" Mac stares at me from his bed. "Go to bed, Bash. We have a big fucking game tomorrow."

No shit. One of the biggest games of my career.

We need to start off on the right foot in the playoffs. Gain some momentum to send us in the right direction. That's especially true with our first two games of the series being on their home turf. But it's impossible to concentrate on the game when all I can think about is how upset Greer looked when she stormed out of her office.

"Do you want to talk about it?"

I glance over at him. "About what?"

"About whatever has you so worked up tonight. You were practically silent on the plane, and now, you look like some junkie incessantly tossing that puck instead of shooting up."

I chuckle despite my dark mood. Maybe that's what Greer is. A drug I just need to kick. I once compared her to heroin, and it seems even more true now. And ever since she asked that question, the different answers have been rattling around in my head. But I can't talk about it with Mac. Even if I skirted around the truth, he could figure out who I'm talking about fairly easily. And if I slipped...

Talking won't help anyway. I need to get the fuck out of here, grab some fresh air somewhere I can think where she just down the hall. "I'm going for a walk."

He glances at the clock. "At this hour? Are you insane?"

"Maybe."

I pull on my jacket and head out the door before he can try to argue with me about it further. The hall and elevator are deserted, and when I reach the lobby, only a few late-night check-ins linger. I slip past the front desk and out into the fresh, crisp air.

Portland is a beautiful city. If I had more time here, I would love to explore it...

With Greer.

The sentence finishes without conscious thought.

Shit.

If I keep going on like this, I'm not going to sleep at all and I'm going to play like total crap. I grab my phone as my feet hit the cement outside the hotel and dial Caleb, the only person I can think of who has any clue what I'm going through.

He answers on the second ring. "Bash, good timing. I just finished grocery shopping."

I bark out a laugh at how domesticated he's become and start my walk down toward the river. "Good."

"What's going on? Shouldn't you be in bed and resting up for the game tomorrow?"

I nod and step up to the railing that overlooks the Willamette River. "I should be, but I can't sleep."

"Why not?"

How do I tell Caleb I'm all twisted up about a woman without him laughing at me? Maybe I can't.

But he's my oldest friend and already knows about my thing with Coach, so if I'm going to come clean to anyone, it's going to be him. "Greer. Things have just gotten...well... shit. They've gotten complicated."

A car door slams, and an engine roars to life through the line. "We've got about ten minutes before I get home, so give me the rundown while you can."

I stare at the moonlight reflecting off the water—brilliant and shimmering like a diamond. "I don't know, Caleb. I've never been so twisted up about a woman before."

He laughs. "I know. I could see it weeks ago when you had just started your thing with her and insisted it wasn't anything serious."

"How did you deal with it?"

"What do you mean?"

"How did you deal with everything during that time when you didn't know where Tara was and if she was all right, or if she was thinking about you?"

Their separation wasn't easy on him by any means, but he never wanted to talk to me about it. He always tried to act like everything was fine. Something I'm struggling with hardcore.

He sighs. "I thought that was what was best. What she wanted. Then I eventually realized how fucking stupid I had been, and by then, I couldn't find her. She had moved. It drove me insane."

"At least I know where Greer is."

"And where's that?"

"Up in her hotel room, probably cursing me."

"Why? What did you do?"

I rub at my aching, tired eyes. "Nothing really."

He barks out a laugh. "Somehow, I don't believe that, Bash. You forget how long I've known you."

He's right.

Caleb knows me better than anyone, and that means there's no point in holding back with him.

"She asked me what we are doing."

He issues a low chuckle. "The dreaded question, and let me guess, you panicked and ran?"

"No. But thanks for the vote of confidence, dick." The vivid memory of her distress in her office fills my head. "I froze...which may be as bad as running, I guess. I just didn't answer the question."

"Well..."

"Well, what?"

"What *are* you doing with her? Is this still just some playful fling like you told me it would be, or is it something more now?"

It would be easy to tell him it means nothing, that *she* means nothing, that it's just great sex. But deep down, I know it would be a lie. Because I do care about Greer. More than I probably should. More than I probably have a right to.

If I didn't, I wouldn't have cared when she said I saw her

as another notch on my belt. I wouldn't think about her when we're not together. I wouldn't give a shit about the potential fallout of our relationship because I wouldn't care what happened as long as I got what *I* wanted.

"I care about her." That's as real of an answer as I can give him right now.

"And is that enough?"

"Enough for what?"

"Enough for you to do whatever it takes to keep you two together?"

"Fuck, man." I rub my hand over my face. "I don't know. For us to be together...I don't even know how that would work. I definitely couldn't stay on the Scorpions as long as she's the coach, and even if I managed to find another team that Bob could trade me to next season, it would potentially be somewhere I wouldn't even play first line or to a team that doesn't have any chance at a cup. And then, we'd be trying to have a long-distance relationship where we might see each other once or twice a month if we're lucky."

He releases a deep sigh. "I know how hard it was on you, Jameson, Rachel, and your mom when your dad would sweep into town a couple times a month during the season, and I completely understand why you would be leery of getting into a relationship where that would happen. So, it sounds like you have your answer."

I jerk my head up. "I do?"

"It sounds like right now, your career is the most important thing in your life."

I guess it is. "Is that selfish of me?"

"I can't answer that for you. It's your life, man. You need to live it. I can't do that for you."

21

BASH

Two games on the Wolverine's turf and two crushing defeats...

Unfortunately, we were the ones crushed.

I don't even know how they pulled it off. Everything is just a haze. One giant, tangled mess of memories of plays and penalties and checks and fights and brilliant goals that gave them the wins and left us heading back to Vegas with our spirits and heads low.

Now, we have home ice where we hold a decent record this season. But the looks I got from Greer during the first two games and the blade of harshness in her voice when she spoke to me is preventing me from getting my head on straight to prepare for next two.

It all felt so wrong, like I was being punished for not knowing what I want.

Greer hasn't said a word to me about what happened and what we said—or what I didn't say. She tried to remain professional, and aside from the looks and tension in her voice that likely only I noticed, she succeeded.

But now we're home. We're going back on our own ice, and I don't know what's going to happen between us next. I can't continue to pretend that everything is fine, that this tension doesn't permeate the air between us and tighten my gut.

I won't be able to play well until we come to some sort of understanding.

It's fucking up my game. Getting in my head and under my skin. It's precisely the reason I've avoided any form of relationship or deep connection to anyone. I can't risk playing shitty like that again. Which is why I'm standing in front of Greer's house, staring at the door like it's going to bite me.

It won't, but the woman inside might.

I force myself up onto the porch and press the doorbell. We have an early practice tomorrow, and I should be in bed, which is probably where Greer already is. But this just can't wait.

The light above the porch flips on, and those beautiful green eyes peer out at me from one of the long panes of glass on the side of the door. Her lips twist into a frown, but she unlocks the deadbolt then swings the door open.

"Bash, what are you doing here?" She stands with her arms wrapped around herself protectively.

What does she need protection from? Me?

"I need to talk to you." I step closer.

She shifts, blocking my entry. "I don't think that's a good idea, Bash."

I grab her arm. "Please."

"Don't."

"Don't what?"

"Don't do things like this." She shakes my hand off her arm. "I'm not sure what you were expecting when you came over here, Bash, but I don't really have anything to say that hasn't already been said."

"Well, I do." I brush past her into the house.

She mumbles something under her breath. Probably unflattering, but I don't even care if she thinks that I'm a dick for barging my way in here. She can't expect me to just walk away and pretend everything isn't crumbling around me.

I have a contract with the Scorpions, and given how well the team played this year, she's going to be their coach for the foreseeable future. We need to be able to work together professionally even if whatever this is can never be more than whatever it is at this moment.

"Just let yourself in why don't you?" The annoyance in her voice carries across the living room.

I turn toward her.

She closes the door then faces me. "What do you need to say, Bash? We have an early morning tomorrow."

"I know. And I haven't slept well in days."

Her eyebrow wings up. "You didn't play well, either."

I sigh and run my hand over my stubbled jaw. "I know. I was so distracted by everything that went down between us that I barely remember those games. I can't go into the rest of this series with all of these things unspoken between us."

She squeezes her arms around herself again and glances at her feet. "Say what you came to say, Bash."

I can't believe she really doesn't have anything to say.

Maybe I've misread this entire situation. Maybe I'm feeling something that's one-sided. She seems way too willing to let this go, to let it end on what I *didn't* say in her office.

"I wanted to tell you that this is not easy for me, Coach."

She peeks up at me. "What isn't?"

"This." I motion between us. "I'm not..." I shove my hand

through my hair, tugging at the strands. "I'm not a relation-ship guy."

She snorts and shakes her head. "No shit."

"This is the closest I've ever come to having a real one."

Her eyes widen slightly. "Seriously? Not even high school?"

I shake my head. "I was busy with hockey in high school." I pause to consider whether to tell her what's really behind my aversion to any type of deeper connection. At this point, why hold back? "And when I was seventeen, my best friend's ex-girlfriend committed suicide after he broke up with her and went to college."

"Oh, God." Greer's hand flies up to cover her mouth. "At that age?"

I nod slowly. "It hit all of us really hard. None of us had noticed anything was wrong. She tried to contact him at school, and he ignored the calls. I saw her a few times after he left, and I just thought she was upset about the breakup, like any teenager would be. I didn't see how much she was struggling, that she was in a really severe depression. Then she killed herself. We all carried the guilt of thinking we could have done something to stop her. It made me not want to have that kind of pain in my life. Why open yourself up to something that could affect you that deeply? That... combined with how I grew up, just tainted the way I saw love and relationships."

Her brow furrows. "What do you mean how you grew up?"

I've avoided her questions about Dad for a long time. I never wanted to tear open those old wounds when telling her wouldn't change anything. But maybe it's time the truth about Mike Fury comes to light, at least to one person.

"My dad was a self-centered asshole, Greer. Still is. We would barely see him all season, then he would show up for a few days and come and go when it was convenient for him during the off-season." I swallow past the emotion threatening to choke me. "It was better when he was gone...because when he was home, he was a complete monster."

Her eyes widen, and she waits for me to continue.

"The man had the same aggression off the ice as he did on it. He hit my mom more than once each time he was home, and I did my best to protect Jameson and Rachel from his wrath, so he hit me a lot, too."

She takes a step toward me. "Bash, I'm so sorry."

I hold up a hand. "I'm not telling you this to get your sympathy, Greer. I'm telling you because I want you to understand that I never anticipated caring about you when we first got together because I've never *wanted* to care about *anyone*. I even pushed Jameson and Rach away because I felt myself turning into my father at times and I didn't want any of that to touch them."

She cringes slightly, but the words had to be said. It would be a lie if I told her I had planned for anything more than a few hot nights sharing a bed with her, and if I lied about that, she would see right through me and believe I was lying about the rest of what I have to say.

Her green eyes soften after a moment. "I care about you, too, Bash. That's what makes this so hard."

The pain shaking her words slices at my heart. A few months ago, watching a woman I was sleeping with cry wouldn't have affected me at all, because I've never given a shit about anyone I've stuck my dick into in the past beyond what they could do for me for a night or two.

But it's so different with Greer.

I close the distance between us and take her into my arms. She buries her face against my chest and wraps her arms around my waist. I wish I could take away all this pain and all the complications, but I can't. All I can do is hold on right now for what might be the last time.

Fuck does that hurt to actually acknowledge.

I pull back slightly and tilt her face toward mine. "You asked what we're doing, and I didn't have an answer for you. I still don't. Because the truth is, we don't have a lot of options here. I can't back out of my contract..."

"And I'm not going to quit my job."

I nod.

She chews on her bottom lip. "So, where does that leave us?"

We stare each other for what feels like an eternity. Her eyes well with tears until they slowly overflow and trickle down her pale cheeks.

I brush them away with my thumb and lean down to press a slow, soft kiss to her lips. "I guess all that leaves is goodbye."

GREER

His words hit me in slow motion and knock me back with their sincerity and depth of their meaning. I never thought Bash capable of showing emotions other than arrogance and anger. Then lust. But it's far more than that flickering in his bourbon eyes.

Fear. Resentment. Longing. Pain. It all lies there, staring back at me and begging me to understand.

I don't doubt for a second that he does care for me, that this is eating away at him the same way it has been me. The way he touches me, the way he looks at me, the things he's done for me to ensure I'm taken care of, even the way he reacted when I suggested I was just another woman in a long line of them that will continue after I'm gone prove he does care.

But that's just not enough.

The revelations about his high school friend and his father explain so much about Bash, about how he's lived his life and why he's reluctant to get close enough to me to open up and let me in. Why he can't just answer the damn question I asked with how he really feels and instead pushes me away and tries to ice me out.

Bash and the rest of his family have been hurt by the person who was supposed to love them the most. While Mike Fury was praised for his violence in the game, he brought it home in a way that damaged Bash in a way that may never heal. Between that and suffering the kind of loss he did at such a young age, it's no wonder the man is emotionally frozen.

Telling me everything he just unloaded started a crack in that wall he's built up.

He cares for me, and he's finally willing to admit it out loud, but the sad, awful truth is...he just cares for himself more.

The bastard.

I push out of his arms and take a step back. "You're so goddamn selfish, Bash."

He raises a dark eyebrow and points to his chest. "Me? Why am I selfish?"

Can he really not see what's happening here?

The man is so dense sometimes, I swear, it's like talking to a child. He has the emotional depth of a five-year-old if he can't see what I'm referring to.

I scoff and throw up my hands. "Are you kidding, Bash? You could probably ask around the league and find half a dozen teams to pick up your contract. They might not be ones with great records or playoff potential, but you'll have a spot on a line somewhere. Whereas, I can't just quit my job. Too many people are watching me. Too many little girls who want to be taken seriously in hockey. I can't *fail* at this, Bash."

He snorts and shakes his head. "For argument's sake, Coach, let's say I find a team willing to pick up my contract, what then?"

"What do you mean?"

He steps toward me, and I move back. One thing I know without a doubt, that the time I've spent with Bash has taught me is, when he's close enough to touch me, I'm in serious danger of making bad decisions.

Only space can ensure a clear head.

Bash stops his advance. "I mean...what then? Let's say I go to New York. I'm in New York, and you're in Vegas. Maybe we see each other once a month, if that. What the hell kind of relationship would that be? How long would it be sustainable? How long would we *really* be happy with the situation?" He shakes his head. "I won't do that to you or to me. It's just setting us up for even bigger pain down the road."

He doesn't explain what he means by that, but I assume it's a reference to how he grew up with his dad playing. Having a family and maintaining this type of career isn't easy. What he went through was awful. There's no denying or downplaying that. But not everyone who plays the game is a shitty father and spouse, and him making that leap is just fucking stupid.

"So, why even bother trying, Bash? That's what you're saying?" I release a little strangled laugh-sob. "You're so afraid of opening up to anybody, of letting anybody in, that you won't even give it a shot. You just assume that the worst is going to happen and assume the worst in *people*."

His defeatist attitude is so opposite of the way he is on the ice. This isn't the confident Bash who does what he wants and takes what he wants. This isn't the Bash who lets his anger out on the ice and off it can be so caring and gentle. This Bash is *scared*.

The man before me is terrified of what will happen if we really give this a chance. If we take on the complications it presents and give ourselves the potential for that kind of joy...and pain.

He growls low and steps toward me again. "I've been through this, Greer. I've lived through it and seen it first-hand. This does not end in a happily ever after for us. It will be us unhappy and unfulfilled and with us rushing through short reunions, fucking like rabbits, or being too tired to even do that. It ends with you pregnant and me an absent father, who, when I am there, is so wiped out from playing that I don't even have the energy to spend time with my kid. Or fucking worse, taking it out on him or her because I don't know how to be a fucking father. It ends with us living in two different cities and me never even *seeing* my child if I haven't destroyed my relationship with him or her to the point that they would even *want* to see me." Anger vibrates his voice, and he clenches his fists at his sides. "I promised myself a long time ago that I would never do that."

That was before me.

The words are on the tip of my tongue. But despite the burning anger in my chest, there's something else there—the acknowledgment that he's right.

We can never live in the same city as long as both of us are doing *these* jobs—except a few off months in the summer.

What kind of relationship would that be? What kind of future?

I don't dare think about kids or the house with the white picket fence. It's all stuff I never thought I would want, and now, this man I couldn't even stand to be near—a man who elicits equal parts desire and rage in me, a man who is looking at me now with so much pain and so much determination—is capable of shattering my heart by denying me those very things.

He reaches out and grabs my shoulders, then leans down until his face is level with mine, making me meet his eyes. Resolve lies in them. "This will never work, Greer. It was incredible, but it was doomed the moment we developed any sort of feelings for each other."

Feelings. Goddamn fucking feelings.

It never would have happened if I hadn't been so weak. So needy. So many of the things I've vowed my entire life *not* to be. This happened because of my failure. I got myself here.

He presses a lingering kiss to my forehead, and I take one final breath of his scent before he pulls away and walks toward the door.

I force myself to turn to get one last glimpse of him like this, when we can still acknowledge the truth, before we have to pretend none of it ever happened.

That's the future for us. Denial and lies.

It should have been obvious.

I always knew it would end with Bash. I just never expected *this* end.

He pauses at the door and looks back at me. His sad gaze meets mine. "I really am sorry, Coach."

The door closes with a loud click, and I drop to the floor and finally allow myself to fall apart.

When did I start loving Bash Fury?

And how do I make it stop?

22

BASH

The shrill ring of my phone fills the inside of my car. I glance at the display, and a smile spreads across my face even though my mood is complete shit. It's hard to be happy after what Greer and I said to each other and when the team has been playing like utter crap.

But things will turn around—at least where the team is concerned. I have to believe that. And Rach is probably calling to wish me good luck tonight.

"Hey, Rach, how's it going?"

"Bash?" Her voice wavers in a way that sends a chill down my spine.

Rach isn't a drama queen and doesn't overreact. The last time I heard this kind of panic in her voice was when Mom was diagnosed with cancer.

"What's wrong?"

She sniffles. "I hate to tell you this...I know you have a game tonight."

"Rachel, what's wrong?" I tighten my hands around the

steering wheel as I wait for her to drop whatever bad news is undoubtedly coming. "Just tell me."

"It's Dad. He had another stroke."

Fuck.

That's number three in the last five years. The first two were minor and didn't kill the old bastard, though. They just made him angrier, more demanding, and even more difficult to deal with. Something I never thought possible.

It's been so long since he's been in my life in any way that I've managed to avoid having to see him, but Rach can't seem to break away from the man even after all he's done to all of us. Her kind heart sees an old man who needs help and family, not the violent drunk he used to be.

Still, I should act like I care. "Is he alive?"

Rach releases a deep sigh. "Yes. But they're worried about him having another one. It doesn't look good, Bash."

"Shit." It's not that I really care if the asshole dies, but it will devastate Rach to lose her only surviving parent, and that alone tugs at my destroyed heart.

"I'm flying back to Michigan tonight."

Of course, she is.

Rachel is nothing if not the perfect daughter. It doesn't matter that she barely saw the man growing up or that when she did, he was distant and aggressive toward everyone—she still takes care of him as much as she can, even though she's in California now and has her own life and career.

"Is Jameson going?"

She snorts. "What do you think? Of course, he's not."

I wouldn't have expected him to show any interest in seeing the old man. I sure don't have any.

So, she'll be there alone...

I rub at my jaw. "Rach, you know I can't—"

"I wasn't expecting you to come, Bash." She releases a

little sigh. "I know how you feel about him. I just thought you should know. Good luck tonight."

She hangs up before I can offer some form of an apology for not caring about the fucking bastard, and a strange mix of white-hot anger and chilling confusion flows through my veins.

I glance up and slam on my brakes. "Shit!"

The tires squeal as the car struggles to stop at the red light I almost drove through.

My heart thunders against my chest, and I'm going to blame that on the near-death experience and not the phone call.

Even if I wasn't playing one of the most important games in my life tonight, I wouldn't be going back to Michigan— that's exactly what Rachel meant. Yet she still felt the need to inform me of his condition.

Why the hell would she tell me now, knowing I'm playing tonight?

The last thing I need is to be worrying about the man who never gave a shit about us when I'm out on that ice. My head is already a mess after my conversation with Greer and our losses in Portland. There's no room for anything else tonight.

If we win these two games, we at least have a *chance* of moving on to the second round if we can keep the momentum going into the final games of the series. It only takes four wins. These two are essential. My complete focus needs to be on playing hard and keeping everything tight. But a vision of Dad in a hospital bed flits through my mind, and I squeeze my eyes shut.

Get the fuck out of my heart, you bastard!

The car behind me lays on the horn, and I glance up at the green light and press the gas.

Get your shit together, Bash. You need to concentrate on this game—not on a woman, or a man who doesn't give a piss about you.

I've never had trouble focusing on the game. *Never.* The game is my life. It's what my heart beats for. What I *bleed* for. Years of hard work, breaking my body for this damn sport, and this is as close as I've been able to get. No team I've ever been on has advanced past the first round. The Scorpions have the ability to do it. We're a *great* team. I'm not fucking it up now that the Cup is within reach.

I drive the rest of the way to the arena on autopilot—left turn, right turn, right turn, left turn, and park my car. The bright afternoon sunlight glints off the windshield and straight into my eyes. I squeeze them shut against it.

For one moment, the silence of the car envelops me, and it's surprisingly calming. Usually, the bustle and noise of the arena and game get me amped up and quiet is the last thing I want or need. But right now, it's slowly helping release some of the tension in my body.

But it can't last forever.

Time to forget everything else and concentrate on slaughtering some Wolverines.

I climb from the car, grab my bag, and jog inside the arena to the locker room. Most of the guys are already here in half-dressed states, and Steve hustles around getting people anything they need.

Mac looks over at me with a raised eyebrow and makes his way across the locker room. "Are you all right, man? You don't look very good."

"I'm fine." It comes out more like a snarl, but I don't need him up my ass right now.

He snorts and shakes his head. "You don't sound it, either."

I sigh and run my hands through my hair. "My sister just called. My dad had a stroke."

And I have no idea why I just told him that.

Everyone has such hero worship for Dad. When word of Dad's other strokes went public, there was a goddamn prayer vigil held for him. Mac is probably a member of the "love Mike Fury" club.

His face falls, and he sits on the bench across from me. "Shit. Do you need to go?"

I shake my head. "No. My dad and I don't exactly have the greatest relationship."

Mac narrows his eyes at me. "He's still your dad, Bash. If you need to go, go. Everyone will understand."

"I'm not going." I shove up and slam my hand against my locker. "Let's just get this done."

He nods slowly, stands, and backs away to continue pulling on his gear. The years we've played and roomed together have taught him when to back off, which is good for his health and my sanity.

I drop down onto the bench in front of my locker again and pull out my gear. Compression shorts. Cup. Shin pads. Socks. Pants. Skates. Elbow pads. Shoulder pads. Jersey. I dress on autopilot. I've done it so many times that I don't need to consciously think about it. I grab my helmet and gloves, and Coach walks into the locker room.

All the air rushes from my chest.

Christ, she's beautiful.

There's nothing different about her today. One of the same tailored suits that show off all her curves hugs her body. Her blond hair pulled back in a ponytail has my fingers itching to tug on it. Those soft, pink, perfectly bowed lips part slightly as she waits for us to turn our attention to her.

Nothing different from how she looks every day, but

somehow, seeing her now sends my heart racing and makes my hand shake. Maybe it's the news about Dad. The realization that he's coming to the end of his life while my career is at its peak. Maybe it's because I fucking miss her so much and want to be able to talk to her about what's going on. Maybe it's because I feel like I got punched in the gut ever since I walked out of her house.

Maybe it's because I love her.

But there's no time to consider the *why*. I need to shake off my reaction to her and focus on the game.

I suck in a deep breath and rise to face her. Her eyes scan the room and linger on me momentarily. They narrow slightly, as if she, too, can see something is weighing on me, but she doesn't approach me, doesn't acknowledge her concern. She just moves to the center of the locker room and whistles to get everyone's attention.

When all eyes are on her, she steps up onto one of the benches. "Guys, we need this win. Losing isn't an option. We can't let these fuckers walk all over us on our home ice. We got this."

Everyone cheers their agreement. It's a straightforward pep-talk, but it's all we need. We all know our roles and what's expected of us. At least...on the ice.

In life? Who the fuck knows? Certainly not me. And certainly not where Greer or Dad are concerned.

But even if my heart is breaking looking at the sadness and concern in her green eyes, I have a job to do.

And I'm going to do it.

———

GREER

There's something wrong with Bash.

The moment my eyes landed on him, I knew. I felt it somewhere deep in my soul.

Bash may be good at hiding his feelings from everyone else, but in the time we've spent together, I've learned to read him enough to know that the darkness lingering in the depths of his bourbon eyes isn't usual.

He's hurting.

Because of last night? Or did something else happen?

My heart may still be shattered from the way he just walked away from me, but that doesn't mean I'm not having to fight the desire to run to him and wrap my arms around him and offer him comfort against whatever weighs so heavily on him. I can almost feel its heavy presence pressing down on my own shoulders, and I don't even know what it is.

I want to go to him, but I can't.

Even if I weren't his coach, it isn't my place anymore. Things between us are over. He made that crystal clear last night. And if there was something else going on, something that affected him or could affect this game, he would tell me. Not as his girlfriend or lover but as his coach.

Then again, Bash is too stubborn to admit he may have a weakness.

The man would probably play with a broken leg simply to prove he could.

I just need to trust he would never jeopardize the team by playing when his head isn't in the game.

It's really all I can do.

So, instead of running to him, I push out of the locker room. The cool air of the arena hits me at the mouth of the tunnel, and I step out into a roar of applause from the fans already seated to watch warm-ups.

The sound envelops me, wrapping around me like a hug from an old friend. All the fond memories of being on the ice and the feeling of contentment being in skates flood my brain, washing away the concern over the man who has occupied far too much of my thoughts with such a big game starting in only a few minutes.

I take a deep breath of the chilly air and step into our bench area.

Upbeat music fills the arena, amping up the already raucous crowd to a whole new level. This team. *Their* team. Has made it to the playoffs in their first season. And these fans have been here since the beginning, since *day fucking one*. This is what they thought could never happen but dreamed of, nonetheless.

The guys file out onto the ice with Bash bringing up the rear.

Shit.

It's not like him to not want to be first out, to not want to be the center of attention for every second possible. The only other times I can remember him heading out last was when *I* was the reason—keeping him back to tear into him.

The unease in my gut returns and strengthens. He doesn't even glance my way as they start their warm-up.

My gaze follows Bash. He flashes across the ice, juggling the puck on his approach to the goal. He whips his stick back and fires.

Shot after shot...each misses the net.

Wide to the left.

Wide to the right.

Off the pole.

Over the net.

Jesus.

Bash skates around for another shot and shakes his head as if trying to clear off whatever is causing this catastrophic string of misses.

This is bad. Really, really bad. Potentially catastrophically bad.

Whatever's going on with Bash has messed him up mentally enough that I don't know if I can trust him to play solidly in this game. It's only warm-ups, but I've never seen anything like this from him. And I'm not the only one who has noticed.

Mac tosses me a concerned look from his place on the ice near Bash, and I force myself not to respond or even acknowledge it. Not until I figure out what to do about it.

We made it pretty far this season without Bash, but he's become an absolutely invaluable member of the team. If he's off, it could throw off his entire line and the entire offense of all the lines—the entire rhythm of the team could be at risk.

I glance over to where Bob sits in the GM's box and fist my hands so tightly, my nails dig into my palms. This is the Stanley Cup playoffs. This is as big as it gets. We've already made history in more than one way, and I don't need it to go down in flames because one of the players was in his own head about something.

This game literally means *everything*. There's no room for hurt feelings or distraction. That's a hard lesson I learned as a player and now has only been reiterated as a coach.

The littlest things can fuck up your mental game. I always knew it was possible. Even when I played. I'd be lying if I said it didn't happen to me a time or two, but when it did, if I couldn't get my shit together, Bob—or whoever was coaching—pulled me.

There's only one way to deal with it—get the liability off the ice.

I'm sorry I have to do this, Bash.

He's going to think this is personal. He's going to believe it's about what happened between us. But it's not.

Don't shit where you eat.

I get the old saying now. My history with him makes these decisions even harder—for him and for me. But it's time to step up and be a coach, regardless of my personal feelings for Bash or how it may look to him. And hopefully, Bob will understand if I explain.

I elbow Marty and nod toward Bash on the ice. "Keep a close eye on Bash tonight. If it looks like he isn't a hundred percent in the game, pull him."

His eyes widen, and he glances across the ice at Bash. "Are you sure?"

Am I?

I close my eyes and let the sounds of the arena fill my head. Pulling Bash will have major repercussions—with the fans, with Bob, and with the other players. But if whatever is going on in his head can interfere with his ability to play, I need to do what's best for the team, not what's best for Bash. And my assistant coach needs to know I'm one hundred percent sure.

"I'm sure."

Marty shrugs and nods. "You got it."

If I end up having to pull him, he'll never forgive me.

But at this point...what does it matter?

Things between us are nothing but dust in the wind. Any lingering feelings we have for each other will dissipate over time. Maybe it would even be a good thing, like a final nail being hammered into the coffin. A sign that we need to keep walking away from each other instead of running right back, which is definitely a possibility, at least for me.

Who the hell knows what he's thinking?

For a while, I thought I did.

I thought I understood him. I truly believed we had come to a point where we *knew* each other, but apparently, it was just lust fogging over the reality of the situation.

That no one will ever really *know* Bash Fury because he doesn't want anyone to.

Only one thing is clear—this game is the most important of my career as a coach, and I won't let anything, or anyone, impede the team's success. Not even Bash Fury.

23

GREER

The message from Bob was very clear: *come to my office immediately.*

Shit.

As if losing at home and being one game away from being eliminated isn't bad enough, I also had to pull Bash, and now I have to explain it to all to Bob.

I don't know if it's worse because I know him so well or if he would be even harder on me if we didn't have such a long history. Either way, this will not be pleasant. Bob's temper simmers just below the surface, and when it rises, you don't want to be in the same room. I've always done my best not to be the focus of his explosions, but tonight, it will be unavoidable.

He's put a lot of faith in me to lead this team, and we're crumbling.

I knock on his door gently, as if doing so will somehow lessen what's about to rain down on me.

"Come in." His voice vibrates through the door, anger hardening his tone.

He isn't happy, and I can't say I blame him.

Neither am I.

I push it open and step inside. Bob glares at me from behind his desk, and I turn to close the door behind me.

"Don't bother. We're waiting for—"

Bash appears in the open door, his wet hair slicked back, and the cool scent of his shampoo and soap filling the air between us.

God, I miss that smell.

I've missed him—all of him—more than I want to admit. But I wasn't expecting him to be joining the meeting. It shouldn't surprise me, though. He played like shit today before I pulled him, and in the last two games before that, and Bob is going to want answers.

I step back from the door, and Bash brushes past me without a word.

"Both of you *sit*."

Bob's brusque order shakes me from my stupor and reminds me of where I am. I shut the door and lower myself into the seat next to Bash. Bob stares at me for a long time. Then, he stares at Bash.

I'm ready for the tongue-lashing we're about to receive. I deserve it. I failed as a coach. That's pretty clear.

"I know why you called us in here, Bob. And I can explain why I had to pull Bash."

He slams his fist onto the desk. "Is that what you think this is about?" He shakes his head. "Yes, your team fell the fuck apart, as did your star player." He points to Bash. "But what I pulled you in here to discuss is the fact that the two of you have been sleeping together."

"*What?*" Both of us jerk to attention.

Shit.

Bash's frantic gaze meets mine.

242

Oh, shit. This can't happen now. We aren't even together anymore. How did he find out?

Bash clears his throat. "Bob—"

Bob holds up a hand to stop him. "Spare me, Bash." He points a finger at him. "You, I should have expected this from." He turns his gaze on me. "But you..."—he shakes his head—"I just can't wrap my head around how you could do something so stupid. With all eyes on you and everyone waiting for you to fail. With my career on the line as much as yours, you sleep with a goddamn player?"

"I-I..." I open my mouth and close it.

All words fail me.

There's no excuse or explanation I can offer that will placate him because none of them are legitimate. There *is* no excuse for what we did.

None.

"Who told you?" Bash's question hangs heavy in the air.

Bob narrows his eyes on him. "Why the hell does it matter? I don't see you denying it."

How can we?

Bob knows I'm a shitty liar, and with Bash's reputation, Bob wouldn't believe him, anyway.

The man who holds our careers in his hands rises from behind his desk, rage flashing in his normally kind eyes. "It was right in front of my face. The way you two suddenly hit it off. You sat here in front of me and mocked me while you were secretly having an affair."

I gasp and shake my head. "It wasn't like that, Bob."

At least, not for me.

He raises an eyebrow at me. "It wasn't?"

Maybe for Bash.

He was making suggestive comments. In fact, it's precisely what we fought about before we fucked like animals in my office.

Bob shakes his head as he sits on the edge of his desk in front of us. "People do a lot of stupid things in their lives, Greer, but this, this has to be at the top for you. I don't even know what to do with you two." His gaze darts between us. "If this goes public..." He shakes his head and drops his face into his palm for a moment before looking back up. "I've managed to contain it. For now. Or at least, I think I have."

Bash clears his throat and leans forward slightly. "What are you going to do?"

Bob shakes his head. "I should fire you"—he points at me—"and trade him the first chance I get"—he moves the finger to Bash.

Bash snarls. "And ruin both our careers."

Anger flares Bob's nostrils. "If your careers are ruined, it's your own doing. Don't try to make me the bad guy here. I'm not."

"I'm just saying—"

Shut up, Bash!

I need to try to salvage this. "Bob, we aren't..."

The words catch in my throat. I just can't seem to get them to come out. Emotion strangles me, tightening like a vise around my chest.

But Bash picks them right up for me. "We aren't seeing each other anymore. So, it's not an issue."

"*Not an issue?*" Bob practically growls the words. "Have you seen the way you played the last three games, Bash? The animosity between you two has been obvious the whole time. If you can't play for her or concentrate on the fucking game because of your former involvement, I can't have you on the team."

"I don't want to leave the Scorpions." Bash's statement is hard and definitive. He glances at me. "This is a good team. I play well with these guys. No matter what happens this season, we'll play well together next season, too."

Bob eyes him skeptically. "So, you're saying you don't want to be traded?"

Bash shakes his head. "I'm not leaving. You can always get a new coaching staff."

Anger heats my skin and has blood rushing in my ears. "I'm not quitting."

Bob scowls at me. He wants to get rid of me. And he would be *well* within his rights to fire me this fucking minute.

I need to remind him why he can't.

"You can't fire me, Bob. You would have to tell the world you fired the first female head coach in history who took an expansion team to Stanley Cup playoffs in its first year. Have fun explaining that."

His jaw tightens, and a muscle there tics. It's the same look he always got when things were going to shit on the ice. "I don't have a fucking clue what I'm going to do with you two. Let's just get the rest of the season over and then I'll figure it out. But until then, you two stay—"

Bash holds up his hands. "No need to worry about that, sir. It's over."

Those last two words feel like the final twist of the blade in my heart. I knew it was over after our last conversation, but hearing the words out of his mouth, hearing Bash tell Bob that his career is more important than mine, is more important than us...

It's too much.

I grit my teeth and clench my fists to keep from crying. He's always going to think his wants and needs are more important than mine. It's who he is. Maybe he had a shit childhood and suffered at the hands of his father, but instead of making him sympathetic to others, it's turned him into someone I can barely stand to look at.

The person I thought he was the day he set foot on my ice.

Bash Fury is an arrogant, self-centered bastard. And he always will be.

I was kidding myself to believe the flickers of the caring man were enough to rescue him from his true nature. Just because he can be sweet and is good with kids and a generous lover doesn't mean he's not selfish when it comes to something having to do with himself, when it comes to giving something up.

Bob waves a hand at me. "Greer, get out of here. I'll talk to you tomorrow."

"That's it?" I glance at Bash then back to Bob.

"I need to talk to Bash alone for a minute."

I push myself up on shaky feet and make me way out of the office with nothing but unanswered questions, a broken heart, and a guillotine hanging over my neck.

———

BASH

I barely managed to get the words out before my throat closed up, and I had difficulty swallowing.

It's over.

Even now, after Greer has already left the office, I can't seem to manage to regain my breath. My lungs don't want to inflate, and the room spins slightly, with little orbs of light closing in on my vision.

It's over.

It's one thing to know it. It's another to say it out loud.

It's over.

It makes things final. Definite. We can't go back now. Not now that we've voiced the truth to Bob—that neither of us is willing to budge and there's no way around the reality of our situation.

I thought walking away from her and saying goodbye was as hard as it gets, that the pain couldn't become more intense, but saying those two little words here, in front of Bob, and seeing Greer's reaction might be the single worst moment of my life so far.

Considering everything I witnessed as a child and the loss of Mom, I didn't think it was possible to feel anguish like this, but my chest feels shredded. Like someone has taken a freshly sharpened blade and gone to town on me with the intent on inflicting the most pain possible.

"You two really fucked up a good thing, Bash." Bob shoves off the desk and walks around to his chair. "I sure hope it was worth it because it sure is fucking with your game."

Worth it? Absolutely.

I can't say I regret a single second I've spent with Greer in my arms.

Not one kiss.

Not one look.

Not one touch.

But Bob can't think she's the reason I've been a mess— even if she was part of it. That will only make him come down harder on both of us, and she doesn't deserve that. She doesn't deserve to lose this job because Bob thinks me and the rest of the guys can't keep it in our pants and play for a woman like her.

He needs another reason, something he can blame my shitty play on while directing his ire away from Greer. And I have the perfect excuse.

No one could blame me for being fucked in the head knowing my father is dying, and since Bob doesn't have any idea about the love lost between me and the old man, he doesn't have any reason to question my feelings on his health issue.

It's the perfect way to focus his attention on anything but that feisty blonde who walked out of here thinking her future is any abysmal black hole because of what we've done.

I swallow thickly and shift forward in my chair, doing my best to display all the turmoil raging inside me when I typically fight so hard to keep it contained. "My father had another stroke earlier today."

Bob's eyes soften momentarily, and he rests his forearms on his desk. "I'm sorry to hear that, but you know we can't have any distractions right now. No excuses."

"I know."

He sighs, sympathy relaxing some of the creases in his old face. "What I need from you right now is to know if you're really here or if you're just a liability to the team at this point. Do you need to go home to Michigan?"

There's no way *that* man is going to be the reason I miss playing in game four. Not after everything else he's done. He can rot there alone for all I care, like he deserves. But Rachel will be with him, even though he doesn't deserve it. She'll hold his hand and let him believe he was some great father instead of telling him the truth during his last moments on this earth.

I grit my teeth and shake my head. "I'm fine, Bob, really. Just had a couple bad games. It happens to everyone."

He narrows his eyes on me. "Are you sure everything is all right, Bash? Can you play for Greer after whatever happened between you two, on top of the situation with your dad?"

Even though it's unspoken, it's clear the next game could be the deciding factor between whether I stay, or I go. It will determine whether I'm more indispensable than Greer. It could be what decides *both* our fates.

I force a smile I don't feel at all. "I'll get them next game, sir."

There isn't any other option. I need to get back to the *old* Bash, the one who just played. The one who did his job well and without reservation. The cold, heartless Bash who used his body to send a message and scored goals as easily as he got willing women into his bed.

The one I was before I met Greer Waterson.

I can do it. I have to do it. Closing my heart off to her and what we shared is the only way I can move forward and the only way we can win.

"You better, son, because you've burned just about every bridge in the league. You're still young, and you know you're one of the best players on the ice right now, but you've let it go to your head. If you hadn't, there's no way you would've ever considered getting involved with Greer. Think with your head and not your fucking dick. Greer is a good coach." He pauses a moment, overcome with emotion himself. After his long history with her, bringing her up onto the Olympic teams and getting her into coaching, seeing her make such a huge mistake must feel like watching his own daughter destroy her career. "Can you separate your history with her from that and just play?"

I nod immediately. "For as long as I have to."

I don't want them to fire Greer. She doesn't deserve to pay like that just because she got involved with me. I can play for Greer. At least, that's what I'm trying to convince myself.

Even though I found myself glancing at her on the bench far too many times. Even though I cringed at every frustrated or angry look she gave. Even though I've imagined her in my arms and under me a thousand times since we walked away from each other.

I can do it.

Bob leans back in his chair and shakes his head. "You two have really put me in a shit position, Bash. You know there's no way I can keep her as coach and keep you here after this season no matter what you both say."

"I know that."

And so does Greer.

We both knew it the moment he exposed us.

The fact that he hasn't decided what he's going to do yet surprises the fuck out of me. When he asked me to stay behind, I was sure it was to emphasize how important Greer is, not only to the team, but also to the NHL and to Bob personally.

They share a long, close history. I thought he would pick her over me, that she is the obvious choice in this situation. But maybe I'm underestimating my own worth here.

The threatening words I said to her during our first confrontation in that tunnel ring in my ears—my jab about my contract and how they would always choose me over her.

Back then, I was so angry and intent on proving a point. Now, bile climbs my throat knowing I might have been right.

"If I brought in another coach, can you shelve the attitude you had with Greer when you got here? I don't want to have to go through that again with a new coach."

I nod. No one will ever get under my skin the way Greer Waterson has. "I want to stay with the Scorpions. I'll do what it takes to make it work."

No more moves. No more trades. I'm staying put. Whether that's with Greer as the coach or someone else is in Bob's hands.

"Good." He waves toward the door. "Then get out of here. And I expect to see a win in game four."

I stand and nod. When I reach the door and turn the handle, Bob clears his throat. I glance back at him.

"And Bash...stay the hell away from Greer unless it's on the ice."

"That won't be a problem."

24

BASH

T alk about an absolute shit show—like watching a train wreck and not being able to look away. Though, it's really impossible to look away when you're part of the team and on the ice.

Game four—our only chance to stay in the goddamn playoffs and my opportunity to prove to Bob he needs to keep me here...and we played like a bunch of fucking ten-year-olds. Actually, those kids from *The Mighty Ducks* movie probably would've done better than us.

Pierre let in six shots in the first period alone, and even though Greer pulled him in the second, it just wasn't enough because our offense sucked, too.

Shots ricocheted off the poles left and right. Pucks flew wide and over the net. It was like we were playing blind and drunk.

Epic shit show.

And to top off an epically horrible night, when Salinski slammed me into the boards in the third period, I really got my bell rung.

My head still pounds like a jackhammer on my brain. Concussions are just a part of the game, and I've had my share of them, but having to get pulled to get checked by medical was the perfect fucking icing on the pile of turd cake that was that game.

Now, the season is over, and I can't wait to get the fuck out of here.

There's no way I'm sticking around for any of the end of the season bullshit. Mac can clean out my locker for me. There's nothing I need in there that can't wait for him to ship it to me back in Chicago.

I just want to get back *home*. I never thought I'd be desperate to get out of Vegas and these swanky digs, but my condo on the river in downtown Chitown is calling my name.

My own bed.

My own TV.

My own stuff.

My own *space*.

Away from Greer and everything that reminds me of her.

Like this damn hotel room that has her scent all over it despite the fact that the maid service comes in daily to clean.

It's psychosomatic. I know it. It's me missing her, but I can't begin to move on with her haunting me like this. I have to get the hell out of here—fast.

I open the dresser drawer, grab a stack of T-shirts, and shove them into my suitcase laid out on the bed. Even hours after the game, I'm still fuming. It wasn't only my fault. We all played like shit, but I expected more out of the team and myself.

Bob was so pissed, he stormed out of the arena without even saying anything to us.

But what he said in his office to Greer and me made where we stand pretty fucking clear—both of our heads are on the chopping block until he decides what to do.

Other than thanking the team for a great season, Greer didn't say shit, either. She just slipped out of the locker room with her tail tucked between her and legs and disappeared.

Which was for the best.

Standing there and giving some long, drawn-out speech wouldn't have changed how things ended. For the team or between us.

I throw open my closet and start pulling shirts off the hangers. It doesn't matter how I pack or what a mess it will be when I get home.

Fuck...I just need to get out of here.

I need to decompress. I need to relax. I just need some goddamn time.

Is that so much to fucking ask?

It seems so because my phone keeps ringing off the damn hook. And there it goes again. I glance at the screen, but this time, it's someone I don't mind answering for. "Hey, man."

"So, that was kind of painful to watch." Leave it to Caleb to make a joke out of my agony.

"No shit." I grab another stack of clothes and shove it into my suitcase.

"You want to talk about it?"

"What do you think?" I down the last of the scotch in my glass and pour another shot.

He chuckles lowly. "I think not."

"You're a smart man, Caleb Carlson."

"So, maybe we should talk about your dad instead."

I freeze and drop onto the bed with my head in my palm. "Dude, don't get started with me."

The only reason I answered the damn phone was that it

was Caleb and not Rachel or one of my teammates. I thought it would be safe with him.

He sighs. "Rachel called me. She told me what's going on."

I rub at my eyes. "Now, why would she go and do something stupid like that?"

"Probably because she knew I might be the only one who could talk you into going."

I snort and lie back on the bed to stare at the white ceiling high above me.

Children screaming in the background has me pulling the phone from my ear. I love Bradley and Ivy, but Christ, those kids have some lungs on them.

"Hold on a second. I need to step outside where we won't be interrupted by a toddler." He opens and shuts a door. "Look, Bash. I know you. You're gonna do whatever you want to do, no matter what I say. But you need to have some perspective here." He releases a deep sigh. "I, of all people, understand the relationship, or lack thereof, you have with him. But I also know what it's like to lose somebody without the chance to say goodbye, without the chance to clear the air and tell them how you really feel. I know what it's like to carry that guilt."

My chest tightens.

Lisa.

Her death affected all of us in different ways, including me, but it almost destroyed Caleb. He cared about that girl, maybe even loved her as much as a high schooler *can* love someone, and he carried the guilt of her death for far too long.

"I don't want you to have any regrets, Bash. I don't want you to look back in twenty years when you have kids and wish there were things that you could've said to him. That's all I'm saying. If you think you can live with never seeing him again, with never clearing the air and telling him how you feel, then great, maybe I'm wrong. I hope I am. But experience tells me otherwise."

I scrub my hand over my face and pinch the bridge of my nose to stop the headache pounding against my skull. "I just want to go home, man, back to my condo in Chicago for a little fucking peace and quiet. I just want some time."

"If that's what you need, then take it. But just remember there's a clock ticking in Michigan. You don't know how much time he has."

No, I don't. And while the thought of living in a world without Mike Fury has crossed my mind over the years, I never really considered what I want to say to him. Now, Caleb's words are bringing up years' worth of memories and anger. None of it makes me want to jump on a plane to Michigan.

"I'll think about it, Caleb."

"All right, man. You know I'm here if you need to talk again."

"I know. Thanks, bud."

"You're welcome. So, how did you leave things with Greer now that the season is over?"

I snort and shake my head. "Well, the GM found out about us."

"Oh, shit."

"Yeah." I sit up and sip my scotch. "He called us into his office and said both of our heads are essentially on the chopping block. We told him it was over, but he didn't make a decision, just said he's going to have to think about it."

"Fuck. So, you might get traded?"

"Yup."

"And she might get fired."

A strange pain hits my stomach, and it's not from the booze. "Yeah. She might."

And the thought of her losing her job and this opportunity all because I pushed her into something she was never totally comfortable with brings up all sorts of guilt I never thought I'd feel over my relationship with her.

"So, what are you hoping for, man? That you stay or she does? Is it really over between you two?"

"Jesus, Caleb. I don't fucking know."

I don't know anything anymore.

GREER

Jill stares at me from over the rim of her wine glass as she downs the last sip. "Are you going to get fired?"

Wouldn't I like to know...

It's been looming over my head like a dark storm cloud, casting everything I do in inescapable shadow since the moment Bob pulled us into his office and told us he knew.

I rest my elbows on the table and drop my face into my hands. "I don't know. Maybe. Probably." I look back up at her, and she raises an eyebrow. I sigh and lean back in my chair. "If we would have won a few games in the first round, or advanced, even if we didn't make it to the finals, I think I stood a chance of keeping my job despite this thing with Bash. Bob would have been lambasted for firing me after bringing the team that far, and he had to think about the public affairs side of taking that action. Something he is *very* aware of."

She nods slowly. "But with the epic crash and burn failure of losing four games in a row..."

I glare at her. "Thanks for being so thoughtful."

The woman who is supposed to be my best friend but who is certainly pushing the limits of that just flashes me a grin. Leave it to her to get to the heart of the matter and state the ugly truth. It's actually what makes her a great friend— never being afraid to say what needs to be said or what I don't want to hear. "Anytime."

I shove up from my chair and walk back into the kitchen to grab the bottle of wine sitting on the counter. Bottle number two of the night, and there's no doubt I'll open a third.

After I left the arena tonight, I knew I was losing the fight against ingesting serious amounts of alcohol. Jill was more than happy to oblige my need to lose myself in pinot noir and meet me here with wine and a bag of Chinese takeout in hand. There's nothing like drowning your sorrows in alcohol and MSG.

I refill her glass and top off mine before I drop back down into my seat. The slightly chilled tannin-filled liquid slides down my throat, and while I had hoped to be seriously buzzed by now, I'm still all too aware of the reality of my situation. "I think I fucked up." *Actually, I know I did.* "Do you think there's any way for me to come away from this with anything positive?"

She sighs and a sympathetic look crosses her face. "Oh, honey. That is a loaded question. Yes, you really fucked things up with the whole job situation, but do you regret getting involved with Bash? Was that really all bad?"

I snort and shake my head.

So much of it was good.

All of it, really, except the end.

The long, steamy nights. The lazy days before we had to go into practice or a game. Sneaking into each other's rooms at night while on the road...

Tears sting my eyes, and I blink them away and take a gulp of wine to stop myself from turning into a blubbering mess.

"At the time? Of course not." I shrug. "But at this point, things are such a mess, I honestly just don't know what to think or how to feel about any of it"

It was great...but at what cost?

I've asked Bash that question, and now, we're finding out that paying the price means potentially losing everything.

She pushes back her chair, grabs her wine, and wanders over to the couch to drop down next to me. "You had a good time with Bash. More than a good time. You're lying if you tell me you didn't have more than just fuck-buddy feelings for him."

I sigh.

When did I become so damn transparent?

"I know."

"And there's no way to fix anything?"

"What do you mean?"

She sighs. "I mean, can you fix things with Bob or Bash, or are both lost causes?"

"I think they're both lost causes. I don't know what I could say to Bob right now that would make any of this okay. And Bash..." I take a sip of my wine. "I think Bash proved how he feels when he ran out of the arena and left town without even saying goodbye. Not to mention how he threw me under the bus in Bob's office."

Jill swirls her wine in her glass and nods slowly. "You did the same to him."

I pause with my drink halfway to my mouth. "How so?"

"Well, you said Bash threw you under the bus, but didn't you do the same thing to him by saying your career was more important than his?" She shrugs. "I'm just saying that if you consider him choosing his career over yours as throwing you under the bus, then that's kind of the pot calling the kettle black, isn't it?"

Shit.

It *is* completely hypocritical of me to be mad at him for choosing his career over us when I did the exact same thing. I could have quit, but that option never even crossed my mind. All I saw was the fight to get to this point and what quitting might say to other little girls in hockey skates. But I could have explained it in a way that made it clear I wasn't quitting because I couldn't handle it or wasn't good at my job. I *could* have chosen Bash.

"I guess you're right. It isn't fair to be mad at him about that."

Jill grins at me and throws up her hands. "Praise the Lord! You finally admitted I'm right for once. I feel like I should write this down for posterity purposes."

I scowl at her. "Don't be a jackass."

Her laughter floats through the air, lifting my spirits despite everything happening. "You know I'm only trying to be your voice of reason."

I nod. "I know, and thank you for that and for bringing the food and booze. I really needed it tonight."

"I figured. So, what are you going to do now?"

"Now?"

"Yeah, now that you might be fired and you're single."

"Oh...well...I guess I wait to see what Bob decides, and if I get fired, I try to find a new job. And as far the being single goes..."—I sigh and take another sip of my wine—"there's really nothing I can do about that. Bash and I were doomed from the start. I just have to accept that it wasn't meant to be. Maybe in another life, in another world or another time, if we were in different professions, in different positions, but not like this."

Admitting that is almost as painful as hearing Bash say the words "*it's over*" the other night.

But it's true.

We can't go back on what was said, on how we hurt each

other, on how selfish we both were. The damage has been done, and he doesn't *want* to change anything.

She nods and frowns. "It's sad."

"What? My love life?"

She snorts and shakes her head. "That you two can't work it out. You were so happy. Even with all the stress of worrying about getting caught. You just seem to really like him."

That's a huge understatement, though I don't have the guts to speak the truth out loud, even to Jill.

I more than like him.

With every sly smile, with every arrogant wisecrack, with every damn heated look and wink...that bastard made me fall in love with him. And he did it knowing it would never go anywhere.

25

GREER

Waiting for the axe to drop is agony.

I thought Bob would've made a decision by now, but it's been a week of sitting and waiting. Wondering how things could've gone so damn wrong.

And of missing Bash.

I don't want to. God knows I don't.

The man is as infuriating as he is handsome, and I want to forget his kiss and his touch and the way he smirked when he had a devilish intention for me. But I can't.

All those things are etched into my brain permanently.

I started to call him a hundred times only to remind myself that there's no point. No matter what we do, one of us is giving up something too important for this to ever work. Plus he said he didn't want to let me in, didn't want me any closer. He flat out *told* me he was pushing me away intentionally.

Which means there's nothing else I can do.

So, wallowing in my pajamas with a Webflix marathon

of 90s television comedies seems like the best way to pass the time until the other shoe drops. It's completely out of my hands now, and though I may want to crawl into a hole and cry, I'm going to settle for the couch and a tub of chocolate chip cookie dough ice cream.

I shove a spoonful into my mouth and try to concentrate on the flickering images on the screen.

The doorbell rings, and I jump at the sound.

Who the hell could that be?

Visitors aren't common for me since I don't have many friends here in town other than Jill. And I'm not expecting anyone today.

I make my way to the door and glance through the glass on the side of it. A delivery man stands on my porch, holding a bouquet of flowers. My heart leaps into my throat.

Bash.

I fling the door open.

"Delivery for Greer Waterson?"

"That's me."

He hands me the flowers with a smile. "Have a nice day."

The beautiful scent of the arrangement, including my favorite stargazer lilies, fills my nose, and I bury my face in them and walk toward the kitchen.

A small white envelope sits nestled inside them. I set the flowers on the counter and tear open the envelope.

I miss you. - S

He misses me.

The sting of tears burns my eyes, and I blink them away so I can read the note again and again. Each time, the words bring with them a tidal wave of conflicting emotions. I'm not the only one feeling this way, but I don't know if knowing that makes this worse or easier. Because it doesn't matter that we miss each other.

Sometimes, love isn't enough.

Bash might not even recognize the emotion if he feels it, and if he does, he'll just push it away to protect himself and —in his head— me.

And there's nothing I can do about it.

I sigh and pull the flowers from the wrapping to put them in a vase. Part of me wants to dump them into the trash. Their beauty only reminds me of Bash and what we've lost. But I can't bring myself to throw them away.

Not yet.

Maybe tomorrow when I get sick of seeing them and breaking down.

My phone rings, breaking through the fog of despair threatening to envelop me, and I scramble back to the couch to grab it. "Hey, Dad."

"Hey, sweetheart. How are you doing?"

He means how am I doing with the loss and being out of the playoffs. How am I doing with the way the season has turned out. Because he doesn't know about Bash, and he doesn't know that I'm on the cusp of being fired.

Goddammit.

He'll be so disappointed in me. He taught me better. He taught me to always be aware of the fact that I'm a woman in a man's world, and therefore, my actions will be scrutinized ten times harder than any man. He taught me to appreciate the opportunities given to me and not to squander them. He taught me all of that, and I *still* made a mess of everything.

The tears well in my eyes despite my best efforts to keep them at bay. "Oh, Daddy. I'm really not doing well."

It comes out on a sob, and I slap my hand over my mouth to keep from completely losing my shit and panicking him.

"Honey, what's wrong?"

Everything!

And I need to talk to the person I trust the most in the world. I drop onto the couch. "I have to tell you something. And you're not going to be very happy with me."

He sucks in a deep breath. "You know whatever it is, we can work through it. We always do. As a team."

I swallow through the emotion clogging my throat. "I..."

How do I explain what happened between Bash and me?

No matter what I say, it's going to be awkward, but Dad had to handle all my teenage puberty stuff by himself, including giving me "the talk" when the time came. If he can do that, I can do this.

It's just like ripping off a Band-Aid.

"Daddy, I slept with Bash Fury." I cringe as I wait for him to respond.

He clears his throat awkwardly. "Okay."

"And Bob found out."

"Oh...I assume that did not go over well."

"That's putting it mildly. He was furious, as he had every right to be. But he hasn't made a decision about what he's going to do. I might get fired. Bash might get traded. Or both."

"Well, shit." At least he understands the seriousness of the situation, and the disappointment in his voice slashes at my already shattered heart. "Seems like you've really got yourself in a jam, darlin'."

I rub at my temple and squeeze my eyes shut. "I know, Dad. I really fucked up everything."

"And how does Bash feel about all this?"

"I don't know. We both took a pretty firm stance that neither of us was willing to give up our career, and we broke up even before Bob ever found out about us. Then we lost all the games right on the back end of that..."

"Do you think one had anything to do with the other?"

Could it?

Bash is an incredible player. I can't see him letting personal shit get in the way of his game. But these flowers are evidence that he's been thinking about me, thinking about us. And he was off the last few games. The last two at home, especially, so maybe he is struggling with this breakup more than I realized.

No.

This is Bash Fury I'm talking about. The man goes through women like most people go through clean underwear. I was just convenient. The flowers are just a game of some sort. Maybe a plea to let him stay if I don't get fired. To try to gloss over any hard feelings so things won't be awkward.

It can't be anything more. Not from a man like him.

"I don't think one has *anything* to do with the other, Dad. We just got beat. He had a few bad games."

Dad sighs. "Is there anything you can do at this point?"

I've been wracking my brain for a week, trying to think of anything I can do or say to make things better with Bob, to get his trust and confidence back. To get to the way things were *before* Sebastian Fury came to the Scorpions.

But absolutely nothing has come to mind.

"Not really. Other than wait and hope Bob doesn't fire me."

"And if he trades Bash instead?" Dad pauses and waits for me to consider the question. "Is that something you can live with?"

"I don't have a choice."

He chuckles, and the familiar soft sound tinkles through the phone and warms my heart in the way only *it* can. "You always have choices in life, Greer. It's just some of them are harder to make than others."

267

BASH

My phone rings as I step out of the car and into the chilly April air. Snowflakes fall around me, a late snow even for here, and it instantly brings back memories of playing in the yard with Rachel and Jameson during the days we got off school because of blizzards and hazardous roads.

I dig the phone from my pocket and glance at the screen, then accept the call and put it to my ear. "Rachel?"

"Look, Bash..."

Oh, here we go.

"I know you hate him, but Dad really isn't doing well. He had another stroke yesterday, and this one was bad enough that it's shutting down his organs. He's on dialysis, and they're saying it could be any day now. He's in and out of consciousness." Her voice cracks, clearly fighting her emotions to make it through this call. "He asked to see you last night."

My steps falter, and I pause for a moment, the flakes falling and whipping around me in the brisk wind. I force myself to start walking again across the parking lot and step through the sliding doors into the building. "Really? That's something very un-Dad-like to do."

The man hasn't shown any interest in what's happening in my life for years. Even playing well in the league, even be named MVP, following in his footsteps wasn't enough to warrant a phone call from the man.

He probably knew I wouldn't answer or would hang up on him, but he could have at least made an effort. In the years since Mom died, I haven't even heard his voice. And that's probably for the best, for both of us.

Any conversation would have only ended with more

pain, the same way it always did when he and I would spend "quality time" alone together when he was home. Nothing was ever good enough. I was never aggressive enough on the ice. Never fast enough. Never *anything* enough...

"Please, Bash, I know how you feel, but just consider coming."

I make my way down the long, tiled hallway and stop outside room 113. "I'll consider it."

Rachel's head jerks up from where she leans against the wall outside the room, and her tear-filled eyes meet mine. She lowers her phone, and her bottom lip trembles. "You're here."

I end the call and shove my phone into my pocket, and she does the same before she launches herself at me and wraps her tiny arms around my waist.

"I'm here."

Reluctantly.

And with a whole lot of reservations about it.

She pulls her head back from my chest and looks up at me. "Why did you change your mind?"

I break free of her embrace and glance up and down the hallway.

It's exactly how I remember it. Though, I wish I could forget those awful days, weeks, months watching Mom slowly slip away.

We've been here before. The same hospital. The same floor. The same smell of death and the cleaning solutions they try to use to cover it invading my nostrils.

We watched Mom deteriorate here. It's where I came to say goodbye to her. A place I never thought I'd set foot in again, yet here I am, standing outside the room of the man the world worships but who I've wished dead more times than I can count.

"Bash? Did you hear me? Why did you come?"

I shove a hand through my hair and sigh. Caleb's words from our phone call echo in my head. *"I know what it's like to lose somebody without the chance to clear the air and tell them how you really feel."*

"Something a friend of mine said."

She grins at me and swats at my chest. "I always liked Caleb."

I chuckle and roll my eyes. She more than liked him. She had a raging crush on him growing up. One of those embarrassing ones where she wrote "Mrs. Caleb Carlson" all over her notebooks and told all her little friends she was going to marry him. He was always a good sport about it, but it took a long time for her to outgrow it.

"Yeah, yeah, yeah. Well, Caleb said I would regret it later if I didn't come."

It may have taken me a week to suck up my pride and store away all my animosity before I could get on the plane and fly out here, but I did it.

I glance at the closed door to our left. "He's not doing well?"

She bites her lip and shakes her head. "No. He asked for you last night, but he's unconscious again, and he isn't awake for very long when he *is* conscious."

I nod slowly as Rachel watches me.

Her green eyes, ones the same color as Mom's, assess me long and hard. "What are you going to say to him?"

"Does it matter?"

She scowls at me and crosses her arms over her chest. "Of course, it matters, Bash. Jameson wouldn't even come. And you're here, but I can already see that it isn't to give him a kiss and hug."

I scrub my hands over my face and shake my head. "Look, Rach, you were too young to really understand what was going on—"

She holds up a hand. "Oh, no. Don't even get started with that bullshit with me. Yes, I was young, and you all did your best to protect me from the worst of him. But I wasn't blind or stupid. I know he made a lot of mistakes. I know he was a shitty father. But he is still *our father*. He's still a human being."

Barely.

"Are you perfect, Bash? Have you made *no* mistakes in your life?"

"Jesus, Rach, I've made plenty of mistakes." But for some reason, I can't put Greer on that list. Even with the terrible way everything has turned out, I can't consider her a mistake or harbor an ounce of regret for the time we spent together. Regret over how it turned out...that's what eats away at me. "There's no need to lecture me."

"I'm not perfect, Bash. Far from it. But it seems you need a reminder that neither are you. He may only have a few days left on this planet. He knows he's made mistakes, so please don't go in there all riled up for a fight like you do on the ice. Or you might be the one who kills him. You don't want that on your conscience."

It's not fair to say that speaking my mind is going to kill the old man, but she's right about my conscience. It's weighed down enough right now, wondering if what Greer and I did, what I initiated, is going to get her canned. On top of knowing I didn't play my best in the last few games and it might have played a role in costing us the Cup.

I can't self-flagellate over that. It wasn't just me; the whole team fell apart. But sometimes, all it takes is one amazing play from one player to turn things around, and I just couldn't be that this time.

Because of Greer or because of Dad? That's up in the air.

There was just too much swirling around my head. Too many unspoken words. Too many unanswered questions. At least I can resolve some of them now before it's too late.

I suck in a deep breath of the stale hospital air and tug Rach in for another hug. "I promise I'll be gentle with him."

She pulls back with disbelief in her eyes. "Your version of gentle or *actually* gentle?"

I grin at her. "I only know one version."

She sighs and shakes her head. "That's what I'm afraid of."

26

BASH

I t turns out Rachel was worried for nothing.

In the long days I've been here, sitting beside the man who caused me so much pain, Dad has only stirred and opened his eyes a few times, and he's never been conscious long enough to even acknowledge me being here.

Watching him cling to life, moving in and out of consciousness for almost a week, has given time for the anger I was holding onto to dissipate somewhat. It will never completely go away. It's in my nature to hold grudges, even against blood, but if he's ever lucid long enough to actually have a conversation with me, it won't be the knock-down, drag-out fight I had pictured in my head when I first came here.

He looks so small, so fragile in this hospital bed, so different from the man I remember growing up. That man was a monster. Huge, muscled, dominating on the ice and off it. Even though it's been years since I've seen him, I didn't think it would be this bad. He's just a shadow of who and what he used to be.

The man lost his career. He lost his wife. He lost his kids. Well, all but Rachel. She just has too big of a heart to leave him despite everything he's said and done. But for all intents and purposes, he's been alone.

He created this world of his own making, though. He chose to be angry. He chose to drink. He chose to bring his aggression off the ice and into our home. I can't ever forget that. And I don't know if I can ever forgive it, either. Even if my anger does fade. Even with him like this.

And maybe I don't have to.

Each day, he seems to deteriorate more, and he may never wake up.

I rub at my tired eyes, push myself up from the chair next to his bed, and wander over to the window for what feels like the hundredth time since I got here. Other than short stints where I went to the hotel to try to sleep, shower, and change, I've been here nonstop, rotating with Rachel to make sure he isn't alone, just in case the inevitable happens.

And it's starting to wear on me.

Stamina on the ice is one thing. Sitting here, watching someone die is completely different. My entire body aches, and I stare out the window at a town I never thought I'd come back to.

The last time I was here was for Mom's funeral. Even though it was only a few years ago, it simultaneously feels like an eternity and only yesterday.

While burying her felt like losing a piece of me, the thought of putting dad in the cold ground Dad feels more like a release of something I've been holding onto for so damn long that I won't even know what it's like to live without that weight.

Saying goodbye to him won't be hard, but still, I would've liked to know why he wanted to see me—what was so damn important that he asked to see me after all these years. But if it doesn't happen, if he never wakes up long enough to say whatever it is he needs to say, I won't hang on to any regret where he's concerned.

The only reason I came was so he could get whatever he needed to say off his chest before he died. The fact that I would get to speak my piece where he's concerned was just an added bonus—one I'm sure I can live without if need be.

Leave it to Dad to get me to fly home to see him then never even talk to me.

The old bastard.

I glance back at the bed and freeze. Amber eyes, the same color as mine, stare back.

"You came." His words are soft and barely audible, but they roll over me like an ice-cold wind in a whipping blizzard.

Goosebumps pebble on my skin, and my throat tightens. I approach slowly, with as much reluctance as the years have left weighing on my shoulders, and stand behind the chair I just vacated. "You wanted to see me."

He nods slightly and motions toward a glass of water sitting on the table next to his bed. I grab it and hold the straw to his lips. He takes a sip, then closes his eyes again.

Shit.

For a second, I almost thought this was it. I set the Cup back on the table, and his eyes flutter open to meet my gaze.

"Why did you want to see me?"

He sucks in a shallow breath. "To apologize."

I snort and shake my head. "For what?"

The list of his sins and things he should be apologizing for is so long, there isn't enough paper or ink in the world to write it all down.

"For what I did to your mother. For what I did to you and Jameson and Rachel."

Something tightens around my chest, and I wrap my

hands around the back of the chair and squeeze to try to relieve some of the tension building in my body. "A little late for that, don't you think?"

He nods and lets out a rattling cough. "I wanted to say that for a long time, but I knew you wouldn't talk to me."

Probably right.

If he had called, I wouldn't have answered, or I would have hung up.

"And your brother isn't coming."

"I know."

"Where's your sister?"

"She went back to your house to sleep for a few hours, but she'll be back. She hasn't left you."

"I know." He offers a sad smile. "She has your mother's heart."

I squeeze my eyes shut and grit my teeth. "She loved you, even though you treated her like fucking garbage."

"I was stupid, Sebastian. I was arrogant and angry." He coughs and then regains his breath. "I let hockey be my life instead of all of you. And I brought my anger from the games into our home. I only wish I could've seen it then the way I do now."

His revelation isn't anything I haven't known for almost three decades. It isn't anything Mom didn't know before she died. It was how we lived every damn day he was under the same roof. The only relief we got was during the season when he was with the team and not in Michigan with us.

Don't tear his head off.

As much as I would love to rip him apart for what he did to all of us, Rachel was right—it doesn't do any good to further destroy a man who is left dying almost alone because of how he lived his life and treated those he should have loved.

I shake my head. "Yeah. Me, too."

"Don't make the same mistake I did, Bash."

"What's that?"

"Letting the game be my happiness instead of the people in my life."

Greer's face pops to the forefront of my mind.

God, I miss her.

The woman is so far under my skin, she's part of me now. But I can't give up my contract, my career now. Not when I have everything I worked so damn hard for. All those five a.m. practices. All those hours on the ice honing my skills and ensuring I would be the best of the best. I can't throw that all away. Even for her.

"I wish it were that easy, Dad."

"Bash..."—he swallows thickly again—"it is." His eyes drift closed before I can say anything else, and his body relaxes.

The machines will keep him alive, but who knows how much longer.

I walk around and drop into the chair. My eyes sting, but I refuse to shed tears for this man. I don't know whether he'll hear these words or not, but I need to say them before he dies.

I'll never forget what he did, how he lived his life, and what he did to us, but at least he was able to recognize the ways he failed even if it was far too little and came far too late.

The words burn on my tongue, but I force them out, tearing my heart apart. "I forgive you, Dad."

———

GREER

My phone beeps with an incoming message from Dad.

Turn on Sports Network right now.

What the hell?

I grab the remote and flip the channel over to Sports Network. The *Sports Time* anchors chatter on, mid-conversation about something. Animated and wide-eyed, whatever it is has left them in a tizzy.

"This is truly shocking."

"There's obviously more to the story here, but whether we'll ever get it or not, is another question."

"I know. It just doesn't make any sense. He's at the height of his career, sitting on a twenty-plus million-dollar contract, and his team just went to the playoffs, yet he's retiring? Insanity."

What the hell are they talking about?

I turn up the volume and lean toward the television, as if getting closer to the damns screen will somehow give me the answer to what could be so important that Dad called me to watch.

"Bash Fury must've lost his mind."

"Or there's some sort of injury or medical situation we're unaware of that means he can't continue to play."

"Hopefully, we'll hear more from the Scorpion camp soon on this matter."

Oh, my God. Bash is retiring?

That can't be right. It can't be.

There's absolutely no *way* Bash is going to give up that contract and playing the game he loves so much. Unless... the anchor is right. Maybe he's hurt. Maybe he's sick.

Acid crawls up my throat, and I gulp it back as every conceivable horrible possibility runs through my head.

What could cause him to retire?

A severe enough head injury could, and he's definitely had a few concussions over his career, but we follow strict protocol now to prevent the kind of permanent damage the old players were exposed to. But...he did have his bell rung in the final game.

The staff checked him out, though, and he was fine. Nothing to worry about. He kept playing and seemed totally okay. Still, symptoms of a brain injury can appear days, weeks, or even months later, so it's possible something major happened that's only presenting itself now.

Why hasn't Bob called me about this?

If Bash retired, for any reason, it means he spoke with the GM and filed paperwork with the league office. Even if Bob is pissed at me, he should have told me about this before I saw something on the damn television.

I have to call Bash.

It doesn't matter that it's been weeks, or that we ended things on hurtful and shitty terms. I need to know he's okay. I need to know why he would do something so stupid.

If he answers.

I grab my phone and call him with a shaky hand. Each ring ratchets my heart rate up higher and tightens the vise around my chest.

"You've reached Bash. You know what to do."

Shit.

BEEP!

I swallow through the lump in my throat. "Bash. It's me. I just saw you're retiring. What's going on? Are you all right? Just let me know you're okay." The words *"I miss you"* sit on the tip of my tongue, but I bite them back and end the call.

Instead, I send the same message in a text...and wait.

I toss my phone onto the end table and meander over to

the kitchen. The pizza that was my dinner still sits half-eaten on the counter. I grab a piece and bite into it.

Eww.

I forgot I hate cold pizza.

My mind is a jumbled mess right now.

I drop it back into the box and make my way back to the couch. My phone rings, and I practically dive for it and glance at the screen.

Bash!

Even after the way we ended things, even after the time that's passed and the losses and the words we said to each other, my body still tingles and heats seeing his name. The memories of every moment we spent together—the good and the bad, the arguing and the making up, the wild and reckless—come racing back.

"Bash?"

"No, this is his sister Rachel."

What?

Why the hell would his sister be calling...unless he is sick...

My entire body trembles. "Is...Bash okay?"

"He left his phone here by accident. I saw that you called and then sent a text message, and I didn't want you to worry, so I thought I would call you back right away."

Fear wraps around my spine and squeezes tightly. "Is Bash *okay*?

Rachel sighs. "I know we don't know each other, Greer, but Bash has said enough that I know something happened between you two. I know things are...complicated. He doesn't care about a lot of people..."

Why isn't she just answering my damn question?

"Rachel, you're freaking me out. Is he all right?"

"Physically, he's okay, but he needs you right now."

Bash has never needed anyone but himself. He made that perfectly clear when we ended things. For his sister to be telling me the opposite has blood rushing in my ears, drowning out the television and every other sound in the house.

"What's going on?"

"Our father's in the hospital. He's dying. It's going to be a matter of days, maybe even only hours..."

Mike is dying?

"Oh, my God. I'm so sorry." Given how difficult things are in their family dynamics, this has to be eating away at Bash from a hundred different angles.

"He needs you here. Can you come?"

"Of course."

The words are out before I can even consider the potential ramifications of what I'm agreeing to.

I have no idea where Bash and I stand. No idea if he even wants me there. All I have is the statement from his sister, who I don't even know. Yet, none of that matters. There's no way I'm *not* going.

If there's even the slightest chance Bash needs me, I'll be there for him, even if I don't think he would do the same for me.

"Text me all the details. I'll find the next flight out."

"Thank you, Greer. I know he'll really appreciate it even if he can't show it because he's a total hardass. I'll see you soon."

I hang up and stare at my phone.

Bash's father is dying.

It *could* explain the timing of his retirement announcement...if we were still in the playoffs and he needed to go take care of family matters.

But even then, why *retire?*

He could have told Bob what was happening and that he needed to leave. Surely, Bob would have understood, and even though it would have been a hit to the team, he wouldn't have forced Bash to choose between his family and his contract.

So why is he retiring?

None of it makes any sense. But the unknowns don't matter. He can explain everything to me when I get there.

A text comes through with the information from Rachel about what hospital Mike is in and the hotel where Bash is staying, and I jump on my computer and find a flight leaving in three hours.

It's just enough time to throw together a suitcase and get to the airport.

This is crazy.

I must be insane traveling across the country for a man who couldn't put me first. This is what stupid, needy women do. And I am neither of those. Yet, I'm tossing random clothes into my suitcase and racing around the house in a whirlwind.

The flowers that were delivered almost a week ago now catch my eye as I drag my bag past the kitchen. My hand hovers over the note from Bash.

He did say he missed me...but is that enough?

Maybe not to make a relationship. Maybe not to solve all the problems between us. But it's enough to tell me I'm doing the right thing by going to him now.

I pull open the door and turn to lock it behind me.

You're doing the right thing, Greer.

My heart believes it, but it may take some convincing of my mind. It's a good thing I have a four-hour flight. God knows I'll spend it replaying every moment we've spent together for the thousandth time and questioning every-thing we've ever said to each other.

I turn toward the driveway and almost run smack into a tall, wide body standing behind me on the porch.

27

GREER

"**O**h!" I jerk back and glance up into the face of the man in front of me. It takes a second before I recognize our equipment manager. After only ever seeing him in the work context, having him standing on my porch throws me momentarily. "Steve? What are you doing here?"

He flashes a smile and glances down at my suitcase with wide brown eyes. "I hope I didn't catch you at a bad time."

A bad time? What in the hell is he doing here?

I point toward my car in the driveway. "I'm just on my way out. Heading to the airport."

His eyes narrow on me, and he fists his hands at his sides. "Where are you going?"

That's not really any of your business.

And I'm not about to tell him about Bash.

Bob said he put a lid on any potential scandal or fallout from our relationship, and opening my mouth now would only worsen the situation.

"What can I do for you, Steve?" I scan the street behind him. "And how do you know where I live?"

As the equipment manager, he shouldn't have access to anything that has my personal information on it. The only ones in the organization who would are people in HR and Bob.

Unease creeps over my skin.

The smile that seemed so friendly from him only moments ago seems somewhat forced now. "I needed to see you. I thought maybe after you got the flowers, I would hear from you."

"The flowers?"

What the hell is he...

Oh, my God.

The flowers. The cupcake. The keychain.

S.

I assumed they were all from Bash...*Sebastian,* but thinking back, he never actually said anything about sending them. He never acknowledged them or confirmed I received them. He never asked if I liked them or if the cupcake was delicious. He didn't reference the single flower and the night we spent together before it appeared on my desk.

We never discussed the gifts.

Because he didn't send them.

"*You* sent me all those things?"

Steve's lips curl into a sneer. "Of course, I fucking sent them! Who the hell else did you think would send them to you? That douchebag Bash?"

I flinch and take a half a step back. "You knew about us?"

He growls, and anger flashes in his darkening eyes. His size was never intimidating before because there was no reason to be afraid of the friendly guy who made sure we all had everything we needed and took such good care of the guys. But now, his barrel chest and large stature create a roadblock between me and my car.

"Are you kidding?" He scoffs. "It was so obvious. When I walked in on you two in your office, there wasn't any question what was going on, especially after the way I saw him touch you at the party."

Shit.

"Are you the one who told Bob?"

"Of course, I told Bob." He spits the words at me and clenches his fists until his knuckles whiten. "He wasn't right for you. It wasn't right for you to be involved with a player."

He isn't wrong but Jesus, this guy's a total psycho.

My keys bite into my palm, and I position them between my fingers, just like Dad always told me to. A make-shift weapon in case I need one. "I'm sorry, Steve, but I have to go."

Get far away from you...fast.

I shoulder past him and walk as fast as my legs will carry me to my car, dragging my bag behind me on the concrete walkway. His footsteps echo behind, and I glance back as I round the hood to the driver's side.

He stands a few feet from the car, watching me with intense, almost black eyes.

How could I never have noticed the way he looks at me?

"I'm sorry I have to go, Steve. We can talk more about this when I get back."

After I inform Bob about this creepy behavior and file for a restraining order.

He grunts a response and clenches his jaw. His hands bunch and flex at his sides.

I drop my bag in the back seat and climb into the driver's side, keeping one eye on Steve. Engaging the locks lets me breathe a sigh of relief, and he stalks away to his car at the curb. I throw the car into reverse and back out of the driveway, while Steve sits in his across the street watching me.

He's a problem I just don't have time to deal with.

I need to get to Bash.

Given how complicated his relationship with his father is, he shouldn't be making decisions about his career when the man is on his death bed. I need to talk some sense into him and get him to realize what a mistake he's making.

But first, I just need to be there for him. No matter what happened between us or how we ended things, he needs to know I'm there. As a friend, of course. Because I care about him in a *friendly* way.

Not because I love him.

He can never know that. It would only hurt both of us. To say it and have him not say it back would break me. I'm going as a friend, nothing more. That's all I can ever be.

I press the Bluetooth button on my steering wheel as I wait at a stoplight. "Call Jill."

She picks up three rings later. "Hey, Greer, what's happening?"

"Bash's sister just called me."

"Oh...that's...odd. What's going on?"

Jill doesn't exactly follow sports, except for what I'm up to, so there's no way she saw the news about Bash.

"Bash is retiring."

"What?" A door slams in the background of the call. "Why the hell would he be retiring? That doesn't make sense."

No, it doesn't.

It's obvious he's not thinking clearly. Bash is a lot of things, but stupid isn't one of them. And retiring now is just *stupid*.

"His dad is dying. That may have something to do with it."

"Oh. Shit."

The light turns green, and I continue toward the airport. "Yeah. His sister asked me to come."

"Wait, isn't Bash from Michigan?"

"Yeah. Michigan. I'm on my way to the airport right now. I need you to watch my place. I'm not sure how long I'll be gone. I'll try to keep you updated when I know more."

"Okay. Does this mean you two are..."

I shake my head as I turn onto the freeway. "No. I'm just going as a friend."

Jill releases a heavy sigh. "Do you think that's a good idea, Greer? Emotionally?"

"I mean..." I shake my head. "No, but his sister says he needs me there."

"Did *he* ask for you?"

Leave it to Jill to get to the nitty-gritty. The question I should probably be asking myself but haven't. Mostly because I know what the answer would be and it would keep me from going when he needs me.

"I don't know, but it doesn't matter. If I get there and he doesn't want me around, I can always come back."

Jill's silence speaks volumes. The farther I drive down the freeway, the more I feel her judgment through the line. I know she means well, but she can't understand the situation. She doesn't know Bash. She doesn't know the relationship issues he has with his father. She doesn't know what it would mean to him to have someone there for him.

"Jill, I know what you're going to say..."

"I feel like this is setting yourself up for more heartache."

"I know what I'm doing. I'm just going to—"

Boom.

Something slams into me hard from behind and to the left. I grip the wheel to try to stop the car from going to the right, but it's useless. The car careens to the side and slams into the guardrail.

The world flips.

Metal crunches.

Glass shatters.

And then...darkness.

———

BASH

I stand and reach toward the ceiling, stretching my lower back to ease some of the growing tightness there. These places were not meant for comfort, and the combination of sleeping on hotel room beds and in hospital chairs for so damn long has my body protesting.

A nurse wanders into the open door and offers me a kind smile. "Any change?"

I shake my head and glance at the bed. "No."

She nods and goes about checking all the machines and jotting something in the file. She turns before she leaves me again. "It will just take time."

"I know."

But waiting sucks.

I'm so fucking sick of waiting. Waiting to make another mistake on the ice. Waiting to know if I'm going to be traded again. Waiting for that tension between Greer and me to finally come to a head. Waiting for her to fully give in to me. Waiting for the next time I could see her and have her under me. Waiting for Dad to die...

And now—I glance down at Greer's blond hair splayed out across the pillowcase and the bruises and cuts covering her pale skin—*waiting for her to wake up.*

I sigh and drop into the chair I've spent the last several

days in. Her small hand rests across her stomach, and I reach out and drag it to me, bringing it to my lips. The warmth of her skin should be a good sign, but her utter stillness makes it feel like I'm staring at merely a shell of the woman who has come to mean so much to me.

"You need to wake up, Coach." I feather my lips across her fingertips. "We have so much to talk about."

As the hours and hours have passed, I've tried my best not to worry. Not to panic like I did when I got the phone call from Jill to tell me Greer was in the hospital. But it was impossible not to then, when I was thousands of miles away and couldn't get to her right away. And it's getting more difficult not to now.

The more time that ticks by, the longer she's out, the more dangerous it is for her. And now that they've stopped the medication that's kept her unconscious the last few days, she should be waking up.

Should be...but she hasn't yet.

I squeeze her hand and drop my forehead against her chest. The steady rise and fall of her even breathing and thudding of her heart offers me little comfort. I'm not sure anything could except her opening her eyes and talking to me.

After all this bullshit, I can't lose her this way. I'm not sure I would survive it.

Losing has been a huge part of my life lately. I've lost more in the last six months than I did my entire life before that. And while I've learned some things need to be let go, Greer isn't one of those.

Not by a fucking longshot.

She's the thing you hold on to, what you cling to like a lifeline in a tempest, and she became mine without me even realizing it. Despite all my bravado, all the strength I portray on the ice and in life, the thought of losing her makes me feel completely adrift, like there isn't anything left for me in the world if she's gone.

You can't leave me...

Her hand twitches in mine.

I jerk my head up. "Greer? Can you hear me?" Her lids flutter open slowly, and she blinks, struggling to focus on what's in front of her from her reclined position. I jump to my feet and lean over her, squeezing her hand again. "Greer?"

Hazy green eyes finally meet mine, and her lips twitch into the tiniest smile. "Bash?"

"I'm here." I grip her hand even tighter—maybe tighter than I should, given her condition. "I'm not going anywhere."

She returns my squeeze, and that tiny gesture sends hope flooding through my veins for the first time in what feels like months. If she told me to take a fucking hike, she'd be well within her rights considering what I've done to her, but she seems happy to see me.

I brush hair back from her face, trying to avoid touching the various cuts and bruises. "Do you remember what happened?"

She groans and tries to sit, but I place a gentle hand against her chest.

"Don't try to sit up." I grab the call button and press it as I keep her prone. "Do you remember the accident?"

Her marred brow furrows, pulling at the stitched cut above her left eye. "Accident?" Her eyes flick above my shoulder, like she's searching her memories, and suddenly widen. "I was on my way to the airport..."

I nod. "Yeah, you were. Do you remember where you were going?"

The guilt that she had been on her way to see me claws

at my chest, just like it has ever since I learned of that little fact.

Her gaze cuts over to meet mine. "To come to you."

I grin at her. "My sister told me. But...babe, that was four days ago."

"Four days?"

I nod and settle back into the chair next to the bed. So many emotions swirl through me, and my shaking legs don't seem to want to support me anymore. The sheer adrenaline that's been keeping me running has finally dissipated, leaving behind sheer exhaustion.

How do I explain everything that's happened?

"Oh, you're awake!" The nurse approaches the bed and smiles at Greer. "I'll alert the doctor and get her in here to talk to you." She presses something on the back of the bed, and it raises Greer into a slight sitting position. "How are you feeling?"

Greer offers a tiny smile. "Okay, I guess."

"Do you remember what happened?"

Confusion crosses Greer's face, and her brow furrows. "I...I'm not sure..."

The nurse pats her shoulder. "It will come back with time. I'll go grab the doctor."

Greer's questioning eyes meet mine. "What happened?"

I don't want to freak her out. She's already been through so much. But she needs to know everything—sooner rather than later.

"You were pushed off the road. Your car flipped. You hit your head and had some swelling in your brain. They wanted to keep you sedated until the swelling went down."

"Oh, my God." She stares at the sheet covering her like she's trying to dig up the memories she lost. "Your dad?"

I brush off the hair that's fallen forward onto her forehead and lean in to kiss her there gently. "He died two days ago."

"Oh, Bash, I'm so sorry...and you weren't there?"

"No." I shake my head and pull her hand into mine. "I was exactly where I should be—with you. He would've understood."

Her hand tightens around mine, and her eyes widen. "Bash...it was Steve."

"I know, Coach."

Her eyebrows shoot up. "You do?"

That motherfucker...

I tamp down my anger so I don't scare her. "He pushed you off the road. They caught his car and license plate on the traffic camera and arrested him pretty quickly. Once he was in custody, he spilled. Apparently...he was sending you gifts?"

She nods gently and winces at the motion. "I thought it was you."

I chuckle and shake my head. "Shit, Coach, you gave me way too much credit. Now I kind of feel like a dick for not sending you anything romantic."

Greer laughs and fights another wince. She smiles at me, and despite cuts and bruises covering her body, she's the most beautiful fucking thing I've ever seen. "No, Bash. That doesn't make you a dick. Maybe not A-plus boyfriend material but not a dick. And as much as I hate to admit it, dick or not, it's just who you are." She tightens her grip on my hand. "You showed me you cared about me in different ways. More 'Bash' ways, and for me, that's all I need."

28

GREER

I t's not an *I love you,* but it might as well have been to a guy like Bash. I was too terrified to actually say *those* words to him right now even if I feel it with every fiber of my being after waking up and seeing him sitting vigil beside me.

I had no illusions of what I was getting into when I hooked up with him—it was never intended to be anything more than a release from the tension between us.

But something happened along the way.

Something strange.

Something scary as hell.

Something totally unexpected—to everyone except Jill who *warned* me it would happen.

I realized he's not a total douchebag.

Far from it.

He's a hard, complicated, fucked-up man who uses his attitude as a shield against anything *real* infiltrating it. No real friendships. No real joy. No real pain. No real relationships. No real *love.*

But the fact that's he's here—that he came *here* to be with me when his father's death was imminent, speaks volumes. Only so does his silence right now...and the fact that he can't look me in the eye.

His gaze drops away from me and centers on our entwined hands. He brushes his thumb back and forth slowly across my palm. The move is both soothing and infuriating because he's doing it instead of talking to me.

Waiting for him to say something is almost as agonizing as the headache I have right now. At least that will go away, though. If Bash rejects me, rejects *this*, after that almost confession of love, I'm not sure how I'm ever supposed to get over that.

Is it even possible?

Now I understand why he was so reluctant to let anyone into his life. Rejection is agony. A kind of pain I never want to feel again. What I felt when he walked out of my house that night after saying we were doomed. Yet, I just threw my heart at him again, knowing what he said only a few short weeks ago might still be true. Knowing he's likely to throw it away again.

Maybe he's not ready for any of this.

Maybe being here for me now is his final goodbye to whatever we had.

Seconds drag into minutes. Minutes to what feels like hours before he finally looks back up at me, his warm bourbon eyes overflowing with emotion and unshed tears. "I know, Coach."

It's not exactly a declaration of love, more an acknowledgement that he understands how *I* feel about him. But I'm not sure what to expect. He just lost his father, and—

"Ms. Waterson, it's nice to see you awake." A woman enters the room with a tablet in her hand, scrolling through something on the screen as she approaches the bed with a smile. "I'm Dr. Burton. How are you feeling?"

I would be a lot better if I could finish this conversation with Bash without being interrupted.

"I'm okay, I think." I take mental stock of my body, shifting slightly to test my limbs which ache in protest but don't seem *too* bad. "My head hurts, and I feel exhausted."

"That's all to be expected after an injury like this."

Bash's hand tightens around mine. "But she'll be okay, right?"

Dr. Burton nods and smiles at him. "She should be fine. The swelling has gone down, and now that she's awake, we can do some final assessments. Do you remember the accident?"

"Yes." I repeat what I just told Bash about my memory of the day of the accident and rub my temple with my free hand. "It's still a little fuzzy, like I'm seeing everything through frosted glass, and I'm not quite sure it's all real."

"That may take some time to clear up, and some people never fully regain all memories. Others do. The brain is weird that way, but everything looks normal in your most recent scans. We'll keep you here another day or two and then send you home as long as nothing concerning crops up."

Bash releases my hand and reaches across the bed to shake the doctor's. "Thanks, Doc."

She smiles at him, and a strange pang of something that feels an awful lot like jealousy hits my chest watching the way her eyes rake over him.

Bash is always going to be the guy who attracts attention from women, and even though Dr. Burton is clearly *not* flirting with him, I can't help the green monster from rearing its ugly head seeing the way she assesses him.

She's probably just a hockey fan.

We both watch her walk out of the room, and Bash retakes his seat in an uncomfortable-looking chair next to me. He must be hurting after spending so much time on that thing...

Shit.

His retirement.

In the confusion of waking, I totally forgot the fact that he announced it before the accident...or that I had every intention of finding out *why* and making sure he corrected what is obviously a huge mistake.

The death of his father probably played a role in his decision. But there may still be something else I'm missing here, some piece of information that will make it all seem like a logical decision instead of some stupid thing he did in the heat of the moment.

"Bash...are *you* okay?"

He presses a kiss to the back of my hand and winks at me. "I am now."

"No." I shake my head, and pain immediately shoots through it. It's probably going to take some time before that feels better. "I mean, I heard you retired. I thought maybe you were injured or something?"

His eyes widen, and then he gives me an awkward half-smile and shakes his head. Slowly, his thumb begins to brush rhythmically over my hand. "I've had days to think about this. Countless hours to consider the words I would use to try to express everything I'm feeling and explain everything that's happened, but none of it ever seems sufficient. It all just sounds like bullshit."

What is he talking about?

Acid churns in my stomach and threatens to make its way up my throat. He's starting to freak me the fuck out here.

Did that hit he took in the final game do more serious damage than we thought?

"I don't understand what you're saying, Bash. But you're scaring me."

He drops my hand and scrubs his palm over his stubble-covered jaw. "Christ, I'm fucking this up." He stands, then sits on the edge of my bed and pulls my hands into his lap. "I'm okay. I'm not hurt...physically." He swallows thickly, his Adam's apple bobbing with the slow motion. "I talked to my dad before he died, and he said something that stuck with me. He said not to let hockey be my life and ignore what's truly important. That and something Caleb said about not having the chance to say how I really feel kind of resonated with me." A heavy sigh slips from his lips, and he leans forward and rests his forehead against mine. "I don't need the fucking money. I have plenty of that. Enough to last me ten lifetimes already. And I don't need the fame."

I grin and chuckle at the audacity of that statement.

Bash Fury feeds off the roar of the crowd and the adoration of his fans. He loves the violence and the speed of the game. Bash Fury *is* hockey.

"I know you think my fragile ego can't live without it, Coach, but I can. And I thought about it. I truly *thought* about what playing means to me, but in the end, my career doesn't mean as much as you do, and your career is important to a lot more people than just you. You shouldn't have to give it up."

My breath catches in my chest, and I struggle to process his words. He can't be saying what I *think* he's saying.

"Wha...what?" I drag my head back to look into his eyes. "Are you saying you retired for *me*?"

BASH

Her words are said with such disbelief that a pang of guilt hits me and twists the knife in my heart a few more times.

Am I really so selfish that it's that hard to believe I would be willing to do this for her?

Is it so hard to see how I really feel?

Apparently, because Greer stares back at me, looking more shocked than she did the first time I skated onto her ice late for practice and full of arrogance.

"Wow." I run a hand through my hair. "I really did a number on you, didn't I? I'm a much bigger asshole than I ever thought I was."

Her eyes widen slightly, and she shakes her head. "No. Well..."—the corner of her mouth tilts up into a little half-smile—"sometimes. But that's all just what makes you...you. You're Bash Fury, the bad boy of hockey."

"I was."

"Don't give it up, Bash." She sucks in a shaky breath, and tears wet her eyes, the absolute *last* thing I want to see right now after what she's been through. "You're too good. You're at the height of your career. It's not worth it."

"No." I reach out with my free hand and force her chin up until she looks me in the eye. "Don't say it's not worth it. That *you're* not worth it. My dad lived his entire life married to my mother but with the game as his mistress. I'm not going to do that. And I'm not going to wait until I'm retired at forty to find somebody to spend my life with. Because I'd be settling."

I capture her cheek in my palm and brush away a stray tear. This damn frustrating woman is going to be the death of me.

I'm sitting here try to pour my heart out to her, and it's going completely over her head.

She just doesn't get it.

"It would be settling, Greer, because I would be comparing every woman I was with for the rest of my life to you. And none could possibly measure up."

Her bottom lip quivers, and she shakes her head. "You don't mean that."

"Yes." I get in her face and press a kiss to her lips, a little harder and harsher than I probably should, considering where she is and what just happened to her, but I need her to understand. I need her to shut the fuck up long enough for me to finish. "I do mean it. You challenge me, Greer—on the ice, in the bedroom, in life. You don't make anything easy, and I fucking love that about you."

I'm acutely aware of the fact that I just said a very important four-letter word. But it isn't enough. Not nearly enough after everything.

"I just fucking love *you*, Greer. Even when you're fuming mad at me. Even when we're fighting for dominance and throwing each other to the damn wolves, I love you. And I love hockey, too, just not enough to give you up for it. So, I quit. I'll find something else to occupy my time, as long as I get to spend it with you."

Tears trickle down her cheeks. "You're serious."

I nod. "Dead serious. One of us was going to have to give it up. It would never have worked any other way. And you worked too fucking hard to get where you are for me to be selfish and ask you to quit. I'm doing this for us, Greer, so that we can have a future."

She shakes her head and swipes at the tears. "B-but...I don't want you to resent me when you start missing it because you can't play anymore. When I'm the reason you have to watch all your friends earn a cup while you sit on the damn couch."

"Jesus, Greer." I shake my head. "I could never resent

you. You're the best fucking thing that ever happened to me. The only good thing hockey ever did for me."

She grins at me. "What about the money?"

I bark out a laugh and shrug. "Yeah, well, the money *is* nice. I can't lie about that, but money isn't everything."

"No. I guess it's not." She sighs and stares at me for a moment. "You're really sure about this."

"Well, I *was*...until you started trying to fight me so hard on it." It never even crossed my mind I might not being doing what she wanted, that this could backfire on me so badly. "Isn't this what you want?"

When I signed my retirement papers, everything told me I was doing the right thing, but I expected Greer to be a little more excited about this instead of trying to convince me that I'm doing something stupid.

She nods. "Of course, it's what I want. Anything that would make it possible for us to be together is what I want. You know I love you, Bash. Probably more than I should. Probably more than is healthy. And what you did for me... for us...only makes me love you more."

The burn of unshed tears stings my eyes.

Fuck. I hate crying.

I squeeze my eyes shut for a moment and try to regain some semblance of control over my emotions. Leave it to Greer to completely unravel me with just a few words. When I open them again, she's watching me expectantly. "What?"

She shakes her head and laughs, then she winces and laughs again. "God, that hurts."

"Then stop laughing and shaking your head."

"I can't." She manages the words through her laughter.

"What's so funny?"

"You." She holds up her hands and waves them. "*This.*

This has to be the least romantic place to have this conversation."

I grin at her. "I can think of less romantic places."

She snorts. "I'm sure you can."

I lean in and kiss her. Slow and sweet this time, the way she deserves to be kissed. I've done everything with her so damn hard and fast, and that was a huge mistake. A self-preservation tactic I hadn't even realized I was relying on until it was almost too late. "I love you, Greer Waterson."

"I love you, Sebastian Fury."

I jerk back and narrow my eyes at her.

Her brow furrows, and she brushes her fingers along my arm. "What?"

I grin at her. "You know that's the first time you ever called me by my real name."

Her eyebrows shoot up, and she shakes her head. "No way."

"Yes." I nod and lean in, stopping a hairsbreadth from her lips. "I kinda like it. You should do it more often."

Bash Fury was a different man. He was self-centered. He was arrogant. He was brash, and he annihilated anything in his path. Bash Fury would've annihilated a problem like Greer, too. He would have made sure she was the one who left the Scorpions, so he could stay on the team.

But Sebastian Fury...he's something and someone else entirely. He's the kind of guy who sacrifices what he loves to do to be with who he loves. And he finally gets what he deserves, even though it meant losing a lot along the way and causing and suffering unimaginable pain.

It's an ending he never saw coming, but it is pucking perfect.

EPILOGUE

BASH

The tension has my body wound so tightly, I might explode at any moment. Every pass of the puck, every shot, every body-check, and every penalty call might as well be happening to me. I can feel every single thing as if I were the one out on the ice, as if it were *my* fate being decided.

Who would've thought watching from the stands could be this stressful?

I glance down at the bench. Greer's laser focus never wavers from the ice or her team—the one she almost lost.

The Scorpions finally did it. They reached the Stanley Cup finals. In only three years, she's managed to achieve something some teams only do once in their entire history.

And game seven is on our home ice, in front of our home crowd, with everyone who has supported the Scorpions here to see this moment.

It's her chance to snatch the thing that eluded me during my career—the Cup.

Caleb elbows me in the stomach.

I glower at him next to me. "What was that for?"

He chuckles and nods toward the rink where the clean-up crew enters to clean off the ice during a television break. "You need to relax, dude. You look like you're about ready to have a coronary."

With only three minutes left and down by one, I might.

This game has been nothing short of World War III. The Scorpions and the Boston Bulldogs are going at it as if their lives depend on it. And I guess, in a way, they do.

For some of the older players on both teams, this is probably their last opportunity to get the Cup. And for the young guys, this is something they've dreamed of their entire lives and probably never thought they could accomplish at this age.

I remember what that was like. The wonder. The excitement. The racing of my heart when I stepped out onto the ice. It still thunders in my chest now, but for a different reason.

A far less selfish one I wouldn't have known I was capable of a few years ago.

I want this so much for Greer.

That woman has busted her ass and worked so damn hard to get here. She's coached an incredible team that came together and pushed through a rough season to end up *here.*

It's her time to win.

A tug at the left leg of my pants drags my attention downward. "Daddy! I want to see Mommy!"

I scoop up Annabelle into my arms and point to the bench just to our left. "See Mommy right there? She's working. The game will be over in a few minutes."

Bringing a toddler to a game is always an experience, but we didn't want her to miss this huge moment for Greer. She may not fully understand what's happening, but we always want her as involved as she can be. It's the only way to ensure Greer doesn't end up feeling like an absentee parent and Anna understands why Mommy has to be gone so much.

So far, it's worked out, with us traveling with the team as much as we can and coming to games even if she ends up sleeping in my arms for most of them.

"Come to Uncle Caleb." He pulls her from my arms and nods toward the game. "Now, you can pay attention."

I clap him on the shoulder. "You're a good friend."

And he's just in time.

Lebedev faces off against Fredericks, one of the Bulldogs' forwards, and the ref drops the puck. Shoulders clash, bodies slam, and the puck flies straight out to Mac, who's waiting right in the slot. He shoots, and it soars over the left shoulder of the Bulldogs' goalie and into the net.

"Yes!"

The foghorn blows through the arena, and the crowd erupts. Even Anna cheers in Caleb's arms and high-fives me. Watching her get so excited at the games makes every sacrifice worth it.

All the late nights. The crying missing Mommy when she can't be with us. Giving up this game I love so damn much.

On the other side of Caleb, Jill, Tara, and Bradley high-five while she juggles Ivy in her arms. Having Jill and my best friend and his family with me to see this moment is more than I could ever have hoped for. If it weren't for him, I wouldn't even be here with Greer. I'd probably be playing in some other city and being a fucking miserable asshole.

But the fight isn't over yet.

All we've done is tie the game, and there's still plenty of time to fuck this up.

My hands itch to be holding a stick and be out on the ice with them. I miss it more than I'll ever admit to Greer or anyone else. There are days when I'm out coaching the youth league team or just messing around on the rink and I have flashes of what could have been.

But what I told her that day was true. None of it would have meant anything. My *life* wouldn't have meant anything if it weren't with her. I could have won a dozen Stanley Cups and never been fulfilled. Seeing her succeed is greater than any success I could have had on my own.

I would have played maybe another ten years. Done untold damage to my body...and been lonely as fuck. I know I made the right decision to walk away from this game, even if every fiber of my being craves to be out on the ice.

"Let's go, Scorpions! Let's go." The chant starts through the crowd until all 40,000 people are screaming in unison.

The entire arena vibrates with anticipation and energy.

Two and a half minutes—a fucking lifetime in hockey.

I glance down at Greer pacing behind the bench. She leans down and whispers something to Hayes. He nods and jumps onto the ice to replace Kasinski.

It's a good call. He's much better in the high-pressure, clinch situations. She needs her best shooters out there together. Where I would be if I were still playing.

"Daddy! Daddy!"

But if I were still playing, I wouldn't have *her*. I reach over and take Anna from Caleb and rest her on my hip as I watch the puck drop again.

This time, the Bulldogs end up with it. My chest tightens as I watch them take it through the neutral zone and into our territory. Their sticks have been quick this entire series, and tonight is no exception.

Only our own stellar defense and an incredible game from Pierre has kept them from having even more goals. This will be one of those games they talk about for years to come.

Mac intercepts the puck and makes a break toward the Bulldog goal.

"Go! Go! Go!" My chant echoes those of the surrounding fans, and Annabelle joins right in even though she has no idea what's on the line, can't possibly fathom what this goal will mean.

He's got him beat.

I played long enough with Mac to know his moves, to see what he sees even from up here in the stands.

He's got this!

I hold my breath, and just as Mac looks left to Hayes to draw their goalie that direction, Knight cross-checks him, knocking him to the ice.

What a fucking idiot.

Now we're going be on the power play for the final two minutes. They would've been better off letting us score than to give us that penalty.

Mac climbs from the ice, unshaken, and grabs his stick.

The ref skates to center ice. "Number 17—two minutes for cross-checking."

Come on, guys.

This is our chance. This is *Greer's* chance.

Don't fucking blow it.

———

GREER

Don't fucking blow it, guys.

I don't need to say it to them. My guys know what this means. They know this is our chance.

We *don't* want to go into OT with the Bulldogs.

We've played like shit in OT this entire season and lost twice in OT to the Bulldogs already this *series*. Games we should have won. Games we had in hand until things went to shit at the last second. We need the *win* now, and we *are* going to get it.

It's times like this, I wish Bash was still playing, that he was experiencing this as a Scorpion, on the ice with his friends.

I know it kills him to watch from the stands, to not be able to step in when he sees something going to shit, when he sees us needing help. And I know he bites his tongue probably more than I could count on things he wants to tell me to do or instructions he wants to give to the guys. But as he's told me multiple times, they didn't hire him as a coach, they hired *me*. The fact that he echoes exactly what Dad once told me always makes me laugh.

Have faith in yourself, Greer.

You got them here.

It took a lot of sweet-talking and begging and reminders of our history to Bob to allow me to stay after what happened. But the conversation Bash had with him when he retired smoothed over things enough that Bob was willing to let me stay. He believed I was still what was best for this team despite my suspect decision-making where Bash was concerned.

Now...here we are. The place we could've been with Bash only a few years ago if things had gone a little differently.

I still wonder if the way the team fell apart that season had anything to do with what happened between Bash and me, if somehow our toxic relationship, though secret from them, somehow leached out into their psyches and made us shit the bed.

But I'll never know what might have been if he had never kissed me. If I had never gone to his hotel room that night. If I had said no or just ran away again.

I don't want to know, anyway. What might have been will never be now. And now is a pretty damn good place to be.

If we don't blow this...

I pace behind the bench as they drop the puck. Lebedev swats it over to Mac, who gets it to Hayes. He circles behind the net and turns toward the goal, but he doesn't have the shot. My nails bite into my palms as he juggles the puck, then he slings it, using the boards to ricochet it back behind the goal to Mac.

The Bulldogs are fast, but so are we.

All we need is one opening.

One split-second is all it will take.

Come on, guys.

I clench my fists at my sides to keep from biting my nails as I watch the puck float back and forth across the ice.

Clean passes, guys. Keep them tight. There you go...

Mac works his way into the slot with the puck and fires. It ricochets off the pole and back toward the neutral zone. Everyone chases after it, and the Bulldogs come away with it and break toward our goal.

Dammit.

I glance at the clock. One fifteen left. Plenty of time to get it closed out and done for either side.

We're *not* losing this game.

We didn't come all this way to lose in game seven.

Not these guys.

Not this team.

As good as we were our first season, we're better now. Stronger. We've lost some excess baggage and gained some new players. We truly are a team to be reckoned with, and I'm not about to lose what we worked so damn hard for. What I missed spending time with Bash for. What I missed putting Annabelle to sleep for all these years.

I stop at the end of the bench and watch intently. My

lungs seize in my chest as Anders fires for the Bulldogs. Pierre's wicked fast hands shoot up, and he catches the puck in an immaculate glove-save.

The arena releases its collective breath, and I do the same.

Shit.

They set up the face-off, and I glance over my shoulder and at the seats along the glass. Bash's eyes meet mine, and he smiles and nods. Even without words, I know he understands exactly how I feel right now.

He's been my rock. My everything from the moment I woke in that hospital until this very minute. And he will continue to be—just like he'll continue to be stubborn, and bossy, and infuriating at times.

I force myself to refocus as the puck drops again.

Thirteen seconds.

Mac takes the puck and manages to sling it over to Lebedev, who drives it straight to the goal. He pulls his stick back, and it's like the entire world slows. The arena's suddenly silent. Then *bam!* His slapshot connects with the puck, and it flies into the net as the final buzzer sounds.

Holy shit!

It takes a second to process it.

The arena erupts with cheers, mixing in the foghorn and screams from the bench in front of me. Arms circle around me from behind, and I'm pulled off the floor. I glance behind me at Marty.

He grins at me, squeezing me tightly. "We fucking did it!"

It takes a second for his words to sink in. He sets me back down, and I turn to find the entire team on the ice celebrating.

We did it.

"We won."

He grabs my shoulders and shakes me. "We just won the Stanley Cup!" Someone tugs on my shoulder, and Mac practically drags me out onto the ice. He yells something, but I can't even hear him over the roar of the crowd and rest of the team.

They surround me, and a stream of cheers and congratulations rumble together. Everything gets fuzzy, like I'm walking through a fog. Time passes but I have no concept of how long has passed.

My legs tremble. I sway, and a set of strong, familiar arms wrap around me from behind.

"Congratulations, Coach."

I practically melt at the sound of Bash's voice and turn in his arms. "We won."

He stares down at me with so much love and pride in his warm bourbon gaze. "*You* won."

Tears stream down my face, despite my best efforts to keep them at bay. "I never could have done it without you."

He leans in and presses a kiss to my lips as the celebration continues around us. "You *did* do it without me."

"No." I shake my head and capture his face between my hands. "Maybe I didn't have you on the ice, but you were always here for me. For whatever I needed."

A shoulder to cry on. Someone to vent to when a player did something stupid. A best friend who understands my job maybe better than I even do and who never questions how I do it even when I know he *wants* to.

He's been *everything* he thought he couldn't be but I always knew was somewhere deep inside him.

"I love you, Coach."

"I love you, Sebastian."

I fall into his arms, and his lips descend on mine again. It's the perfect end to an amazing season and only a hint of things to come for us. The Scorpions may have the Stanley Cup, but we're the ones who truly *won*.

———

I HOPE you enjoyed *Dirty Pucking Player*. The Fury Family Series continues in *Fabulous Filthy Friend*, Rachel Fury's steamy best friends to lovers story!

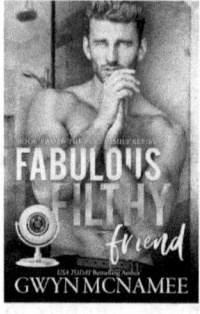

Get your copy: books2read.com/ FabulousFilthyFriend1

To stay up to date on news, sales, and releases from Gwyn, join her newsletter here: www.gwynmcnamee. com/newsletter

ABOUT THE AUTHOR

Gwyn McNamee is an attorney, writer, wife, and mother (to one human baby and two fur babies). Originally from the Midwest, Gwyn relocated to her husband's home town of Las Vegas in 2015 and is enjoying her respite from the cold and snow. Gwyn loves to write stories with a bit of suspense and action mingled with romance and heat. When she isn't either writing or voraciously devouring any books she can get her hands on, Gwyn is busy adding to her tattoo collection, golfing, and stirring up trouble with her perfect mix of sweetness and sarcasm (usually while wearing heels).

Website: http://www.gwynmcnamee.com/

Facebook: https://www.facebook.com/AuthorGwynMcNamee/

FB Reader Group: https://www.facebook.com/groups/1667380963540655/

Tiktok: https://www.tiktok.com/@authorgwynmcnamee

Newsletter: www.gwynmcnamee.com/newsletter

Instagram: https://www.instagram.com/gwynmcnamee

Bookbub: https://www.bookbub.com/authors/gwynmcnamee

www.ingramcontent.com/pod-product-compliance
Lightning Source LLC
Chambersburg PA
CBHW070549260626
47161CB00002B/555